COMPLETE

LEGATUM - BOOK 5

LULU M SYLVIAN

GRIFFYN INK

I wouldn't have made it this far without the help of so many:
Steve, the girls, Heather, Sarah, Suzanne, Suzanne, Alana, Eli,
Dana, Victoria, Kat, Erin, Lea, Lea, Liz, and everyone I ever had
a conversation about paranormal romance with—thanks for
sharing what you wanted to read.

PROLOGUE

The road to Haven wasn't the best, and Ramona's little red Scion rattled and jumped over the patched-up pavement. She was fairly certain she had taken a wrong turn. Nothing looked familiar.

She had been here just a few days ago with her father. He'd insisted on driving the rental truck down, packed with her few belongings. Of course traveling with her father, she had been distracted by his tales and not paying proper attention to the route followed.

Daddy kept pointing out that if they were back in Scotland, they would be in Wales by now. But here in Texas they could drive the equivalent distance across Europe and still be in the same state.

She was going to miss him and Mami. She hadn't lived at home for years, but there was a huge difference to living on the other side of Dallas from her parents versus living almost three hours away on the edge of hill country.

She needed out of Dallas; she needed her own space; she needed to find out where she belonged. If she couldn't find space to be herself in Texas, her only other options were another state, another country, or Mars Colony. Oh right. Mars Colony wasn't a thing yet. Wasn't going to be a thing for at least another twenty years, if even that soon. So another country.

Mexico was out. That would alienate Daddy. Scotland out, same thing, Mami would be hurt. When her parents had met years ago at an economics conference in Italy, it was love at first sight. After less than a year of traveling back and forth in a long-distance relationship, they cast their academic nets to the US, and UT Dallas bit. So Texas was where Ramona and her older sister, Lorena, had been born and raised, with healthy doses of Scottish and Mexican heritage.

The rental truck had bounced and rattled with such ferocity she was certain that everything she owned would be broken. Daddy had helped her to unload all the boxes, and what furniture she had. He slept that night on her small couch, and they drove back to Dallas together in the morning. He prattled on and on the entire time, keeping her happily entertained.

She should have left earlier in the day. But the route to Haven was easy. At least it had been the last two times she had driven down here. It was getting dark, and this road was not right. The screen on her GPS had turned to gray over an hour ago. Last time it had guided her straight into town.

She hit a crack in the road and bounced. Her car had to have better shocks than that rickety moving truck. Maybe her shocks weren't as good as she thought. Or was it struts? She never knew. It always seemed like each mechanic was telling her something different.

Her little car bounced along, full of the very last things she needed to move. Including a cooler of frozen tamales.

Ramona wasn't complaining; Mami made the best tamales. Only these came with a hefty side of guilt.

Ramona had promised her mother she would come home for a few days before summer school, and again before the fall classes started. When your parents were international economics professors, it made perfect sense to be a math teacher.

The car bucked and began making a *thump thump thump* noise. Steering became difficult.

"Hijo de puta," Ramona spit.

She eased on the brakes and stopped. Pressing on the hazards, she slid out of the driver's side and walked around her car. This was so frustrating. It was too dark to see properly, but that tire did not look right. She reached back into the small car and grabbed her phone from the dash. Stupid GPS with a pin plopped right in the middle of nothing. She pressed a few buttons, and the useless GPS on her phone turned into a flashlight.

Yeah, that tire was definitely not happy. It actually didn't much resemble a tire anymore. All that was left was a flap of tire-like material and a doughnut of steel belting. How long had it been in the process of shredding before it completely gave up?

She cussed again, a liberal sprinkling of *bloody hells, Jesus Hs,* and *cabeza estúpidas.* Her car did not have a spare. The flat-fix-it kit required that the tire be in one piece, not three. She kicked the closest tire. That was a bad idea; all it did was hurt her toes.

She slumped down in the driver's side seat, her feet swinging at the rocks in the road. She wasn't going to cry. She wasn't going to cry. She angrily swiped at a tear as it ignored her resolve to not cry.

Okay, what did she need to do? She didn't have a spare,

she didn't know where she was, and that bastard Devon was the one with the stupid auto club membership.

It wasn't until all the noises of early night stopped that Ramona realized just how loud the bugs were. She heard a huffing noise, like a large animal. Great, she was probably in the middle of some ranch, and her little red car looked like a challenge to a local bull. She heard a soft lowing and the shuffle of bodies moving away from her. *This is so not good.*

Once the cows moved off, she continued to hear a rough chuffing noise. Crap, there were coyotes out here. She flashed her light up the road. Two intense lights reflected back. Jesus H, she was either going to be abducted by aliens or eaten.

She kept the flashlight on the animal as it approached. It wasn't nearly as far away as she had originally thought.

"You're one hell of a big coyote."

The animal cocked its head to the side as if it was actually listening to her. Ramona pushed herself slowly back into her car. That wasn't a large coyote. It definitely looked more like a wolf. A really big one.

"Okay, Lassie. Why don't you go tell Timmy I need some help with a stupid flat tire, and I promise not to scream or tell the village there is a man-eating wolf out here scaring the cattle."

The door closed with a firm *click*, and Ramona let out a deep sigh.

The wolf circled her car.

"Seriously, doggo, the car isn't going to be tasty. I don't care if it has a soft crema filling."

As if in reply, the wolf gave a deep woof and left.

Ramona rummaged in the back seat. Mami had insisted she take her old bedspread. Ramona wasn't exactly certain if it was a guilt ploy, to make her homesick, or if Mami just wanted it out of the house once and for all. Ramona was glad for it and wrapped up. It was going to be a long night. In the morning, in the light, she would be able to hike back out to the main road and find out where she was exactly, and find some help.

Just as she was dozing off, the deep rattling sound of a diesel engine pulled her back to consciousness. Flashing yellow lights had her out of her car and waving like a maniac.

What were the odds that a tow truck would be out on this road?

"I can't believe y'all are here," Ramona gushed. "How on earth?"

Two of the tallest, broadest, good-looking men stepped from the truck. The one from the passenger side had a head full of hair like some kind of rock star. He went straight to the other side of her car and to the flat, as if he knew what he was looking for. The driver, wearing a Tire World ball cap, approached Ramona.

"We saw your hazards from the main road. What are you doing out here?" he asked.

"Being lost." Ramona practically cried with relief. "I made a wrong turn somewhere. My GPS is for shit."

"Hey, this car doesn't have a spare," the deep voice from the other side of her car called out.

"I have a few random tires in the back. See if I have something to fit. Otherwise we'll tow 'er back to the shop."

Ramona rained down praises and thanks as the men happened to have the right size tire.

They replaced her blowout while telling her it wasn't a problem. No charge. Glad they could help.

"Let me turn around and you can follow me back to Haven."

Again she thanked them, offered to pay, considered offering other means of gratitude—they were that good-looking—but refrained. It was one thing to think it. It was something completely different to actually follow through. It wasn't until she was back in her car, bouncing down the road on her way to Haven, that she realized she hadn't even asked them their names.

1

Ramona sucked in a quick gasp as two men came crashing out of the bar and stopped inches from where she stood. Maybe this wasn't the best idea, meeting her hairdresser in a bar. What did she know about the woman? Not much, only that she had magic fingers when it came to hair washing, and she'd managed to convince Ramona that she needed to come on out and make new friends.

Khendra had texted that she was already inside while Ramona sat in her car building up the nerve to do this. She had already had the nerve to up and move mid-semester to a new place. A small town; it might as well be a foreign country, it felt so different from Dallas. But Texas was Texas, she told herself. And it didn't get much more Texas than a big, burly bouncer carrying a middle-aged drunkard out the swinging doors of a roadside bar next to the train tracks. Right? Well, there could be cows.

Ramona tiptoe danced backward out of the way as the drunk man staggered into her space, rounded, and swung at the bouncer. This wasn't going to be a fair fight. The bouncer was huge and somehow familiar. Biceps strained at the material of his T-shirt. Judging by the number of spectators who followed them out of the bar, there was going to be a brawl.

Ramona scanned the gathering crowd. They were almost all women. She took another look at the drunk. He wasn't anything special, a typical-looking guy in a polo and khakis. When she looked at the bouncer, she sucked her breath in for a second time. No wonder he was familiar. He was one of her miracle roadside assistance guys. She had seen enough of him that night to know he was hot, but he was more than hot—he was glorious in a wild, untamed way.

He had almost as much hair as she did, only his was dark gold. It fanned out around him. He tossed his hair over his shoulders and followed with a smoothing motion of his hand over his brow and back.

His eyes glowed with intensity from all the neon. He dodged the arm swung at him and caught the other man around the chest, pinning his arms in place.

One of the women stepped up to the big guy and handed him a wide-brimmed cowboy hat. "Here's his hat, Bobby."

Bobby. The glorious man had a name. He settled the drunk on his feet and handed him his hat.

"Gimme my keys," the smaller man slurred.

"Walk it off, Coach," Bobby directed.

Coach lunged for Bobby again. "I said gimme my keys." He missed his reach, and Bobby caught the man from falling on his face.

Bobby looked up at the crowd of women. "Y'all go inside. There's nothing to see here," he barked.

They left with a twitter of giggles. "You just let us know if you need any help, Bobby."

The comment made Ramona think they were out there to watch Bobby and for no other reason.

"I'm gonna tell the sheriff you stole my car," Coach slurred. He was barely able to stand upright on his own, but he managed to stagger toward a large white SUV.

"You do that, and you'll spend the night in jail again," Bobby called out after the retreating figure.

Bobby twisted back around, and his gaze locked with Ramona's. She froze in place like a deer caught in the head-lamps of a Peterbilt.

"You okay? We didn't crash into you?" His voice was smooth like bourbon over ice.

"No, you missed me," she managed to say. "You're just gonna let him go off like that?"

They were both ignoring the protestations of the drunk man.

The giant held up a fistful of keys. "Yep, he can come back and get them after he's walked this off. More likely, he'll walk home and in about an hour or so his wife will swing by and pick up his keys."

She hadn't appreciated just how huge Bobby was the night he'd rescued her. He loomed over her. He gestured for Ramona to precede him inside. "I hope this doesn't stop you from coming in." He pulled open the door for her.

"Thanks." She felt immensely out of her depth. She didn't do bars. She was a coffee-shop kind of girl.

"Welcome to Ray's."

She paused just inside the door. It smelled exactly like she expected a bar to smell, a hint of stale cigarettes—more a memory than an actual smell—grease, and beer. Ramona shuffled out of the bouncer's way as he stepped past her. She scanned the room, focusing on locating Khendra and her friends. Her gaze swept over the tall round tables and long bar. Her eyes found the big guy again. He really was incredibly good-looking.

She waved as she made eye contact with the hairdresser and approached the table. Khendra had not been joking when she invited Ramona out for drinks and said Ramona would like her girls. Debbie was short and bubbly and worked as a clerk in the local police department. She had a sassy, short haircut that emphasized her heart-shaped face and perky nose. Vanessa was cool with an easy smile, a dental hygienist who looked more like a movie star with perfect shoulder-length flat hair. Upon meeting them, Vanessa announced she was going to make a play for Bobby.

"The big guy?" Ramona asked.

Debbie sighed. "Bobby is pretty much why we are here. Us and every other single girl in town."

The four sat at a tall round table in the middle of the bar. Ramona looked around, pool tables were located behind her, the walls were lined with booths. There was a long bar with a kitchen behind it. It looked like a typical local bar hangout, at least based on what she had seen on TV.

"Y'all need menus?" a short waitress in jeans and a tight T-shirt asked.

"I do," Ramona confessed.

The waitress handed over a folded and grease-stained piece of paper.

"Drinks?"

Everyone ordered a different cocktail.

"So, my girl Ramona here teaches math over at Raven-Croft and is recovering from a bad romance." Khendra provided a little back ground.

"Maybe we should let her have a go at Bobby. He's fabulous for rebound sex," Debbie cooed.

Vanessa squinted her almond-shaped eyes at Ramona as if in challenge.

Ramona held up her hands in self-defense. "Oh no, I'm staying away from men for a while. I'm in recovery. Got burned."

"So you gonna tell us about this tragedy that drove you here?"

Ramona thought about it. She knew that talking to friends was always good therapy. She missed that currently, and these ladies seemed nice enough. They could be her friends. "Oh hell, why not. Bad breakup, really bad. He was my boss. I needed to get away from him and everyone involved. We were secretly engaged. I know stupid, right? So to everyone back home it's just a breakup, but to me my whole future changed."

"Ladies," a smooth, deep voice interrupted as a round trayful of drinks slipped onto the table.

Ramona's mouth went dry. Up close she could admire his features better. She had to be careful so he didn't catch her blatantly staring at his chiseled jaw.

"Hey, Debbie," he said as he handed over a bright green margarita on ice.

"Thanks, Bobby." Debbie giggled.

"Khendra, you the Long Island iced tea today?" His voice was liquid gold.

Khendra reached over and took the drink from his offering hand.

"I'm the sex on the beach tonight," Vanessa purred.

"Of course you are." He chuckled as he winked at Vanessa. "That means you're the spiced rum and Cherry

Coke," Bobby announced as he placed Ramona's drink in front of her. All she could do was nod mutely.

"Bobby, this is our friend Ramona. She's new in town." Khendra said.

Bobby offered his hand. Tentatively Ramona took it. His hand was large and warm. She could hardly look him in his big amber eyes. "Nice to meet you, Ramona." Bobby smiled. Ramona couldn't help but to return the smile.

He let go of her hand. "Ladies." He nodded and left.

Ramona was dumbfounded. "Jesus H. He's the bouncer? He's beautiful."

Debbie giggled. "Told ya."

"You're gonna hit that?" Ramona asked Vanessa.

"I sure as hell am gonna try. I've got on matching delicates. I'm in need of that man. It just depends on who else is Bobby hunting tonight."

"Damn." Ramona shook her head. "Isn't he, um, hard to acquire? I mean..." She looked around the tables, trying to find him again. Her gaze rested on his back. She raked her eyes up and down his form, admiring the view: tight, muscular buns in formfitting, faded jeans; a tight T-shirt stretched across broad shoulders. "Doesn't he have a girl-friend or something?"

"Bobby Cray is the most eligible, available, and easy man in this town," Vanessa answered.

"Yeah, he's a man slut, but oh he is so worth it," Debbie gushed.

"So I take it you, ah...?" Ramona asked Debbie.

"Yes. I ahed and ohed and screamed a little bit. That man is good. I'm not joking when I say he's really good for rebound sex. After I broke up with Derrick last year, I got with Bobby. And I swear I didn't give a rat's ass about Derrick anymore. Forgot all about his skinny butt."

"And you're okay knowing he's a man slut?"

"Honey, everyone knows he's a man ho. It's part of the charm. Kind of a rite of passage to the women in this town," Khendra explained.

Ramona's inner flame over Bobby quenched. He was something to look at, but she had no interest in sharing the communal germs and STDs he must have.

Ramona followed the student out of her room. She leaned against the doorjamb and watched him strut down the hall toward his friends. She shook her head. Cocky and full of ego with nothing more than testosterone to back it up. Poor kid, he was clueless. She smiled to herself. Then again, weren't most men clueless?

Well, when it had come to Devon, she was the one to have been clueless.

She returned to her desk and began straightening papers. One pile for assignments to check, another for things she needed to take care of. Three days on the job and she was already sinking under paperwork.

Someone cleared their throat near the door. Ramona looked up. "Hi, Dr. Grover. How are you today?"

"I was going to ask you that very question, Ms. Campbell. How has your first week been going?" He stood just inside her classroom door and didn't enter all the way into the room.

"So far, I think it's going well. I've pretty much figured out who my know-it-alls are and who my troublemakers are going to be."

"And the lesson plans?" He continued to hover by the door.

She picked up a stack of papers and wagged it back and forth. "I have everything right here and plan on putting those together tonight, just like you asked. You wanted my first two weeks by Friday, right?" She tried to keep her voice chipper, but putting together lesson plans was not high up on her favorite things to spend her free time on. Especially since they always required such precise language. She couldn't say she was going to teach a simple algebraic equation where the students solve for X. No, she had to say the student would demonstrate learning of how to solve for X by method blah blah blah blah. And that she would teach them to solve for X buy implementing standards boring point boring boring. And inevitably the lesson plans would be returned to her decorated with loads of red pen marks as if she were a student again.

Fortunately, she had copies of all her previous years of lesson plans, already corrected by Devon. She taught to state standards, and RavenCroft High used the exact same textbook she had been teaching with for the past two years. Hello, computer files and copy/paste function. There was no reason Dr. Grover should know or even care.

"And how about Trey Shelton?" Dr. Grover asked.

"Who?" Realization dawned on her—the student who had just strutted from her class after asking for clarification on the homework assignment. "Oh right, him. What about him?"

"I was wondering what you may have said to him recently? I overheard him in the hall making claims that you would be going on a date with him? I want you to understand that while you—"

Ramona laughed, a sharp cackle, and let the stack of papers in her hand fall back to the desk. "That's rich. I think I may have actually said, 'see you later.' If that's some secret code around here for going on a date, I misspoke. But, no. He's a student; why would I even? No. Dr. Grover, I am a teacher. I work with children. Children. They may think they are adults, but I do know the difference. Trust me."

"Well, you are a young, single—"

Ramona cut him off again. "I'm not as young as people think. I am a professional, and I am offended. I'm sorry if anything he said raised some concerns for you. I may have suggested after-school tutoring as an option for him in needing help understanding this course, but I did not volunteer my time."

Great, she did not need to deal with this. So what was it? The smile? The hair? The willingness to listen and genuinely want to help her students pass this course? It was bad enough when she got a whiff of this from the students, but to actually have an administrator question her about it... She sighed.

"Trust me, Dr. Grover, I'm currently not interested in joining the dating world of Haven. But when I do, I will pick from a pool of men over the age of eighteen and who have graduated high school."

Dr. Grover seemed to relax, wilt a little. Had he really thought he had come into her room bracing for a show-down? "Well, just so that we're clear."

An involuntary shudder ran down Ramona's spine. Had Dr. G dealt with that in the past? Ew.

"Dr. Grover, so that you don't have to worry about this too, I won't even date a teacher from the same school where I teach." That was a lesson hard learned, and she knew she would have no problems ever repeating it.

Ramona sank into her chair and buried her face in her hands after Dr. Grover left and closed the door behind him.

Three days in and she was already being questioned regarding interactions with students.

The bell to dismiss teachers from the building rang. Ramona kicked back, groaned, and reached into her bag. She picked up her phone and flipped the ringer on.

The phone began vibrating as a series of texts came rolling in.

Do you do Wednesday church?

Ramona knit her brows together. That was an odd question coming from Khendra. She did not, but if her new friend was inviting her, maybe she should go, just to check it out.

Not typically, she answered.

Good, want to join our Wednesday revival meeting?

Excuse me? Ramona typed in response.

Revive our senses, give us something to lean on for the rest of the work week! Come on, you need to join our Wednesday Bobby study, Khendra explained.

You mean Bible study? Ramona asked.

Hell, gurl! I mean Bobby. Have you forgotten him? Oh, you so need a refresher course.

Ramona laughed out loud at Khendra's reply. She had definitely not forgotten Bobby.

What I really need is a big fat hamburger and a beer, Ramona countered.

See you at Ray's at 7.

Hamburgers! Ramona pounded at the letters on her phone.

Ray's, hottest damned waiter and the best hamburgers in town. See you at 7.

Ramona let her arms hang at her sides. She shook the tension out. A juicy hamburger and some serious eye candy were exactly what she needed after her encounter with Dr.

Grover and his implications of her being interested in Trey Sheldon. Her whole body shook in revulsion. Teenage boys were disgusting. She had even thought so when she was a teenager. That's why she'd never dated then. Boys were icky. Who was she fooling? Men could be pretty icky too.

2

The wheels made an annoying *chunk-thump* sound as Ramona pushed her buggy through the aisles at the IGA. She was tempted to go back and get another one, but she was already half full of frozen dinners and easy meals. She couldn't exactly roll the full cart outside to the buggy corral, shift everything over, and then come back in.

She sighed and reminded herself to try to check the cart next time. She always seemed to win at bad-buggy roulette. She turned the corner at the end of the aisle and froze.

There was that Bobby guy from the bar. Damn, he was even better looking in the bright lights of the grocery store. That wasn't something that could be said for most people. His cart looked like it had been careened into and pinned up against the boxes of cereal. Ramona could only see the back of the woman who was applying herself to him like plastic wrap. He didn't seem to mind.

Bobby was smiling down at her. It was a long way down. Either the woman was extremely short, or Bobby really was that tall. Ramona couldn't help but stare. She had never seen such a blatant hookup being arranged in the middle of a grocery store before. She should skip this aisle and come back to it. But she kept staring. The woman gave a loud giggle, and Ramona noticed how his hand trailed up and down the back of her arm.

Ramona felt voyeuristic and tacky just standing there and watching the mating rituals of this little town. She managed to pull herself away, twirling her buggy around and heading down the paper goods row. She was going to need paper towels, TP, oh, and paper plates, at least until the landlord fixed the kitchen sink and the dishwasher.

She didn't know what had happened. Everything had worked beautifully when she moved in. The landlord said he had updated a few things and even slapped a fresh coat of paint on the walls and cupboards. Less than a week later and the dishwasher blows up. It took all her towels to keep the flood limited to the kitchen. But it wasn't just the dishwasher. Somehow all the drain pipes from the kitchen just stopped and backed up.

Fortunately the bathroom still worked, but she couldn't really do her dishes in that tiny sink or in the shower. When she'd ducked out this afternoon to do some shopping, it was day two of the sink and all the knobs and hoses and pipes spread out across her kitchen floor.

As long as the freezer and the microwave still worked, she would be fine for a while. She looked at the contents of her cart and ticked off the items on her fingers. She should have made a list. Grapefruit cups, check, *chunk-thump*; bananas, check, *chunk-thump*; peanut butter, check, *chunk-thump-rattle-rattle*. This really had to be the oldest cart in the whole store. Five frozen dinners, a bag of cheapo frozen burritos. Mami would kill her if she knew she was eating those. But they were so good. A block of cheddar, two jars of chunky salsa, Tapatío sauce, *chunk-thump, chunk-thump.* Crash.

Ramona looked up in shock. She had been so focused on making sure she had enough food for the next few days for dinners and school lunches that she had not seen the other shopper's cart.

"I am so sorry," she said with a gasp. She looked up into a pair of warm amber-brown eyes and froze. Her throat went dry as she took in that chiseled jaw covered in dark golden stubble.

"Yeah, well, I'm already busy tonight." His voice was smooth and even, and his words made absolutely no sense.

"I'm sorry, what?" Oh shit, maybe he was on the phone and he had one of those invisible ear thingies in. She stepped back and pulled the buggy with her. *Chunk-thump, rattle, squeak.*

"I'm busy. Someone else already crashed into me."

Ramona felt her eyebrows try to join in the middle of her forehead. "It was an accident. I didn't see you." She was pretty certain they were having two completely different conversations.

"You sure? It seems to be a pretty common occurrence at the IGA. Crash into me, see if I'm good for a hookup. I don't do afternoon delight, and I don't do married."

Ramona's eyes went wide. They were definitely having two completely different conversations. This time she hauled the buggy back and took several steps distancing herself from him.

"That was an accident. Not a... No offense, but no thank you. You have a good day." She spun and pushed out of the aisle as fast as she could chunk-thump.

She spun around the end cap and stopped. Why had she told him to have a good day? No one else was down this row, at least for the moment. Her heart pounded. That had been nerve-racking. Embarrassing. Khendra had said he was a hot commodity, but was he so in demand that he actually expected a buggy crash to end up with a proposition?

"Hey, I should probably apologize."

Ramona screamed and her arms went flailing. She felt like she should be claws-deep into the acoustic tiles on the ceiling, she jumped so high. She pressed her hand against her chest. Her heart was trying to crash through her rib cage. If she didn't slow down on the huffing and puffing, she would go into a full-blown case of hyperventilation.

Bobby rested a large, hand on her shoulder, and she felt warmth melt through her system. Her breathing eased up a bit.

"Are you okay? Man, you jumped like ten feet."

Ramona continued to let her breathing slow. She finally looked up at him. "Bloody hell, you scared the ever-loving crap out of me."

"I didn't mean to. I wanted to apologize. You were saying we accidentally crashed, and I made the wrong assumption."

"Well, if you were expecting one result and you got another, I can understand why you reacted the way you did. I'm not gonna be trying to hit on you while I'm out grocery shopping. A cartful of toilet paper really isn't very conducive to flirting. At least not for me."

Bobby tossed his mane of hair back and followed the movement with a sweeping gesture from his hand. He captured the hair at his brow and pulled it all back from his face. Damn, he had beautiful bone structure. "You'd be surprised what some people will do in the middle of the frozen food aisle."

"I believe I saw you making date arrangements in the cereal aisle." She raised her brows at him.

He laughed.

She did not expect that rich sound to come rolling out of his chest.

"I'm Ramona. I think we had a bit of a misunderstanding." She held her hand out to him.

Bobby engulfed her hand between both of his. "That was you in the little red car with no spare? Khendra's friend, rum and Cherry Coke. I haven't seen you here before, have I?"

A woman, a few years older than either Ramona or Bobby, pushed her buggy past their conversation. She stopped and rested a rather possessive hand on Bobby's arm. "I'll see you later, Bobby." She cut a side-eye glare at Ramona.

Ramona openly stared back. The woman had the same short dark hair she had seen in the cereal aisle.

"Yeah, swing by the bar. We'll see how it works out." Bobby nodded at her.

She gave him a broad smile and batted her eyelashes. She gave Ramona another glare.

Bobby returned his attention to Ramona. "You were telling me why I haven't seen you around before."

"I just started shopping here," Ramona mentioned.

"You know you should get the ice cream last, that way it doesn't melt." He indicated the items in her cart.

"I'm still figuring the natural path of this store out. It feels backward to me," she confessed.

"I wouldn't know. I think I've been shopping at this IGA my entire life. You'll get used to it soon enough." He nodded in understanding and began to push his non-dysfunctional buggy. "See you around."

Ramona stood and watched him wheel away. She didn't know if she was going to be able to get used to a town this small. There were only two grocery stores, and this was the one close to home. The other one was closer to the high school. She'd check it out one day after school.

She chunk-thumped to the register and was happy to leave that buggy behind.

Bobby leaned back on the old couch from the living room, his long denim-clad legs stretched out in front of him. Brad stepped over his boots and handed him a cold brown bottle of beer. Brad dropped onto the couch beside him. The threadbare piece of furniture sat on the back deck in front of a dilapidated, half-full pool. The deck was mid-remodel. Piles of flagstones sat in a corner waiting to replace the broken-up concrete around the edge of the pool. The barbecue pit and outdoor bar were finally starting to look as if they might actually, one day, become a functional outdoor kitchen area. The hose spit water into the pool so the kids could use it for the summer. Hopefully it would hold out for a few more months, until it got resurfaced next winter. Wordlessly the brothers clinked their bottles together.

"Oh no you don't, Bradley." A shrill voice from behind, carried from out of the house.

A woman with perfectly coiffed shoulder-length ash-blonde hair, a deep, even tan, and pink lipstick stepped out onto the deck where the men sat. She was dressed in all black, her dress falling just shy of her knees. Her name tag was still pinned above her left breast, her feet tucked into fuzzy pink house slippers. "Don't drink that beer, baby, not until you spit in this."

Perfect pink manicured fingers held out a test tube to Brad.

Brad sat up, rolling his eyes up to peer at his wife.

"It's that DNA thing. Spit up to the line."

He took the tube and began spitting into it as directed.

Bobby looked at her quizzically.

"Since you and Bradley don't know much about your parents or grandparents, I'm hopin' this DNA test thing is gonna work like they say it does on the website."

"DNA? What website?" Bobby asked.

Brad handed the spit-filled tube back to his wife. "Melissa is doing a family genealogy search. Using one of those ancestor things online."

Bobby shifted his focus from his brother back to Melissa. She nodded. "I'm using that GeneoloTree site. They help you find birth records and who your great-great-great-granddaddy was. My cousin Cindy has our side of the family back past the Oklahoma Land Rush. Maybe we can find something out about you two. It supposedly finds genetic relatives. DNA matches. I researched it, and this is from one of the few companies that includes Native American DNA. The kids will want it someday. Who knows"— she gestured toward Bobby—"you might actually settle down, and your wife and kids would be interested."

Bobby shook his head as his sister in-law stepped back through the sliding glass doors into the house.

"And you just spit in the tube, like that?" Bobby focused on his brother's bearded face.

Brad took a long pull on his beer. "Hey, it keeps her happy. A happy wife makes for a happy life."

"You are happy, aren't you?" Bobby asked.

"I can't begin to tell you how happy she makes me.

Almost twelve years, and I have never doubted marrying her was the smartest thing I ever did."

"No seven year itch? I know you don't even look at other women. She that good?"

"Be respectful of my wife, little brother. I can still take you."

Bobby held up both hands in surrender, his thumb holding the neck of his beer. "No harm, no foul. Seriously, you used to be a horndog. What gives?"

Brad chuckled. It rumbled deep in his chest. Both men had smooth, low tenor voices and similar looks. Brad wore his thick, wavy hair business short, with a close-trimmed, full beard. His wife, Melissa, claimed it emphasized his warm brown eyes. Bobby's eyes were lighter, amber, his jaw was covered in a few days' scruff, and he wore his hair long down his back.

"I was nothin' like you."

Bobby tilted his head in acquiescence. He had a reputation as the leading womanizer in town, a veritable man ho. He knew it, he accepted it, he was getting tired of it. "I'm gettin' to where I don't want to be nothing like me."

"Something about her made me want to change. What really makes it last, it's not the sex, not the love, not the kids, it's that she's my best friend, Bobby."

"Not the sex?"

"Best I ever had. Seriously. I'm not joking, though. I knew something was different the first time I met her. By the end of that first week..." Brad shook his head. "I just wanted to hang out with her, be near her. She was waitressing back then. I would go sit at that restaurant every night just to see her, say hi. Anything. Took a while to convince her to go out with me, but she did. I was a perfect gentleman; I didn't touch her for weeks, didn't make one single play. Stopped hooking up with other girls. Wasn't interested. Really got to know her. You should try it. You need to find the right woman."

"I'm jealous, I really am. I don't think I'm ever going to meet the right one." Bobby felt mournful. "It's going to take an angel to put up with the likes of me."

"As long as you still have that bag-'em-and-tag-'em attitude, ain't nothin' gonna change."

"Hey, I'm just accepting what's being offered," Bobby deflected.

"If you're looking for the right one, she might not be offering. Just saying." Brad gave his brother a knowing nod.

3

The intercom system crackled, and Ramona heard her name.

"Yes, ma'am?" she said to the ceiling.

"Dr. Grover would like to see you in his office. Schedule says you're planning, right?" The voice fuzzed and popped.

For a fairly new system in a building less than three years old, the intercom certainly sounded as if it were going to crap out any day now.

"I'll be right down."

Ramona sighed. At least the system wouldn't allow the person on the other end to be able to hear her audible frustration. She would think that being a teacher would make those annoying nervous flips in her stomach not happen every time she was called down to the principal's office.

So far, Dr. G had really turned those nervous flips into something to be dreaded. He had been in her classroom or called her down to his office way more than was necessary these first few weeks. When Devon had been her principal, those nerves were thrilling. How many times had he called her down to his office for a planning make-out session? How many times had they actually had sex on his desk? Not as many as she would have liked, and way more than she now wished she had.

She was going to need to work harder on separating Devon from any and all principal-related thoughts.

She walked into the office and paused at the long desk.

"Dr. Grover called me down?" she asked whoever might be listening since Marge, the head secretary, was not paying any attention.

"Head on in," Marge said without looking up.

Ramona stepped around the desk and walked down the administration hall. At her last school, the principal's office had been at the end of the hallway, well away from the front office—one of the reasons she and Devon could have a quick tryst. Here at RavenCroft, Dr. Grover's office was the first door on the left. Something she forgot as she walked right past it.

She turned around, hoping no one saw that little faux pas, and knocked on the open doorjamb.

"You wanted to see me?" she asked.

"Come on in. Close the door," the older man directed.

That couldn't be good. What could Dr. G need to discuss behind closed doors? She hadn't made any of her students cry yet. Or maybe it was Sophie complaining about too much homework. Or Trey was running his mouth again about some date he at one point fancied taking her on. She'd signed a year lease on her tiny apartment. She couldn't afford for Dr. G to be letting her go already.

Ramona smoothed down the back of her dress and took a seat. She didn't bother to wait to be asked. Door closed. This was a conversation that was going to require her to be seated. It always did.

"How are you acclimatizing to Haven, Ms. Campbell?"

That was an odd question to start with. "So far fine. I really haven't gotten out much. I found a hairdresser and the grocery store mostly." She wasn't sure what else she needed to add. It wasn't any of his business that she had been to Ray's four or five times since she moved in three weeks ago.

"Well, I have heard from some concerned parties that you might be keeping company with some more questionable citizens—" Dr. Grover started.

"Excuse me, what?" Ramona knew her voice was a little louder than it needed to be. "Questionable citizens? So you're telling me that Debbie, who I know works for the police department, and Khendra, who owns the salon I went to, and Vanessa, who works at some dentist office, are questionable? What exactly does questionable mean?"

"I'm sorry, who?" Dr. Grover asked.

"The friends I've made in Haven. How are they questionable? Look, Dr. Grover, I guess I don't clearly understand how the people I am becoming friends with are any of the school's business? They aren't drug dealers or on some predator registry that I'm not aware of, are they?" Ramona was furious. So far this man had jumped to conclusions based on overhearing an overly hormonal teen, and now this.

He blustered and huffed before he began talking again. "No, no, no. None of those women are of any concern. At RavenCroft we want to make sure you are not taken advantage of. We understand that you transferred for this job, and thus are not fully familiar with the citizenry of Haven."

Ramona bit the inside of her mouth to prevent her from rolling her eyes. Dr. G was referring to himself as *we*, and used the term *citizenry*.

"It's... well... I'm not going to bandy about the bush here.

On Saturday you were seen at the IGA speaking with Bobby Cray, and he has a certain—"

Ramona bit the inside of her lips. She wanted to cackle. She wanted to laugh. This was the funniest thing she had heard in ages. But Dr. G wasn't Devon, and she needed to curb her tongue around him a bit more. There was actually some bitty in town either keeping tabs on who Bobby Cray was talking to, or spying on schoolteachers.

"I'm sorry, Dr. Grover, but seriously? Someone saw me talking to some guy at the grocery store, and you feel the need to chastise me behind closed doors?" She licked her lips and no longer cared if Dr. G was about to end her contract. This treatment was ridiculous. "I'm an adult, and I'll speak to whomever I want at the grocery store. Unless Bobby Cray is an active criminal element or underage, my talking to him really—"

"At RavenCroft we do not want our teachers to become the subject of town gossip." Dr. G's voice was lower, gruff. He did not assert himself particularly effectively.

"Dr. Grover, by listening to some busybody calling the school to report the actions of your teachers while they are out causing no harm to anyone, buying groceries, you are the one entertaining town gossip." She wanted to continue, she wanted to grill him further and ask if his informant also told him that she spoke with one of their students who works at the IGA? She had to ask him where aluminum foil was, and only realized he was a student when she saw him in the hallway on Monday. Did his informant mention her lengthy conversation about the broken kitchen sink with the checkout clerk? Did they tell him that Bobby Cray was crashed into by some woman with dark hair in the cereal aisle, and they arranged some hookup?

"Dr. Grover, this is a small town, and I live here. So yeah,

I'm going to go to the grocery store and talk to people there. I might also join that new gym on the other side of town. How are you going to react when someone calls to tell you they saw me in sweaty workout clothes? Do I have to limit my actions to school and home, and that's it? Because that is not what I signed up for." So much for watching her tongue.

"Ms. Campbell, I think you are taking this all the wrong way." Dr. Grover seemed like he was back peddling.

Ramona stared at him. Was Central looking for a new math teacher? How far away was the next town over? Could she get out of her lease? Maybe finding a small town to hide out in had been a bad idea. She should have headed into Houston or San Antonio. She could have stayed in Dallas, but as big as that city was, it just did not feel big enough, not with Devon being a principal.

"How am I supposed to take it?"

"Bobby Cray has a certain reputation—"

Ramona shook her head. "It doesn't matter. I haven't acted in a way that should be scrutinized like this. Dr. Grover, do you not see how this is going to make me paranoid to have any conversation ever outside of the school environment? The school district doesn't pay me enough to get to control who I speak with. I could be dating him for all that matters, and it still really isn't any business of whoever called you."

"Well, I just think someone needs to warn you about that young man," he finally said. Dr. G had called her down here to reprimand her because Bobby had a reputation that she knew about after only three days of living in this town.

"I am well aware of who he is. And I believe this was a misplaced discussion of concern. But I still don't appreciate having to feel as if I am being spied upon while selecting what brand of toilet paper I want to purchase." She stood up before she was dismissed. "If that's all, I have to get back to my lesson plans. My students are struggling with material Mr. Hagen seems to have missed before his stroke."

"Good conversation, Ms. Campbell. I'm glad we're seeing things on the same page." Dr G. stood as she left.

She shook her head. That man confused her, he mixed his metaphors, and she was fairly certain they had just had two completely different conversations. That seemed to happen a lot in this town.

Ramona was frustrated.

She wanted to throw the stack of grading across the room. She could not get Dr. G out of her head. How dare he call her to his office because she had been talking to Bobby? That was ludicrous, nuts.

And it only compounded the frustration she felt at the homework results from her students. What had Mr. Hagen been teaching?

Her table was too small. She needed to spread out.

She should head over to the library. They would have nice big tables where she could work. But she also wanted, no, needed a drink. And she was hungry.

She shoved everything into her tote bag. Screw any semblance of organization she had. She was going to have to redistribute everything anyway. She shouldered the bag and looked at the clock before heading out the door. She didn't remember the dismissal bell ringing, but it was already half past, so it had rung. Dug deep into her own head, she'd missed it.

She was probably the only teacher here this evening not coaching some team or running after-school practices of some kind. She usually stayed until all the grading and all the lesson plans were done. It was a habit she had gotten into after her student teacher mentor had told her to never take schoolwork home with her. She didn't know if it was such a good idea anymore. The halls of the school were creepy, quiet and empty.

She tossed everything into the back of her car. The tires crunched on the gravel of the teacher's lot, and again when she pulled into the gravel lot at Ray's.

She figured no one here would care if she spread out at one of the booths. It was early enough that she wouldn't be too much in the way. At least she hoped so.

She blinked as her eyes adjusted to the dim interior after the bright daylight.

"Have a seat anywhere. What can I bring you to drink?" Bobby called out from behind the bar.

Ramona glanced up at him; he hadn't looked up from whatever he was fiddling with.

"Hard cider, please, and can I get some fries?"

She located a booth with good lighting and slid in. Ray's was practically empty. A few serious day drinkers were at the bar, and a couple was playing pool. It was quiet, and she could work and have someone bring her food.

Panic quickly washed over her. It drained away as she scanned the other people in the bar. Who in here was going to call the school to tattle that she was day drinking while grading? Who was going to be overly concerned that she was seen talking to the bartender? No one.

Dr. G was overreacting, but damn it, if she was going to be busted for talking to Bobby, she might as well enjoy the process with a drink.

Bobby placed a tall, frosted glass in front of her. "What you working on?"

"I'm grading."

He slid into the booth across from her. "So you're a teacher? What subject?"

"Remedial math and algebra one." She smirked.

"Over at Central?"

"No, I'm at RavenCroft," she said.

"So if you've been teaching at RavenCroft all year, how come I'm only now seeing you around town?"

So he had remembered running into her at the grocery store.

"I just started after spring break. The previous teacher had a stroke."

"Oh yeah, I heard about that." He nodded. "Their football team isn't half bad. Now if they could get that new stadium finished..."

"I really wouldn't know. But I do have half of those boys in my class, and..." She shook her head. It wasn't her place to gossip about her students.

"Hey, I understand. I was one of those boys back in my day. Didn't want to learn anything; didn't think I needed to. Good luck with them. I'm sure they are a cocky bunch."

Oh, he had no idea. Cocky seemed like an understatement.

He stood. "I'll leave you to your papers. Should be back with your fries in a minute. You want anything else?"

"Now that you ask, I could really use a burger."

"What do you want on it?"

"Well, what I really want is a BLT, with no tomato, an actual quantity of bacon, not something stupid like four strips, cheese, grilled, with extra mayo, and pickles on the side." She gave him a sheepish grin.

"All that on the burger? You aren't asking for much. Want that batter fried and with avocado slices?"

Ramona opened her mouth to protest.

"I'm joking. I think I can handle a BLT, no T, extra B. If it's grilled, the lettuce won't survive."

"Skip the lettuce. And yes, on a burger. Most places just can't make it with enough bacon without charging me a car payment, so the burger is basically bacon filler."

Bobby grinned, giving her a flash of startlingly bright teeth. His whole face lit up, those high cheekbones got a little higher, and his eyes seemed to pick up some of the neon in the bar and flash. Ramona shivered. She could see why the women of this town followed him around.

"If I can give you enough bacon and not charge you any more than a double, would you rather only have bacon?"

Ramona nodded. "And more bacon."

Bobby clearly understood the requirements of a good bacon sandwich. And his timing could not have been more perfect. She drew another red circle around another red F and added that homework to the ever growing pile of *clearly this kid doesn't know what a number is*.

Her eyes went wide when he slid her grilled BLT, no L, no T, onto the table. It was stacked high, with at least an inch of crispy, thick-sliced bacon. Melted cheese cascaded down the crinkly edges.

"One cholesterol bomb."

"Are you judging me?" She lifted her eyebrows and gave him one of her best I-don't-have-time-for-your-stories teacher looks.

"You're grading papers in my bar, drinking before five PM, and about to eat a half pound of bacon covered in cheese. Of course I'm judging you. I'm also thinking about joining you and having one myself."

∾

"Uncle Bobbeeee." With a squeal three small bodies impacted against his legs. He leaned over and scooped all three children into his arms and stood up. More squeals and almost too much wriggling for him to hold.

"Do you want me to drop you on your heads?" This brought a giggle from the girls, who knew he was joking.

The youngest howled, "No."

"Then hold still." Bobby shifted his grip and walked farther into the house. This was why he tried to show up early on poker nights. These kids, the best damned nieces and nephew a man could ask for.

"Where's your daddy?" he asked, not seeing his brother. Instead he found his sister-in-law lining up rows of beers and chips on the kitchen counter.

"Brad isn't home yet. Has an employee issue," Melissa explained.

With an exaggerated oof, Bobby deposited the kids back onto the floor. The toddler, a towheaded boy in a blue tutu, sat on Bobby's foot and wrapped himself around his uncle's leg. Bobby faked the extra effort it took to walk around with his nephew plastered to his calf.

Employee issues. That meant Brad would be in a foul mood tonight. Damn, Bobby wanted to win tonight, but it looked like he would be throwing a hand or two.

"Let me help." Bobby opened the refrigerator and began pulling out the sandwich fixings.

"Oh good, you're better at that than I am," Melissa said. "I need to get ready. Can you handle the kids and sandwiches?"

Bobby gave her a side-eyed glare. Could he handle some sandwiches and the kids? "You do know what I do for a living, right?"

"Of course." Her tone chastised him. "But Princess Pete can be, well, he's a toddler and—"

"And easier than most drunks I have to deal with. Go get yourself ready. Abby will be here any minute."

Melissa gave him a head shake with a soft smile. He chuckled. That woman ruled this roost, and he could see why his brother loved every second of it.

He arranged the dinner rolls, slicing them in half with a large dual-purpose knife. He didn't care what anyone said, this sold-on-TV blade was the best kitchen tool. It could slice through anything and still cut a tomato. Mayo, mustard, that tomato he easily sliced, and then piles of cold cuts and cheese, he made a mountain of sandwiches, all with his nephew still wrapped around his calf.

"Hey, Bobby." Abby's soft voice announced her presence.

He wiped his hands on a towel and turned with a smile. Slender and young, with her hair worn in two pigtails, Abby set her son, who had been balanced on her hip, down to stand on his own.

"Abby, Tyler!" Bobby smiled at the newcomers.

When Abby had been nine or ten, Brad dated her mom. And through a complex twisting of relationships and events, Abby had ended up becoming a member of this family.

With the announcement of the arrival of Tyler, Petey was off Bobby's leg. Both boys ran away from the kitchen and straight to the toy bin in the living room.

"Oh no you don't, mister," Abby announced as she scooped up Tyler.

Bobby was on her heels, gently removing the toy from Petey's hands.

Petey's face began to melt. Before a wail could escape his lips, Bobby flipped the child up and blew raspberries on his exposed tummy. The toddler giggled and squirmed as the air bubbles made rude sounds.

Melissa came rushing out from her back bedroom, the twins following behind. She patted at her hair, which had transformed from a ponytail into a large pile of a hairdo. She gave Abby a quick cheek-to-cheek air-kiss. "How you doin' tonight, sweetie?"

"Good. I talked to Maxfield this morning." Abby's husband was currently deployed overseas. "He said it's been real quiet. That's good. I want him to be bored over there." Abby hiked her son onto her hip. "You ready?"

Melissa herded her kids toward the front door, picking up her purse. "See you later, Bobby," she called as they all left out the front door to head to the Family Fun Zone. Bobby wasn't sure exactly how much fun it was hauling the kids around, but Melissa was a charm taking them once a month so Brad could hold poker night.

Bobby waved goodbye as the door closed. A second later it slammed back open.

"You missed your wife," he called out, his attention on customizing one of the sandwiches with some hot pickled peppers and shredded cabbage.

"I am my wife."

Bobby looked up to see Melissa scurrying back inside. She hustled back to the bedroom and returned with a box. "Do me a favor, get Brad to do this spit test. They messed it all up, and I need him to do it again before he has any beer tonight."

"Sure thing, Melissa."

The next time the front door slammed open, it was Brad, and he was in a foul mood.

He glowered at Bobby the entire time he spit into the tube.

"Hey, it's not my fault the lab screwed up your results."

Brad growled as he packaged up the sample. He stormed down the hall to the his bedroom and stormed all the way back, his feet stomping with heavy thuds.

Bobby sat at the kitchen table and began shuffling cards. "Work got you on edge?"

Brad sat heavily onto one of the chairs, his legs kicked out in front of him. He ran a bottle of beer over his forehead. "I had to fire the new guy. He was a real cutup, lots of fun to have in the shop. Crappy worker. It would have been easier if he had been an asshole." He groaned, stood up, and grabbed the bottle of aspirin they kept on the back of the sink. "How's the bar?"

Bobby shrugged. "Changed out the hoses on the drinks machine. Made the biggest bacon sandwich for the new math teacher over at RavenCroft."

"Since when are bacon sandwiches on the menu?"

"Since she asked and batted her eyelashes at me."

Brad squinted at Bobby. "You ducking out of the game early?"

Bobby huffed through his nose. "I don't sleep with every woman I meet. Naw." He shook his head.

"Losing your touch? Should you get tested for low T?" Brad asked in fake sympathy. "There's a pretty new teacher in town, and you haven't slept with her."

"Asshole." Bobby pitched a poker chip at his brother's head. "Who said she was pretty?"

"You did when you made her a bacon sandwich because she asked."

Brad was more right than Bobby cared to admit. Ramona was pretty. She had a mass of thick black hair, full sensual lips, and bigger eyes, and was so feminine in those dresses she always seemed to be wearing. Maybe he was losing his touch. After all, she'd declared herself not interested that afternoon at the IGA. Or maybe she wasn't the type to mess around.

The front door crashed open. "S'up? Are you ready to lose all your money to me tonight?" A booming voice announced the arrival of Derrick. He wore a flak jacket, jeans, and a polo, no uniform in sight. That meant he was out to win tonight.

4

"You look so official," Ramona said as Debbie slid into the booth. She wore a sky-blue short-sleeved button-down with the Haven town crest embroidered over the left breast. It almost looked like a police uniform with the black slacks, but she was missing all the other arm patches and the standard utility belt and sidearm.

"Yeah, every so often Chief actually wants us all to wear the uniform. Probably someone from the state coming through. I didn't really pay attention. Oh, I have got to tell you, Derrick finally asked me out again." Debbie grinned as she settled in.

"Isn't he the guy you had make-up nookie with Bobby over?"

"Yeah, but we've been on a serious break. And I've been dropping hints. Derrick doesn't seem to know it yet, but I'm going to marry his skinny ass one of these days."

"Hey, girls." Jenna greeted them with menus. "What can I get started for you?"

Ramona looked at Debbie. "Are we drinking? 'Cause I'm drinking."

Debbie nodded. "Just a light beer for me."

"She'll have a hard cider, and I'll have a Guinness." Ramona ordered. "Oh, and a basket of fries please."

Debbie rolled her eyes.

"Don't give me that. If you're gonna drink beer, drink real beer. Otherwise it's like watered-down horse pee. Don't do that to yourself."

Debbie laughed. "You crack me up. Little miss school-teacher, always in those prim floral dresses, and giving me what-for over beer."

The noise level at the bar grew louder.

"Looks like Coach Shumer has been tossing them back for a while," Debbie commented.

"Isn't he the football coach over at Central? 'Cause he wouldn't have had time to get over here and get that wasted by the time school got out."

"Oh, honey, he walked in the door lubricated. Central didn't do too good last season, and he's feeling the pressure. The team needs to make playoffs next fall or he doesn't have a job."

Ramona made a face. She knew what that meant, knew that feeling all too well. The Sword of Damocles, just waiting for the principal to come in with that form, letting you know your contract would end with the end of the school year.

As coach in this town, at that school, he had a certain reputation to protect. Central was used to making it to the playoffs, and to state on a regular basis. That hadn't happened last year. But she thought this coach had taken the team to the playoffs in the recent past. Probably not recent enough.

"Are you saying he's drinking at school?" Ramona leaned over the table and whispered.

"He drinks at games. That's not water in his water bottle," Debbie informed her. "He knows his days are numbered. I guess he's just adding fuel to the fire."

Ramona turned and watched as soon as she heard Bobby's low rumble of a voice. There really was something soothing about that man, but he was firmly off-limits. Even with his good looks, his proclivity toward sleeping with anyone was a definite no.

"When was the last time you ate something, Coach?" Bobby was even calm in handling the bar drunks.

He got a mumble-cuss type reaction Ramona couldn't hear.

"I'm cutting you off." Bobby placed a cup of coffee in front of the other man. "I want you to drink that, and eat something before you leave. You are in no shape—"

Bobby's words were cut off by Coach grabbing his hand and shaking it.

Coach suddenly got very loud. "Where is your ring, boy? Don't you have any respect?"

Bobby pulled his hand away. "Drink your coffee."

Ramona turned back around to face Debbie. "What ring is Coach talking about? Bobby isn't married, is he?" She was glad she'd put him in the big pile of *nope*, especially if it turned out he was married.

"His championship ring. Central won state Bobby's senior year."

"Bobby played football?" Of course he had. She knew that was a stupid question the second she asked it. How could he not with shoulders like that?

Debbie laughed. "He sure did."

"I bet he deflowered the entire cheerleading squad." Ramona snorted.

"Funny thing is, I think Bobby was a virgin in high school."

"Bullshit." Ramona made that fake cough noise the boys in her class did. "You're telling me the town man whore wasn't a player in high school?"

Debbie shook her head. "He was two years ahead of me, and he had one girlfriend the whole time. She was a preacher's daughter, really good, not wild. Not the kind of preacher's daughter you get in the movies, but a real good, pious girl. His brother, Brad, now he was the town gigolo back then. Things kinda flip-flopped after Bobby went away and came back."

"You certainly seem to know a lot about them."

More raised voices from the bar pulled Ramona's attention.

Coach was on the floor, having fallen from the stool. Bobby was hauling him back up and easing him toward a chair. "You are going to sit here and eat that damned hamburger and drink more coffee, and then I'm calling your wife."

"I can drive myself," Coach grumbled.

"You sure as hell cannot. You have spring practice. You want your team to get anywhere? You start cleaning yourself up."

Coach grumbled some more and picked up the hamburger.

It looked like the show was over.

Ramona asked Debbie again, "How come you know so much about Bobby and his brother?" She hadn't even known Bobby had a brother. Hell, she just found out he had been on one of the town's championship teams.

"Easy, I was trying to get Brad to pop my cherry."

Ramona felt her eyes get wide. Debbie certainly didn't seem to have secrets about her sex life.

"You don't get to fuss at me about booze and then look at me like that about sex. Brad was just as easy to look at back then. Hell, he may have been better looking than Bobby. He slept with anyone willing. Of course I found out that was anyone seventeen and up. He didn't want any underage complications. Go figure; I was fifteen, and the town man-meat had scruples of a sort."

"And you didn't go after Bobby for the job?" Ramona asked.

"I'm not kidding. Bobby was in deep with that chick. What was her name? Her daddy preached at that little Baptist church, the white and brick one out past the dam." Debbie tapped her fingers on her lips, thinking.

"Sorry about the disturbance, ladies," Bobby said as he delivered their basket of fries and drinks.

"Hey, Bobby, what was the name of that girl you dated in high school?"

Ramona felt her stomach drop as Debbie asked.

"You mean Taylor? Why?"

"Just giving the new kid in town a little area history. She was asking what Coach was on about with your ring," Debbie explained.

"Oh, right. He does that every so often. Comes in here and gives me grief over a ring. It doesn't matter that high school was a long time ago for me, and I'm not the same skinny kid. Can't tell him the ring doesn't fit on my fat fingers. Not when he's still in the middle of it every day."

Ramona glanced down at his hands. They were not fat or meaty. Bobby had long, elegant hands. Sure they were big, but those hands looked like they could be delicate and soothing just as easily as they could fist up and break something.

"Excuse me, I need to go make sure he sobers up some before letting him leave."

Both women watched Bobby walk away. Ramona was sure Debbie was admiring his backside just as much as she was.

"So, yeah, Taylor. He even followed her to OU for college. Apparently she broke his heart, and he, well, that's when he got stupid for a bit. When he came back, Brad was dating Melissa—she's his wife—and Bobby stepped up to the plate on sleeping with the women of this town."

"So I'm dying over here." Ramona shoved a few fries into her mouth. "Who did you get to pop your cherry?"

She couldn't admit it to Debbie, but she was a bit jealous. She had been that good little Catholic girl in high school. She hadn't dated. She'd just crushed on Devon for years before he paid attention to her. She was fascinated that Debbie had such a casual attitude.

Debbie sighed, a small little smile on her face. It must have been a good memory.

"I haven't a clue. I was drunk off my ass. I remember that much. Some party out by the dam. I'm pretty sure it was some guy from St. James. That chi-chi private school out past Meridian. There were a bunch of them. Jeez, I haven't really thought about it much. I can remember thinking it was such a burden to be a virgin. And then I wasn't and it wasn't really that big of a deal. I don't think I had sex for something like three more years after that. Not until I was at college. I went for two years in Killeen. What about you?"

"College? I went to UT Dallas."

"Girl, you know I am not talking about college. Now spill."

Ramona cringed. She felt like such a fool, having let Devon play her the way he had. She was fairly certain her cousin, Joanne, hadn't been the only girl he had cheated with, and there was Ramona, the faithful, hopeful, stupid girl next door.

"I've only been with one guy." She felt the blush burn her face.

"No? Not the guy who screwed you over?"

Ramona nodded.

"Oh sweetie, that sucks. I bet you really loved him too. Did you sleep with him before or after he said he would marry you?"

Ramona shrugged. She'd thought she had loved him, maybe she'd just really loved the idea of him. "After. I wouldn't have otherwise. Well, he didn't really love me, so in the end that's what the takeaway was. Right? I mean, if I expected to be signing up for a lifetime commitment, maybe I should have waited for that ring and the white dress. But if I had, I'd still be waiting. I learned a big lesson. I was delusional and put my expectations on the boy I grew up in love with. You know, he was literally the boy next door."

"And you were going to get married. Ramona, that's all kinds of sweet and romantic. You weren't delusional. He was an asshole. How did your parents take the split up?"

Ramona shook her head. "They didn't know. I mean, I'm sure they knew that Devon and I had a thing. But they didn't know we were engaged. You would think that after eight years of keeping it a secret, I would have clued in. I'm an idiot." Ramona took a long drink of her beer. This conversation wasn't feeling very good anymore.

"We both were. You for holding out hope for love, and me for thinking I needed to have sex so people would accept me. High school students are hormonal and dumb. You should know this. You teach them." Debbie giggled.

Her smile and friendship maybe made this conversation not as bad as Ramona had started to think.

Khendra slid into the booth next to Debbie. "Hey, y'all. Oh my God, I have to tell you what I heard from my chair this week! Nola Wilson said that her niece was on her bike, and that big red wolf came on in and knocked her down not five seconds before some idiot ran the stoplight up at the elementary. Saved her life."

"Seriously? That's like the second time this year I've heard about that wolf saving some kid," Debbie said.

"Wait, what?" Ramona asked. They could not be talking about the same wolf she'd seen when she had her flat.

"Yeah, it's either some big dog or some people say it's a wolf. But you'll hear about some mysterious animal rescue around here from time to time. I'd say it's like a local legend," Debbie explained.

"But Nola Wilson! She doesn't go around spreading rumors. That animal is real, y'all. I'm telling you. So what were you talking about?"

"Losing our virginity," Debbie said as if they were talking about the cost of avocados at the grocery store.

Khendra snorted. "I win. Twenty-two, white dress, honeymoon. Should have taken that man for a test drive first."

"I didn't realize you were married," Ramona said.

"Key word: was. Not anymore. That lasted three years too many. Thank God it's over. Never trust a man who prefers virgins. It just means they don't know what they are doing either. So is this us for the Bobby admiration society meeting?" Khendra asked.

"I think so. Vanessa hasn't been coming since Bobby turned her down," Debbie said.

"Girlfriend got drunk. She should know better. Bobby won't mess with you unless you are sober and know what you are getting into. She's been pouting over it ever since. But she did say there is a fine new specimen over at the Roadhouse. We should go check him out sometime."

Ramona guided her buggy into the line. The conveyor belt was already full of the items from the person in front of her. She stared at the magazines and glanced around the store, wondering if Dr. G's spy was in this morning.

"My, you certainly have a full cart. It looks like you are stocking up," a voice behind her said.

Ramona turned and smiled at the silver-haired old lady behind her. Tiny and frail, with a large, infectious grin, her line neighbor pointed to Ramona's full load of groceries.

"I kind of am," Ramona confessed. "Right after I moved in my kitchen broke. The landlord finally got everything fixed, and I hate an empty kitchen. You don't have nearly as much as I do. Do you want to go ahead?" Ramona began to pull her buggy back to let the woman through.

"Oh, no need for that. But thank you. Where did you move here from, sweetie?"

"I'm from Dallas. I teach math at RavenCroft." Ramona reached over the groceries and offered her hand to the lady. "I'm Ramona."

"Nice to meet you, sweetie. You starting this late in the year? That's unusual, isn't it?"

"It's more common than people realize. But it was a

surprise to me too, a good surprise. I didn't expect to be able to find another position when I needed one."

"I'm sure they'll be glad to have you. Welcome to Haven. I'm Mrs. C, Cordelia Neighbors. How'd ya do?"

"Nice to meet you, Mrs. Neighbors," Ramona cut in.

Mrs. C waved her hand dismissively. "I haven't been called Mrs. Neighbors since before my grandkids were born. I'm Mrs. C to everyone."

Ramona unloaded her items onto the belt while Mrs. C offered advice on how to properly stock up for canning, since all the fruits and vegetables were coming in fresh.

"I'd like to learn that someday." Ramona thought about how she would love to have a house with a garden. Nothing too large, but preserving vegetables from her own garden would be wonderful.

Ramona turned her attention to the cashier and then turned back to Mrs. C. "It was lovely to chat. I'll be sure to say hi next time I run into you."

"Every Saturday, that's my routine." Mrs. C. gave her a small wave as Ramona pushed the full buggy into the parking lot.

Ramona lifted bags into the back of her car. That sweet Mrs. C from the checkout line waved as she rolled past.

"Mrs. C, you have the makings for your famous peanut butter cookies in there?" a friendly male voice asked with a laugh.

Ramona smiled. Would Dr. G's spy be calling Mrs. C to let her know she shouldn't be seen talking to Bobby at the grocery store? She overheard him offer the older woman help with her shopping.

"What I really need is help at the other end. Putting everything into the car is easy; getting it into the house, well..."

Ramona glanced up before rolling her buggy back to the cart corral. She felt a little guilty for listening, and a lot curious to see how Bobby looked this morning. Would his hair be down or up in a sloppy bun?

Damn, if she couldn't just stand here and watch the show. Bobby Cray bent over and placed Mrs. C's groceries into the back of her car. He bent over again. Ramona sighed. That was one fine backside. No wonder he was on the top of the to-do list of every single woman over the age of eighteen in this town.

Ramona remembered she, in fact, could not stand here and gape at the man all day. Ice cream was melting in her car as she drooled. Wistfully casting a silent farewell to Bobby, his messy top knot, and his backside, Ramona slid into her car and drove home.

She needed to make two more trips out to her car to unload everything, and then she would spend the rest of the day putting everything away and rearranging the cupboards until her kitchen felt right. It was nice to finally have her kitchen be fixed and functional. She had barely unpacked before and hadn't yet achieved that natural organic flow to the layout of the cupboards.

"Ugh, fix your muffler. I'm so impressed." Ramona sneered as she jumped down her stoop and onto the walkway. She hated that low grumble feeling in her chest from cars that sounded like they needed engine work instead of being that authentic muscle-car big-engine noise. The engine stopped. Ramona looked up to glare at the driver, not that they would ever know they had met with her disapproval.

A matte black Charger with a shiny black roof had pulled in front of one of the houses across the street. And double damn if unfolding from the driver's seat wasn't hunk of the hour, Bobby himself.

Ramona hadn't seen his car on this street before, so she knew he didn't live here. Maybe it was girlfriend du jour's place. And maybe Ramona was being a judgmental ass. She was pretty sure that's what was happening, especially when Bobby walked straight over to the car in the driveway. The same car he had been putting groceries into at the IGA. He popped the trunk and loaded his arms full of plastic grocery bags. Mrs. C opened the front door, and Bobby disappeared into her house.

This time Ramona decided she did have time to stop and watch. She was curious. Was Bobby really the kind of man to follow an old lady home just to help her with her groceries? It certainly seemed like it. So there was more to him than good looks and rumored fine bedroom skills.

She ran the last bag into her small kitchen, tossed the ice cream into the freezer, and returned to her stoop. Bobby's car was still there, but no sign of him. Ew, he wasn't helping Mrs. C out in other ways too, was he? Well, he did have a certain reputation, and there was no reason why a much older woman wouldn't appreciate some... "Oh just stop, Ramona," she chided herself and stood up, wiping the small pebbles and other bits of dirt from the back of her jeans.

Before she could turn and reenter her apartment, Mrs. C's front door swung open. Bobby followed the older lady back outside. She handed him what looked like a plate of cookies covered in plastic wrap. He took the plate, kissed her on the cheek, and waved before disappearing into his car and loudly pulling out.

Mrs. C made eye contact with Ramona and waved. Ramona waved back. Mrs. Neighbors was her neighbor.

Five minutes later Ramona was staring at a row of open

cupboards and a countertop stacked with plates, glasses, and canned food. Her doorbell rang. Ramona jumped.

Heart pounding in her chest, she opened the door.

"Hello again, dear. I didn't realize you lived across the street." Mrs. C announced while holding a plateful of cookies covered in plastic wrap, and a jar of what looked like preserves. These must be the famous peanut butter cookies Ramona had heard Bobby mention in the IGA parking lot.

"Mrs. C, I didn't either. Please come in." Ramona stepped back to allow the older woman to come inside. "I'm still moving in. Don't mind the boxes."

"When I realized it was you across the street, I decided to bring you some cookies. I'm sorry it's not a full batch, but I gave half of them to Bobby Cray. Have you met him yet? Very popular with the younger ladies. He's a good boy. I don't believe everything I've heard about him. Played football with my grandson, Carson."

Ramona nodded. She didn't want to lie, but was *Hi, I'm your waiter; my name is Bobby* exactly meeting a person? Spending several hours giggling and ogling over his finer attributes with Debbie wasn't the same as having him tell her he played football. "He works over at that bar, Ray's. I accidentally crashed into his buggy the other week at the IGA. I guess we all shop there."

"Yes, that's him. Such a sweetie, he drove all the way over here to help me unload my groceries after running into me in their parking lot." She swept her glance over Ramona's kitchen. "Now what are you thinking about putting where? I really think you might like your glasses to the right of the sink, unless you're a leftie. Are you a leftie?"

5

"What can I get you today, Ramona?"

She raised her head at the familiar voice. Bobby looked at her quizzically.

She sighed. Dr. G was having her complete more paperwork than she could ever remember filling out as a first-year teacher. And of course he required a different format than any of the lesson plans she already had written. Everything needed restructuring. Her students were struggling. The papers in front of her needed grading. She really wanted a drink, but drinking and lesson plans and grading did not mix. "I need a clear head. Just a Cherry Coke this time." Bobby turned to head back to the bar. "And a basket of fries please."

He gave her a thumbs-up in acknowledgment.

This shouldn't be this hard. These papers should be easy to grade. This was basic algebra, yet her students were mangling the equations. According to Mr. Hagen's grade book, they had been doing so well before spring break, and now it was like they didn't even grasp the concept of two plus two equals four, forget about finding X. It looked like tomorrow, they were going to start this entire unit over again. The students were not learning—time to review, revise, redo. Hopefully they could make up for lost time later. They wouldn't be able to do those later lessons if this one wasn't mastered first. She continued to mark the incorrect homework, giving up on showing corrections to the work, indicating the wrong answers.

Bobby arrived with her drink, carefully setting it down so that it did not rest on any of the papers she had scattered before her.

"Homework?" he asked, sliding into the booth across from her.

"Yep, grading. I was hoping a change of scenery and some food would make this easier." She rubbed the back of her neck.

"Sounds like it's not working."

"It's not. I don't know." She rested her cheek in her palm, elbow on table. "The students need an algebra brick upside their heads, and I need a bubble bath."

"The thing that always helped me with math was context." Bobby leaned back, looking at the other customers, seeing if he was needed. He was. "I'll be back." He stood and left.

Ramona was still staring at the papers. She hadn't moved when he returned with her french fries.

She popped a hot fry into her mouth and chewed.

"As I was saying, context. I could care less about watermelons, but when Brad helped me, he always put it into terms of the shop. How many cars, how many parts, how to know what to order next. Have you tried that yet?"

"I need to. They were talking about that at my last school. How to prepare for the zombie apocalypse, food storage and stuff. How many cans of peaches to survive the first winter. How fast your gun shoots, how many bullets you need. That's not a bad idea actually. I'm going to have to go over all of this again, so why not. Thanks, Bobby." She popped another fry into her mouth and smiled. "I'm going to need a burger for while I grade the rest of this."

"BLT or you looking to branch out?"

"I'm going to live dangerously. I'm gonna go with a double bleu and grilled onions."

Bobby chuckled. "You are living dangerously."

Ramona picked up the next paper in front of her. Teaching math with zombies might actually work. She just hoped it wouldn't get her into trouble with Dr. G. He seemed to like to keep a tight rein on standards and how lessons were presented. The homework assignments only got worse as she continued grading.

Bobby arrived with her hamburger. "You still look stressed." He put the sandwich down in front of her, then reached behind her and began kneading her shoulders. Ramona felt like melting. Bobby's hands were large and warm. His strong fingers dug into the tense muscles supporting her neck. "Your neck is like a rock."

Ramona suppressed a groan. The massage felt so good. All her muscles turned to Jell-O. Bobby did know how to touch. Okay, this wasn't the touch her friends seemed to seek out, but she would take it.

"You need to go home and soak in a hot tub. That will help." His thumbs continued to press circles next to her spine.

Ramona could barely think. "Ahh, I don't have a tub, just a walk-in shower. It sucks."

Bobby continued working his hands over her shoulders.

"I think you missed your calling. You would make a killing as a masseuse," Ramona almost purred.

His hands stopped. He patted Ramona on the shoulder. "I have a tub you can borrow."

"What? Really? I don't want to impose, but Jesus H really?"

"Yeah, be right back."

Ramona sat stunned. Bobby had a tub, and he was going to let her use it. *Oh no, he's hitting on me. Wait, Bobby never does that. He doesn't need to.* Her thoughts raced from the joy of a tub, to being worried if it was a come-on, and if she really wanted to be another notch on his belt or not. He was good-looking and nice, and that massage had felt so good. She wouldn't mind a full-body rubdown. All the tension he had managed to work out of her neck returned. She shook her head. *Stop overthinking, girl.* She focused on eating her hamburger.

"Okay." He was back. "I have an outdoor tub."

"A hot tub?" Oh, that would be perfect.

"No, just a tub. A really big tub. It's hot as long as you fill it with hot water, but no bubble jets. I'm here all night, so if you want, you can go over and use it."

"Are you serious?" Ramona's eyes felt as if they were large saucers as she eagerly looked at Bobby. A tub! A bath!

"Yeah." He chuckled. "Look, my dogs will be out, but they won't bother you. Just tell them to shut up, use their names so they think they know you." He picked up the pencil she had been marking papers with, tore off a sheet from his order book, and scribbled down his address.

"I'm out on East 2280, dented white mailbox just past a red cattle gate. Una is the big brown hound. Deuce looks like a white pit. Tre is the gray mutt. They are all bark. Like I said, use their names tell them to shut up, and they will calm down. Tre might jump a bit, but they're harmless."

Ramona took the scribbled address. "Your dogs are named one, two, three?"

"And the cat is Cat." He smiled, a charming half grin that pulled up his lips to one side.

"Seriously? Thank you." Ramona placed her hands palms out as if to stop herself. "I'm going to finish this, then go reward myself with a bath."

"Remember to drain the tub. I don't want the dogs trying to drink bubble-bath water."

"Oh absolutely." Ramona's spirits were soaring. A bath and it hadn't been a come-on. Bobby was going to be at work all night.

Bobby returned to working as more people started coming into the bar. Ramona forced herself to focus and continue grading while she finished her food.

Ramona packed up the completed grading and left cash on the table covering her food and a generous tip. This evening overtipping was required—a bath.

"You overtipped me again," Bobby said as he cleaned off the table while she packed.

"That's for the tub. Thanks." Without thinking Ramona leaned in and gave Bobby a quick kiss on the cheek. Electricity zapped through her body as her lips touched his skin, and she realized what she was doing. Embarrassed, she quickly mumbled a "bye" and rushed out of the bar.

Ramona repeated, "I can't believe I kissed him," to herself over and over as she drove home, put away her grading, and grabbed a few towels. She had an unused bottle of bubble bath from a gift basket from one of her students this past Christmas. She rummaged in her hall closet, finding the bottle.

The mantra of embarrassment was replaced with joy at the prospect of a bathtub.

Ramona drove out of town and found the white mailbox past a red cattle gate, just as Bobby had described. She pulled over and got out of her car. The property had a long driveway behind a gate. After closing the gate, she drove up to the small house. It looked like a cabin with a stone chimney and an extended porch that seemed to wrap around the side and to the back, away from the drive. Three dogs raced around the side of the house barking. She leaned out her car window and told them to shut up. As soon as she said their names, the barking stopped and the tail wagging began.

Ramona got out of the car. The dogs' tails whipped frantically back and forth. She thought their bodies were going to wiggle in half, they were wagging so excitedly. She petted each one and used their names again. Bobby hadn't said where the tub was, just that it was outside. She walked around the side of the house and to the back.

The view from his back porch was breathtaking. Rolling green hills with patches of bluebonnets and red paintbrush extended out toward the horizon. The sun was just about to set, the colors lighting everything on fire.

Once she was able to break away from the view, she found the tub. It was large, brown copper with white enamel lining, clearly a luxury model. The back and sides were tall, allowing for deep water. She would be able to submerge completely. Not only was there a huge freestanding tub, but an outdoor waterfall shower tucked behind a bamboo wall.

She twirled the taps to begin filling the tub with hot water. The space design was functional, yet it was beautiful in its stark simplicity. A side table sat next to the head of the tub. Stand-alone towel racks were next to the bamboo wall.

On the other side of the wall, two wooden Adirondack chairs with footstools were positioned facing out toward the view. Ramona nosed around as the tub filled. The outside bathroom wasn't complete; it did not have a toilet.

She tried the door; it was unlocked. The interior of Bobby's home caught Ramona off guard. The stark simplicity of his outdoor furnishings continued to the interior. The space was small, but it felt large with the open floor plan. There was a large-screen TV and shelves with movies and video games. The blue couch and the matching side chair looked like hand-me-downs, a bit worn. But everything was tidy. Just to the left was the kitchen. Not big but well planned. Ramona noticed there were no cabinets. Instead open shelves lined the walls, and the tile counters were over open wood stands. There were no drawers. Instead the lower shelves were lined with baskets. A few dishes sat in the sink, but mostly everything was clean and organized. She turned the other direction, peering into an open room—Bobby's bedroom.

Ramona paused. It wasn't what she'd expected. Of course she realized she didn't know what she had expected. She hadn't really given Bobby's bedroom much thought. It didn't look much like the suave seduction palace she would have thought it to be. The room wasn't large, and the bed was actually small, just a double. The headboard was polished oak. It matched the side table and the single dresser. The style made Ramona think this was probably the furniture he'd had as a kid. Not an extravagant bedroom set, but a set bought with the intent of providing quality furniture that would last. The walls were a dark taupe, and his sheets forest green. A large picture window let in the view she'd admired from the porch.

She finally found the bathroom. It was larger than she'd expected. It was nothing fancy, but there was room to move. A standard single sink on a wide tile counter similar to the wood stands in the kitchen took up one wall. The towel rods were industrial piping. A large walk-in shower with a bench, and most importantly for her needs of the moment, a toilet.

Outside, Ramona sat and admired the sunset as she waited for the tub to finish filling. She felt a little nervous stripping on Bobby's back porch, but there was no one for miles, and the dogs didn't seem to notice or care. After the initial excitement of her arrival they lay down in the dirt just off the decking of the porch.

The water felt perfect as she dipped one toe in. She sank into the depths and felt her muscles melt. She could get used to this life. Everything was a little less complicated in Haven compared to Dallas. Now if she could just settle into a routine, maybe she might find this was the right space for her to belong in.

She let her eyes close and reminded herself to not fall asleep in the warm of the water.

Ramona needed to thank Bobby. She wanted to thank him for the help with reframing algebra for her students. The concept of making things more relatable was really working. Not that zombies would ever be applicable in the real world, but the students certainly grasped the concepts. She also wanted to thank him for use of the tub, and to be honest, see if it would be okay for her to use it again.

His smile was warm and friendly when he said of course. She was welcome to use the tub at any time. His schedule at the bar was pretty stable, so if she knew he was there, no reason for her to not make use of the tub.

Ramona took this as permission to be in the tub every chance she could. She realized she was spending too much time eating and just hanging out at Ray's when she actually knew his schedule and only had to confirm it a few times. She did this by driving by the bar. If she saw Bobby's car, the matte black Charger, in the parking lot, she would continue over to his house and soak in the depths of the tub.

After the second time in the tub she left him homemade cookies as a thank-you. With every visit she felt the need to do something: she would finish the dishes in the sink, straighten the living room, leave home-baked treats. And she always made sure she cleaned the tub.

Ramona sighed contentedly as she slipped into water. She had given the dogs new rawhide bones and did the dishes while the tub filled.

She had purchased and brought an inflatable pillow to rest her head against. She closed her eyes and let the stress of the past few days soak out of her bones.

A low rumble approached behind her. Her eyes shot open as she realized it must be Bobby's car, though it sounded as if he'd gotten that muffler fixed. The dogs abandoned their chew toys to run and bark. Panic struck. She was stuck naked in the tub on his back porch. She tried to remember what day it was. It was Thursday. Bobby always closed the bar on Thursdays. The towel and her clothes were too far away; besides there wasn't time. Where could she hide? She felt like she had been caught doing something she shouldn't be, even though Bobby had said she could use the tub. The car parked and the engine stopped. She could hear him telling the dogs to shut up.

She sank as far down into the water as she possibly could.

"Hey, Ramona!" he called out.

"Hey, Bobby." Her voice cracked. "I, ah, sorry, I thought you worked today. Um, I can leave, but..."

"You're fine. The schedule changed. Didn't even think to tell you last time you came by." She could hear a chuckle in his voice. "I can't see you from here. Stick your head up a bit."

"Hi." She dragged the word out as she peeped over the edge of the tub. Bobby was standing on the other side of the bamboo separating wall, his head turned to the side.

"Hi." He smiled when they made eye contact.

That smile, while she was naked, felt sinful. She ducked back down a bit farther.

"I'm not gonna peek. So you can stay in there as long as you want. I have cold beer over here, so you just tell me when you are going to get out and I will go hide or close my eyes or something."

"You won't look?"

"Promise."

Ramona felt a little disappointed that he didn't even tease or flirt about peeking.

"I'm gonna sit here and watch the sunset."

She heard him pop the cap from his beer and sit.

"Hey, you got the dogs new bones."

"Yeah."

"You don't have to do that."

"It's nothing. You let me use this tub. I've become addicted to watching sunsets from in here," Ramona admitted. "It's just a little thank-you."

"I'm glad it's getting use. I put it in for just that reason. Then I took on more nights. I'm glad someone is enjoying it."

They sat in silence watching the fading sun.

Ramona stretched. She needed to get out of the tub, but Bobby was right there. Okay, he was on the other side of the dividing wall, but he was right there. If she told him to go inside, he might look out a window. This felt like a trap.

"Hey, Bobby."

"You ready to get out?"

"Yeah, and ah..." She bit her lip, thinking of a strategy.

"I can close my eyes or take the dogs for a walk up to the road. It's on the other side of the house. I won't be able to see you. I'll whistle so you can hear that I actually am not hiding to take a gander at you, okay?"

"Would you really?"

"Yep." He whistled sharply to the dogs as he stood up. Ramona could hear him whistle a simple, unidentifiable melody as he walked away. The dogs barked and ran off around the side of the house.

Ramona moved quickly. She toweled off and damply slipped into her discarded clothes.

She rubbed the towel over her hair as she walked around the side of the house so she could see Bobby. He and the dogs were about a third of the way up the drive. He paused to throw a stick. She admired the smooth, fluid motion with which he moved. The dogs playfully ran and fought for the prize. He continued up the driveway.

She took in his long limbs as he moved. She sighed. Having a crush on Bobby Cray was not the smartest thing to do. Of course it didn't help that he was being nice. She thought about that—he wasn't acting nice, he was nice. It was in his nature. And so was sleeping with any woman who threw herself at him. No, crushing was not a good idea.

"I'm out!" she yelled, waving her hand over her head, letting him know it was safe to return.

Ramona perched on the front one of the chairs, working a brush through her hair. A fat tabby rubbed against her ankle. "You must be Cat. Nice to finally meet you."

"Here." Bobby handed her an open beer. She looked at the beer in one hand and the brush in the other, realizing that she was going to have to put one of them down. Brushing her hair was definitely a two-handed job.

Bobby pulled the brush from her. "Move." He indicated for her to sit on the footstool instead.

He sat behind her and slowly worked the brush through the ends of her hair. He sectioned her thick hair off and began working on just one area.

Ramona couldn't help it. A moan escaped her lips. Having someone else brush her hair felt delightful, almost as good as having someone else wash her hair. She took a drink of the beer and closed her eyes, reveling in the sensation. "Where did you learn to brush hair?"

"Years ago. Mom had thick blonde hair down her back." His voice was wistful as he recalled something long ago and far away. "She broke her arm one year, and I had hair-brushing duty. She taught me how to start at the bottom and work my way up, and not to pull." Bobby worked the brush through Ramona's hair, pushing finished sections in front of her shoulders.

"You were clearly a good student." She hummed in appreciation.

"And I do brush my own hair. I'm pretty good at braiding too. You want?"

"Sure, why not." This was unreal. Here she was on Bobby's deck, drinking beer, admiring the evening, and getting her hair brushed and braided. *I shouldn't allow myself to get used to this.*

"Crap." She heard the rumble of a car engine approach the house, and the dogs started running and barking. Caught in the tub again. She'd forgotten about the change to Bobby's Thursday schedule.

"Hey, Ramona!" Bobby called as he got out of his car. She sank down in the tub.

"Hi, Bobby. I'm sorry I forgot your schedule changed."

"Don't worry about it." She heard him go into the house through the kitchen door. He made a few trips back and forth. *Must be unloading groceries.*

"I got you some Cherry Coke to keep in the fridge," he called from the car. "They are yours whenever you're here."

"Seriously? Thanks."

"I also got something else for you." His voice was closer. He had moved out to the back deck.

"Here, my eyes are closed."

Ramona turned to look at him. He stood just past the bamboo wall, holding what appeared to be a large, pale blue, fluffy towel.

"Oh wow, thanks," she said unenthusiastically. "I've got plenty of towels."

"It's not a towel." Bobby let the soft fabric fall as he held up a thick bathrobe. His eyes were still closed. "I'm not looking, I promise." He turned around and walked into the tub space backward. He sidestepped to the towel rack and draped the robe across the top. "Now you don't have to get dressed so fast while you're still wet."

"You didn't have to do that. That's really nice."

Bobby stepped out of the tub area and behind the bamboo wall.

"I figured you wouldn't wear mine if I offered it. One caveat, you have to leave it here. That's your tub robe."

Ramona sat in front of Bobby, watching the sunset. She

was wrapped in the blue robe he had given her, and he was brushing her hair. This was becoming entirely too comfortable. It was becoming a habit, Thursday tub and conversation, then letting Bobby brush her hair while she was wrapped in nothing but a robe. He was always a perfect gentleman, never made an advance or untoward comments. Ramona appreciated that. She really didn't want to become a conquest. She knew he didn't do relationships. She should skip coming next week, but she was a junkie, she knew it. She lived for that soak, especially now that the end of the year was quickly approaching. Students were getting antsy, their focus gone. Could she really forgo the tub? No. She would just show up when she knew he would be at work. The brush caressed her scalp. Ramona stifled a moan. It wasn't just the tub she was addicted to. She decided to skip the hair brushing next week, but not the tub.

6

The door to the bar swung open. No big deal. So why did it catch Bobby's attention today? Maybe a change in the light. He didn't know. All he knew was he looked up and the woman walking in glowed. A radiant light surrounded her. More than that, she looked like an angel.

How had he not seen it before? Her hair was a bit disheveled, not unusual after a long day at school for her. She wore her typical style of dress with the flowers. Her heavy book bag hung from her shoulder.

Ramona had walked into his bar before, and she never caught his attention this way. She never radiated light this way.

How had he not noticed before? Was she an angel?

The glass in his hand slipped from his grip.

He registered the sound of the crash but didn't move until Chareese shrieked. "Oh my God, Bobby, what the hell? You dropped my drink."

Bobby felt muzzy-headed. He blinked a few times. The door behind Ramona swung closed. The radiance did not diminish. The glow around her pulsed in time to his heartbeat.

He shook his head and looked at the floor. When had he dropped that?

"Oh hey, sorry about that. Glass was slippery. Let me get you a new one and clean this up." He ignored the rest of Chareese's bitchy commentary and bent over to pick up the larger chunks of glass.

He felt like a zombie, moving with staggering, jilted steps. Angel. The light had caught the dust in the air and fanned out around her like a blaze of wings. No, Bobby, hell, that was just the light coming in the door. He had always thought she was pretty. He shook his head, trying to clear the image of radiance and beauty that he had never recognized in Ramona before.

The small grin on her face seemed more like her typical resting expression. Ramona did not have "resting bitch face." She had a pleasant expression when her face held no emotion. She didn't look any happier than any other day she'd come in here to work.

Hell, maybe she was knocked up. After all, pregnant woman were supposed to glow. Bobby shook his head. No, between Melissa and Abby he'd been around enough pregnant women to know that glowing was just an expression and not an actual thing. But that did make him realize, Bobby had no idea if there was a special person in Ramona's life. He would like to think that because she took baths at his place and allowed him to brush her hair, there wasn't. He needed to know for certain.

He needed to know everything about her, and that need hit him with a rush and a wallop. Bobby ran his sleeve across his forehead, suddenly beaded with sweat. He asked

Jenna to make another mojito for table eight, and he returned with the mop bucket.

"So, Bobby, you have plans for tonight?" Chareese's voice felt scratchy to his ears. She must have broken up with her most recent boyfriend if she was leading in with the fastest pickup line in town.

Bobby swept the glass fragments into a dustpan.

"No, Chareese, I don't. And I think I'm gonna keep it that way."

"Oh," she pouted. "Are you already booked?"

Bobby sighed. Right now being the easiest lay in town felt like a chore he should have taken care of years ago. He ran the mop over the floor under her chair. "Yeah, Chareese, I'm booked. Thanks, Jenna," he said as the waitress placed the newly made drink in front of the blonde.

Bobby took a hard look at her, nodded, then pushed the bucket back to the utility closet. He had just turned down thirty-eight double Ds, a thirty-two inch middle, and miles of long, slender legs. Chareese loved to dress up in see-through and lacy things, and she wasn't a bad package to unwrap, having unwrapped her a few times in the past.

What the hell had he been doing with someone like her? Had they ever actually had a conversation? She only wanted him for his body and, well, his dick.

No, he didn't need that right now, not tonight, not ever again.

He washed his hands and dried them on a few paper towels.

"Hey, Ramona." Why did his own voice sound like it had a nervous quaver to it?

She smiled, and that body part Chareese was interested in throbbed. He never throbbed around women—well at least not anymore. Hell, Ramona still glowed, and she was astounding.

Her eyes were his favorite shade of green. No, blue was his favorite color. He was letting this whole angel thing run amok with his brain. He slid into the booth opposite of her.

"How was your day?"

"Oh, it was pretty standard. You know, nothing went as planned. The principal came in with someone from the county, and they did observations. I wasn't prepared. The students went a little nuts."

"You still doing the math with zombies?" he asked.

"It's working really well too. Now I'm having them calculate what it's going to cost to stock up a bunker. They are given a supply list with prices, and"—she pulled a handout from her bag and slid it across to Bobby—"they are told what they would need for an average day, and then they have to calculate how much of everything they need for a year. They also have to calculate the costs associated with it, and how long it will take them to stock up on supplies based on randomly assigned jobs."

Bobby laughed. That sounded like real-life math. Except he wasn't stocking up a survivalist bunker, he was saving to complete the build-out on his own house, complete the buyout on the bar, and pay for the new AC system he knew was going to need to be installed next year. That was the kind of math he could have used in high school. "Now that's math they can use."

"Yeah, but you should have seen the look on Dr. G's face," she sighed. "He's going to come talk to me tomorrow, I can just tell. I kind of wish he would let me teach and not worry about all the other crap. I don't know. I still need to keep everyone focused and not have class dissolve into whose house, or which warehouse, or if the school would be the best safe-hold. I hate to say it, but I'm not teaching the best or the brightest."

"No, but you are making a difference. Even if you only get through to one or two of them, this will make a huge difference in their ability to function out in the real world. You're doing good. RavenCroft is lucky to have you."

"Thanks, sometimes I wonder." She looked over her shoulders, right then left, before leaning across the table to whisper. "Dr. Grover seems pretty paranoid about what I do with my life outside of school, and—"

"Grover is your principal?" Bobby rubbed a hand over his eyes. He shook his head. "He taught social studies when I was in school. Heard he worked his way up to vice principal over at Central. You sound like you need a little lift in your Cherry Coke." He smiled. He could tell by the way she rubbed at her neck that she needed a massage. Grover was lucky to have a teacher so caring about her students. Those kids were going to actually learn math because of her, and having been that kid in that class, he knew too darned well how easy it was for the teachers to just give up on the students who were having problems.

"Yeah." She sounded defeated. Ramona took a deep breath. "His actions don't speak well of extending my contract to next year."

"You don't plan on going back to Dallas when school's over?" He didn't want her to leave Haven.

Ramona shook her head. "I'm still contracted for summer school. I moved here to try something new. The people here are really sweet, and so far I really like this town. Going back to Dallas next school year will be a defeat."

Bobby leaned back. "You don't have to worry about

Grover. He is always overly concerned about everyone else's business, but he never actually does anything."

She nodded. "Can I get a BLT, extra B, hold the T?"

"Piled high, with cheese and extra mayo?"

The smile she gave Bobby was subtle, but there was a new sparkle in her eyes that made Bobby catch his breath. He wanted to touch her, to hold her, to rub the stress he saw out of her shoulders. He wanted to take care of her. What the hell was going on?

She catches some random ray of light walking into the bar and all of a sudden you want to give her flowers. Maybe he should go bang Chareese. Maybe he was getting sick.

He slid back out of the booth to go make Ramona's sandwich. So if it was the sun catching dust motes that caused her to look like she had wings, how did he explain to himself that she still glowed?

He placed the BLT, extra B, hold the L and the T, with cheese, grilled, extra mayo and a side of pickles in front of her. "This has a little extra boost to it," he said as he set the large drink next to the sandwich. "And this should help keep you focused while you grade," he said, putting an ice cream brownie sundae down.

She sat up and squirmed a little straighter. Had he even noticed that she had boobs like that before? Perfectly round, with a bit of bounce. Christ, he felt like he was fourteen and just realizing that girls were shaped amazingly different. Of course he'd known Ramona had breasts before. She was a woman. They tended to come with them.

"When did you add this to the menu?" Ramona's large eyes were bright and happy as she took in the chocolate concoction in front of her.

"It's not on the menu. It's special order only, and only if I feel like it. You looked like you could use a little extra."

She turned her sparkling eyes to him. "Thank you."

Her pink tongue peeked out from behind her teeth.

He suppressed a groan and felt a pull in his gut. He held his breath and let it out slowly. "When you're done here, I want you to go use the tub. Get a good long soak in. I'll be here late."

"Hey, Bobby, is she what you're up to later?" The voice was sharp and piercing.

He cringed. Chareese sounded like she'd already had one too many. He had better go check on her, make sure she wasn't popping some pills in his bar and washing them down with the mojitos.

"I'll check back on you in a few." He didn't want to leave Ramona's side, but he still had a bar to run, still had customers to keep happy. But he couldn't take his eyes from Ramona and found that she distracted him from every task he attempted.

Women had been a major distraction in Bobby's life ever since he could remember. But never one like this, never one who he could be happy just to be near. Was this what Brad had been talking about, being friends first? He knew what that mass of black hair felt like under his fingers. What did the rest of her feel like?

Bobby felt a pang of emptiness in his chest. Ramona hadn't walked into Ray's yet this evening. If she wasn't here by now, she probably wasn't coming. He wondered if she was at his place, puttering around in his house, waiting for the tub to fill. He liked that thought. He could picture Ramona soaking in his tub. Her golden-cream skin would be slick with water. Bubbles would be strategically piled to hide her buoyant breasts from his view. They were always hidden from view; he looked every chance he got.

He almost felt as if he could be content with brushing her hair for the rest of his life. His chest tightened. His groin throbbed. Who was he trying to fool? Yes, he could brush her hair forever, but he wanted so much more. Did she have any idea how much he wanted to touch her, hold her?

He tried not to picture her lips as she smiled. Damn, just thinking about her was making it hard to breathe. When had any woman gotten under his skin so completely?

"Jenna, I'm headed out. You got this tonight?" he asked as he rang open the till and gave it a quick, cursory count.

"Yeah, there's no reason for you to hang around if you have something better to do."

He definitely had something better to do.

He pulled a few of the larger bills. In the back office he swapped them out for more change. He wanted to get out of here, but he wasn't about to leave Jenna and Rob up a creek without a paddle.

He felt like a grinning idiot when he saw Ramona's ridiculously small red car parked next to his house. The dogs were so content around her they barely lifted their heads to acknowledge his arrival home. He understood. Being near her made everything right.

He stopped just beyond her line of sight. Her arm languidly rose up from the tub as she sluiced water over it with a washcloth. What he wouldn't give to bathe her. To be the one running the washcloth over her skin.

He breathed deeply—he could smell her, or rather he could smell the bubble-bath scent, which he associated with her. Honey and roses.

With his next step, he had every intention of walking up

to her and pulling her from the tub. He wanted to lift her into his arms and claim her lips and then her body.

He couldn't move. He didn't have a clue how to seduce her properly. He didn't want to seduce her for only one night. He wanted her to fall in love with him.

Panic. He couldn't do it. Bobby banged into the kitchen and grabbed a beer. He flipped the twist top off and downed the cold amber liquid in a few gulps. His woman was out in that stupid tub, the one he'd put in to share with someone. The tub no one else even knew about. He let out a silent laugh. Ramona wasn't his, she was her own woman, but he was definitely hers. That tub was big enough for both of them, and he wanted nothing more than to slide in with her and watch the sunset with her in his arms.

He grabbed another beer, toed off his boots, and stepped outside. He twisted the cap off and took a long pull.

Hi, Angel, mind if I join you? The words were so clear in his head, but nothing came out of his mouth.

He slid his hand into the water and down her spine.

Ramona let out a small gasp.

God, her skin was so soft. It took no effort to slip her forward. Without a word Bobby climbed into the tub behind her. He sighed and leaned back. His denim-clad legs wrapped around her sides, he rested his ankles on the edges of the tub. He silently pulled her shoulder back to lean against him.

She was warm and perfect against his chest. He rested his arms on the sides of the tub and took another long pull of his beer.

His woman, his house, his land. Yes, this was what it was all about. Ramona liked her tub water a little on the hot side. The breeze coming in from the west felt cool in comparison.

He couldn't seem to move his arms to wrap around her and hold her. At first her body was still, then she sighed and nestled against him.

What the fuck was he doing? She deserved so much better from him. She deserved a proper long-game courtship.

He mumbled, "I'm sorry," pushed her forward, got out of the tub, and slogged his way into the house.

He stood in the kitchen, dripping, staring into the open refrigerator as if it held some mysterious oracle that had answers for him.

"Bobby? You okay?"

"I'm sorry. The tub, you, it looked like it would feel good. Be relaxing." He couldn't face her. "You're my friend, right?"

"Yeah?" Ramona sounded concerned.

"That was inexcusable." Bobby turned to face her. Wrapped in her fluffy blue towel, surrounded by that mysterious light, he saw his future. His chest tightened. "I shouldn't have done that."

Ramona nodded. "I'm gonna change and go. You need me to not come back. I understand."

He couldn't move. Her words felt like a knife in his gut. He wanted her to come back as often as she liked. He wanted her to stay. Ramona turned to get her clothes. When she came back into the house to change in the bathroom, Bobby was still in the kitchen. He didn't know how to fix what he had just messed up.

"Ramona, you're still welcome to use the tub whenever you want. Okay? That won't happen again. My word on it."

"Okay, Bobby, thank you." She was blushing.

What had he done?

She mumbled a quick "bye" as she obviously ran away.

7

The phone rang. Ramona slid it out of the back pocket of her shorts. "Hello?"

"Hey, Ramona, it's Bobby."

She almost dropped the bag of groceries she carried from the car.

"Bobby? Um, hi." Butterflies twirled in a spiral in her stomach. Why was Bobby Cray calling? She hadn't seen him since the tub incident on Tuesday, and she still wasn't certain what she felt about the whole thing. Did she feel violated that he'd climbed into the tub with her, even if he only touched her back? It was still an invasion of her space while she was naked. Or did she feel rejected because he hadn't touched her at all and she was naked? Bobby was beginning to confuse her brain. She was attracted to him, she could admit that. After all, there was no denying he was extremely gorgeous. But his reputation skeeved her out. He had already slept with one of her friends. And Debbie was not shy about sharing just how skilled he was at delivering the big O.

"Look, Ramona, I owe you a huge apology for the other

day. And I want to ask you something. Can I buy you lunch today? I've made reservations at Cavenaugh's. Can I pick you up at twelve thirty?"

Cavenaugh's was the premier elite restaurant in town. The waiters wore tuxedos for the dinner service, Valentine's Day reservations were made at least a year in advance, same for other big occasions. Last week hundreds of teens celebrated their graduation dinners at Cavenaugh's. Those reservations had been made by their parents when the kid entered the eleventh grade. Cavenaugh's was a restaurant for wedding proposals or major business deals. Clearly a weekday lunch, not around a holiday, would be easier to get in, but still. Ramona was floored.

"Cavenaugh's, that's pretty swank."

"I'm really sorry." Bobby emphasized the *really*.

"Um, okay, sure. I just got home from the IGA, so that's just enough time to get ready. You know where I live?"

"Up the street from Mrs. C, but not beyond that."

Ramona described the row of single-story apartments about half a block up. She was the third unit in from the right.

Her doorbell rang. She had just finished a quick shower and had put on a red dress with a black floral pattern. It was one she did not wear to school, saving it for more formal occasions. Cavenaugh's indicated this was indeed a more formal occasion. Ramona opened the door.

Standing just in front of the stoop was Bobby. She swallowed hard. All moisture left her mouth and headed south between her thighs. Bobby Cray looked fine in the jeans and the tight T-shirts he seemed to live in, but Bobby Cray in a suit and tie was a vision. Stylistically the suit was a few years out of date, a little long in the jacket, a little full in the pants, but it was tailored to his form. The suit was dark blue and framed his shoulders, the jacket was unbuttoned, but she could tell when it was buttoned it would emphasize his slim hips. The stark white of the shirt showed off his natural tanned skin. The gold power tie wrapped him up like a bow on a present.

He held up a bouquet of mixed flowers. "I am so sorry, Ramona. I overstepped boundaries."

She waved him inside, taking the flowers. "These are lovely. Let me put them in a vase."

Bobby hovered around the front entry. "I confess I have an additional motive for taking you to lunch. I have a little business proposition to ask you about."

"A business proposition? Now I'm curious."

"You'll have to wait until we get to the restaurant."

Ramona slid her eyes sideways at him. "All right, I guess."

"Have you forgiven me about Tuesday?"

"You'll have to wait until we get to the restaurant," she mocked as she walked past him and out to his car.

Bobby chuckled. "Fair enough." He closed her door.

They rode in silence to the restaurant. Ramona was too nervous to really think of anything to say. She was sitting in his car. What on earth did he mean by a business proposition?

The hostess sat them at a small, intimate table and handed them their menus.

"This place is fancier that I expected," Ramona whispered. "Have you been here before?"

"Once or twice, but it's been a long time."

Ramona nodded, letting her gaze wander around the room. She was glad he had told her where he was bringing her. Afternoon and the dress code was still formal, although the lunchtime waitstaff only wore black pants and stark white shirts with bow ties, and not complete tuxedos.

"So do you forgive me?"

"I'll tell you over dessert, so let's do lunch backward." Ramona grinned mischievously.

Bobby chuckled.

When the waiter arrived, Bobby informed him they would like to start with the dessert tray, then they would make their meal choices.

Ramona selected a decadent chocolate torte with raspberry sauce, and Bobby ordered the bread pudding with hard sauce. Her mouth began salivating when their selections were delivered. She moaned in guilty pleasure after she closed her mouth around the first forkful of chocolate.

Bobby cocked an eyebrow at her response to tasting the dessert.

"So, do you forgive me now?"

Ramona eyed the bowl in front of him, drawn forward by the rich aroma. "Can I have a bite of yours?" she practically pleaded.

"Of course."

Her eyes closed in pleasure as she took a bite of the warm bread pudding. "Hmmm, yes, Bobby, I forgive you." She sighed, contented from the sugary goodness.

Ramona continued to make happy little moans as she ate the dessert. "So good," she repeated.

"So tell me about this proposition. It's not dirty or anything?"

"Dirty? After that show you just gave eating dessert?"

"What? I was enjoying it."

"I could tell." He chuckled. "I don't think I have ever seen you eat anything that enthusiastically before."

"Bacon is not chocolate."

"I will keep that in mind."

The waiter arrived to remove their plates and take their meal order.

"We are friends, right?"

"I like to think so," she answered, uncertain where he was headed.

"Clearly I have issues with what's appropriate among friends—Tuesday, for instance. And since you're a teacher, I was hoping you could help me out."

"How so?" Intrigued, she took a sip of water.

"I want you to teach me how to be a friend. Brad said the key to a successful long relationship is being friends first. I don't think I know how to do that. I don't know how to be a friend with women. I know how to sleep with them but not be a friend. I always mess it up somehow."

"So you're asking me to be your friend tutor?"

"Yeah, you see, someday I'm going to want to settle down. Meet a woman, get married, have kids. But I just have no idea how to get started. And I thought you could show me how."

Ramona was instantly torn. Part of her heart felt deflated. He would never see her as a woman to be romantically interested in, and that hurt, even though she knew she shouldn't even want him to think of her that way. Part of her was angry—how dare he ask her to help him be a better man for another woman. And part of her was up for the challenge of teaching Bobby the Slut Man Cray how to be a better human.

She stared at him through squinting eyes, rubbing her hand across her jaw in concentration.

The waiter delivered their meals. She still stared at Bobby, thinking.

"You want me to help you learn how to be a friend, so at

some point in the future you can be a better man for another woman?"

He winced and then nodded.

"I'll do it. But this means you have to listen to me, and I might even give you homework."

"Really?"

"Hell, why not? Bobby, I think that is the weirdest thing anyone has ever asked me to tutor them in."

He held up his glass to her. She clinked hers against it in toast to their new venture.

"Step one to being a friend: don't climb into a bathtub uninvited."

"Yes, ma'am."

"Step two: don't call me ma'am."

8

B obby never felt like working whenever Ramona was around. And she was around a lot these days. He wasn't complaining. After all, he was the one sitting down in her booth every chance he got. She still glowed with some aura of white light.

He wasn't convinced that she wasn't an angel; she sure looked like one. He never got tired of staring into her eyes. He was pretty certain she was human. At least he hoped so every time he found himself staring at those lips. The perfect shade of kissable pink. Maybe she was an angel sent here to put up with him.

At least he hoped she would put up with him.

He wasn't convinced that his idea for friendship tutoring wasn't completely harebrained. It did give him an excuse to take her out, with no pressure. Their non-date night had been entertaining. He did not pick her up at her apartment. He did not offer to pay for dinner. He did offer to cover the popcorn and candy if Ramona paid for the tickets. He spent most of his time trying to remember how to act on a date so that Ramona would have an opportunity to correct him.

About halfway through the movie Bobby reminded himself not to yawn and stretch and put an arm around her. It may have been a typical middle-school-level maneuver, but he felt like a kid around her. She messed with his sense of reason; she made him feel like he should be staring at his shoes, kicking the dirt, and saying things like *gee, shucks*. She also made him want to peel her clothes off with his teeth.

He coughed and adjusted himself before his jeans got too tight.

She munched on fries and graded papers. Her summer school students didn't seem to frustrate her as much as the group she had before the school year ended. She seemed to dance and hum as she worked. Did she know that she danced when she was happy? Could he take her dancing and still have it be a friends thing? Probably not, especially since he wanted to hold her close and dance slow. He didn't even know if this town had dancing.

The doors to the bar swung open. His attention reluctantly left Ramona. Brad stood inside, scanning the room.

"Hey, Bradley," Bobby called out.

His brother's head pivoted toward him, and the rest of his body followed in a rushed stalking motion.

"We need to talk," Brad practically growled.

That didn't sound good. Brad wasn't the type who would leave work to have a minor confab with his brother unless it was something serious.

"Yeah, sure. Is everything okay?"

Brad cut his eyes toward Ramona and then back to Bobby.

He understood. Whatever this was, it was personal. He scooted out from the booth. "I'll come back and check on you in a bit, okay?"

She nodded.

He led the way back into the office. As they passed through the kitchen, he paused to ask Rob to keep an eye on the front.

Brad stalked into the small office and instantly began pacing before Bobby had a chance to close the door. He thrust a wrinkled piece of paper out to Bobby.

"What's this?" Bobby asked, taking what looked like an official letter from Brad.

"Remember when Melissa had me redo that stupid DNA test? Well, turns out they offered to cover everyone I was related to"—he stabbed his finger into the middle of the letter Bobby held—"concerning a genetic anomaly and a link to genetic relatives. Apparently I share some DNA with Pete that they would like to meet with me in person about."

Bobby sat down slowly. What genetic anomaly? "Of course you share DNA with Petey. He's your kid. Has Melissa seen this?"

"Hell no! She would be a crying mess if she had seen it first."

Bobby scanned the letter. "Non-life-threatening, onset with puberty, the girls don't have it." He shook his head and looked up at his brother.

"Melissa didn't tell me they offered to test all my immediate blood relatives. And I didn't ever see the last letter these people sent to her." Brad continued to pace back and forth. His cage was rattled fairly hard over this.

"So Melissa had the kids do the spit test, and you redid yours, but she didn't tell them about me. You think this is about my, ah, gift?" Holy crap, what if his special talent was trackable? Brad didn't have it. He couldn't shift. "What are you going to do?"

"What if it is your gift? Does this mean Petey is going to

be able to do what you can? How the hell do I tell Melissa? She'll divorce me and take the kids. I'll never see my girls again. Bobby, I won't survive if she leaves me."

"Whoa, Brad, hold on. Melissa isn't going to leave you. And nothing in this letter says it's referring to shifting. Maybe it's some weird-ass genetic thing that makes your dick curve off to the right like it does, and Pete isn't gonna know about having a funky penis until he wants to use it for something other than a security handle. Chill out for a minute."

Brad finally stopped pacing. He stood in the middle of the small space, breathing heavily.

Bobby read over the letter again. *DNA anomaly not recorded for the girls.* Okay, maybe this meant it was a male-only thing. *Onset with puberty.* Yeah, that was a little too close to home. *The medical industry is not currently aware of this set of data. Recommends not consulting with a physician.* Oh yeah, that definitely sounded like his shifter skill. *Were there more blood relatives that were not tested?*

He held the letter back out to his brother. "Look, there is a phone number and an e-mail. Why don't you get in contact with them? See what this is all about. And then tell Melissa. I know how you are about not keeping secrets from her or lying. But maybe keeping this one on the down low would be best for her sanity. At least until you know what it is."

Brad huffed. "What am I supposed to tell her if these people show up?"

"Why not tell her you were contacted by a genetic relative. Tell her you sent an e-mail and are waiting to hear back. That's not a lie. You just don't have to tell her about Petey having something in his DNA." Bobby stood.

"But it's gonna affect Pete, what if it's something serious?"

"The letter said non-life-threatening. Look, I don't remember if you were in the room or not. But after Mom left, Dad said something about it must have skipped a couple generations. He said he couldn't do it, and figured it had to have been some old story his granddad had told him, and he didn't think it was real. You couldn't do it, and then one day, there I was, shaking into a different skin. With fur. Maybe it didn't really skip you? But it's not switched on in you. I don't know."

Brad started pacing again. "We can't tell Melissa."

Bobby shook his head.

"Shit, I have to get back to work." Brad yanked the office door open.

Bobby followed him out through the kitchen. He slapped Brad on the back of his shoulder. "Give the kids a big hug from me. I'll be over in a few days."

Brad pushed out through the door. Damn, what did that letter really mean? If it was about shifting, did this mean Petey was going to be able to turn into a wolf in ten years?

He shook his head. He needed to take the advice he had given his brother. Find out more before making any decisions.

He looked over at Ramona. If this went the way he hoped, he was going to have to tell her. He knew exactly how Brad felt. If Ramona couldn't handle him being able to shift, he would be gutted, completely gutted.

She looked up and smiled. He felt her smile in his chest. He nodded as she held up her empty glass.

He closed his eyes and sighed. She wasn't flirting. She wanted more drink. He smiled at her before heading back behind the bar. He asked Rob to drop another order of fries.

He didn't have to tell her anything just yet. When the time was right, he would know how to tell her. He didn't need to worry about it right now, not when she radiated light like that.

9

The cool darkness of Ray's felt good. The last hour of class had been miserable as the AC system at the school slowly died. And of course since it was summer school, there wasn't a full maintenance staff around to get it fixed. Opening windows hadn't helped, and there were no extra fans in the office. Running around after school in the heat going from store to store trying to track down a few fans for her classroom hadn't helped.

Why was every shop in this town out of fans? One big box store, one drugstore, and two hardware stores later, Ramona was now the proud owner of two completely unstylish, highly functional box fans.

Ramona piled her hair on top of her head and hoped a cool drink and Bobby's calming presence would even out her temperature and her mood. The heat always made her cranky. It didn't matter that she had grown up in it. It just got hotter every year anyway. Thanks, global warming.

Without paying any attention to anyone, Ramona went straight to her booth. She was a creature of habit, and this was her preferred spot. She was such a cliché. Not only had she become a regular at a bar, but she had her set spot too. Next thing she knew she would start spouting random facts that were completely wrong, but she would spout them with laughable authority.

Someone opened the emergency exit by the bar. The bright rectangle of light hit the corner of her eye, and she winced. It let in unwelcome light, and the steady thrum of a passing train. No one was allowed to use that door. It was called an emergency exit for a reason. Silhouetted against the glare was a young woman on the phone. Ramona scanned, looking for Bobby. How was he letting this happen?

A few feet away Bobby was preoccupied with a toddler sitting on the bar.

Was that Bobby's kid? Ramona felt the sudden flash of panic on her skin, followed by the cooling effect as the shock dissipated. She wasn't physically hot anymore.

Why hadn't he mentioned that he had a kid? It had to be his. The way he let the kid sit on the bar, the way he had all his focus on the toddler. The way they had the same color hair.

"Huh?" Ramona blinked and noticed Jenna in front of her. How long had she been waiting for an order. "Sorry, Coke, lots of ice."

"Hot out there today?" Jenna asked.

"Yeah, makes me wish I had a pool."

"That's why I'm headed out to the dam when I get outta here," Jenna said.

"Can you swim at the dam? I keep hearing everyone talk about it, but I've never been."

"Totally. You don't want to go to the top of the dam, but to the lower dam. It's the best swimming. Or you can wade if you don't swim. People hang out and float around.

The trees keep it nice and cool. There aren't any trees up at the top. There's more fishin' up there, but no good swimin'. No easy in and out of the water. You should go. You'd like it."

Once Jenna left, Ramona instantly forgot about how nice the dam sounded because the damn Bobby was playing with a toddler. Maybe it was his brother's kid. Hadn't she heard his brother saying something about kids?

She shook her head and closed her eyes against the stupid glare. Would that chick close the door already?

"Rough day?" Bobby's voice was soft and soothing, just as she had hoped it would be. It felt like fingers reaching up into her hair massaging her scalp.

Ramona didn't open her eyes. "Could you ask that person to close the back door? The glare hurts my brain."

Bobby huffed. "Abby was on the phone. She needed better reception. It's closed now."

No explanation as to who Abby was.

Ramona cracked open one eye. A tall iced drink waited in front of her. Beyond that Bobby sat in the booth. He had some sun pink on his cheeks and nose like he had been outside all day.

"You're sunburned," Ramona stated.

"Spent the morning up at the dam."

"Oh." So, maybe the woman with the toddler was who Bobby needed to learn how to be friends with. Maybe Ramona needed to be a bit more professional; after all Bobby was her trainee, not her crush. She adjusted so that she sat more upright and opened her eyes

"Jenna was just telling me about the dam. The lower dam sounds lovely. Is that where you went?"

Bobby nodded. "Tyler and I spent the morning picking up rocks and throwing them at the water."

"Sounds like the simple things in life can be quite satisfying," Ramona commented.

"They are when you're four."

So Tyler was the toddler hanging out on the bar. She wanted to bombard Bobby with questions. She wanted to know if that was his kid. What did it matter to her if Bobby had a kid? What did it matter? No, the question Ramona needed to focus on was why. Why did it matter?

She didn't want it to matter.

"I've never been."

"Oh, we need to fix that. Next time we go out, I'm taking you to the dam. We'll swim, drink beer, it'll be great."

Ramona did not want her stomach to flip at his smile, but it did. "You work nights, and I teach during the day."

"You forget, I control the schedule. Next weekend we're going to the dam."

"You pretty much do everything around here, don't you?" she asked.

"Well, yeah, that's what happens when you're the owner. You do everything." With those words he did that little tap with his fingers he did right before he got up to leave, and went back to work.

Ramona hadn't moved. She paused in her action, soda sucked halfway up her straw. At least she didn't choke on it.

Bobby owned the bar. That made so much more sense now. Why he was always here, why so many women were after him. He was tall, good-looking, and a successful restaurant owner. Why hadn't she clued in that he was more than just the manager?

She felt like an idiot. A hot, sweaty idiot.

She couldn't stay. She needed to hide under covers, or better yet, soak in some bubble bath.

She tossed three bucks on to the table and approached

Bobby at the bar. She gave the young woman who had been standing in the door a shy smile.

"Hey. Bobby, is the tub open?" She leaned over the bar to ask.

"Anytime you want, Ramona, anytime. Enjoy." His reply didn't really calm any of the stupid thoughts in her head. His girlfriend—mother of his child?—whomever Abby was, she didn't say anything. At least Ramona didn't have to worry about his girlfriend showing up. She was at the bar with Bobby.

~

She could tell by the width of the path and the lack of grass, this was a well-worn trail, traveled repeatedly for years. She followed Bobby, her eyes focused on his broad shoulders. He'd pulled his hair up into the sloppy top knot he always wore. His faded blue T-shirt showed dark in the middle of his back with sweat.

Ramona was feeling the humidity today as well. Her hair was braided down her back to keep it from absorbing the moisture and turning into a bush on her head. She couldn't wait to jump into the water. So far everything anyone had told her about the lower dam made it sound like paradise. She should have worn better shoes. No one had told her they would have to park along the side of the road and hike in.

The path followed downhill, while the land split and rose to form a cliff to one side and a canyon of boulders and scrub. The water was a trickle of a creek, not the river she was expecting.

"You said we can swim, right?" There really didn't look

like there was going to be enough water for anything. And she was getting hot.

A group of teenagers heading the opposite direction walked toward them with towels hung over shoulders and wet hair. They fought each other with long foam pool noodles until they reached Ramona and Bobby. Once they passed by, they were giggling and laughing again. The kids were wet; there was water somewhere.

She hitched the bag higher on her shoulder and kept walking.

Bobby turned back to her, the cooler in his grasp preventing him from rotating all the way. "You're gonna want to watch your step through here. It's less path, more rocks."

Bobby leaped with the grace and agility of a mountain goat. Ramona wasn't so graceful. Someone—cough cough, Bobby, cough cough—really should have mentioned the shoes.

They followed a bend in the trail, and Ramona stopped.

"Oh." It was beautiful, and it felt as if the temperature had dropped ten degrees, maybe even fifteen.

The path opened onto a lush garden of swimming delights. The lower dam was roughly circular, with a tall, curved cliff wall along one side. A small waterfall cascaded into the pool. The water was clear and as blue as the sky. Ramona had only ever seen pictures of water this color from the Caribbean. She hadn't known it existed here in Texas. Of course the only natural swimming holes she had ever been to were always a dark muddy green color.

"Let's head over this way." Bobby moved away from the cliff wall and toward the lush green trees. Large flat rocks created islands in the water up to the edge, where live oaks provided relaxing shade.

They were clearly not the only people to have thought of this as a good escape from the heat today.

"This is good." Bobby sat the cooler down in a clearing that provided shade and a flat spot for Ramona to lay out the towels.

He whipped his shirt off over his head and wiped the sweat from his face.

Ramona froze. She could no longer function. Part of her brain had known that Bobby had to be well-built for his clothes to fit the way they did. She knew he had muscles to spare the way his arms and shoulders strained at tight T-shirts. She just never really put any thought into the way hair would snake up from his waistband and twirl around his belly button. Or how his abs would ripple and cast shadows over his golden tan skin. Her gaze could not leave his midtorso and scan up to take in the rest of him. Her eyes would not move so she could focus on his face as he said words. Incoherent words as she stared at his belly button.

She managed a noise, something like, "Uh-huh," in response to whatever Bobby had just said.

He tossed his shirt behind her, turned, and with a "Wahoo!" took a running jump into the water. Cool droplets sprayed in her face; she was able to function again. Barely.

All that skin. Those golden hairs, sun bleached. Her mouth went dry.

"Put the towels down and come on in!" Bobby called out to her.

Again, his physical appearance nailed her in place. He looked like some kind of god emerging from the water. Wet hair plastered down his head and over his shoulders, broad shoulders, naked chest, and again those perfect abs. Ramona forced herself to focus on his face, his smile, his lips. His tongue darted out and licked his lower lip. Maybe focusing on his mouth was a bad idea.

He stood there waiting for her. Watching her. She spun around and pretended to be fussing with something in the tote bag of towels. Self-consciousness over-came her like a steamroller. She wore a bikini under this oversized gray mess of a shirt. And the shorts she had on were not meant for getting wet. What would Bobby think as he saw her almost naked? Why had she worn such a small bathing suit?

Ramona took a deep breath and turned back to Bobby, pretending to pay particular attention to the removal of her flip-flops. She'd worn the small bathing suit because it was the only one she owned, and until five seconds ago she had never had a self-conscious moment in it. It actually covered her entire butt, not some tiny string bikini. And her breasts were fully contained in a halter-style top, no danger of side boob falling out. If she could wear the same bathing suit around Mami, who was as judgmental of a mother as they came, and Lorena, the older sister who thought she was Ramona's second mother, then she could wear the thing around Bobby.

She slid the shorts off first. Maybe she could claim fear of sunburn and keep the shirt on?

Okay, so that was something her father could get away with. But he was a pasty-white Scotsman who grew up never having his skin exposed to the sun. Ramona could not claim that. Her coloring took after Mami and their Mexican heritage. Sunburn was only in her vocabulary because of Daddy.

Besides, she had to remember, Bobby had some woman in mind that she was training him for. Probably that Abby. She could see that, Bobby being interested in a single mother. If Tyler was his kid, maybe Bobby needed to learn how to get along with his son's mother.

Right, Bobby and his sexy-as-hell treasure trail of belly button hair was not going to care one way or another what she looked like in a swimsuit. She dropped the gray shirt next to his, and mimicking his actions, she took a running jump into the water.

She surfaced with a laugh. The cool water lowered her body temperature. She swam in closer to where Bobby stood. Her toes touched down on a slippery rock bottom. She had to bounce to not be covered by water. Bobby grabbed her arm and hauled her over a few more feet. It was shallower yet, and she could stand. Maybe she should move back into the deeper water? Give Bobby more opportunity to touch her.

"This place is amazing. But I thought we were going to the dam?" A dam in her mind was a smooth wall of concrete built to contain water flow. She didn't see anything like that around here.

Bobby pointed up at the cliff face where the waterfall sprayed down. "That's the dam. It's a natural break in the river, not a man-made dam."

"Oh, all this time I thought it was a man-made dam everyone was talking about. This is so much better."

"Yeah, it's pretty great. The water gets deep by the wall, and out that way"—Bobby gestured along the tree bank, opposite of where they'd hiked in—"it gets shallow and is good for wading."

"And throwing rocks into the water?" Ramona asked. She tried to keep the bite out of her tone.

Bobby laughed. "And throwing rocks into the water. But I thought that really only appealed to four-year-olds."

"Or people mad at the water." Something Ramona

understood at the moment. She could throw rocks at the water and get her frustrations out. She could not throw rocks at Bobby, or Abby. Ramona really needed to curb this jealousy. Bobby was friend with a capital F. She jumped deeper into the water and swam away. Floating on her back, she let the soothing water relax her.

She watched as some of the more daring kids climbed the face of the cliff wall. They would spring away from the face, twist midair, and dive into the clear water. People were laughing and splashing. She noticed more than a few were using those long foam noodles to float around on. She was going to need to pick up a few this week. Those were a great idea.

Bobby swam up beside her. "Boo."

Ramona twisted so that she was no longer floating. Her feet beneath her, she treaded water. "What's up?" she asked.

"What are you going to teach me today?"

The question caught her off guard. What did he want her to teach him, what exactly...? Oh right, she was on the clock. This was an official training session.

"I think today"—she rotated in the water, looking at the people around them—"is going to be about observation. Who is here on a date, or with someone they have a crush on? Who is here with friends? What do you see that is different in the way those people are acting?"

"Why does that sound like a book report?" Bobby groaned.

Ramona adjusted her motions and rested on her back, floating. "It's more like a long five paragraph essay." She chuckled.

"This is going to require a beer. Want one?" Bobby asked.

"In a bit, right now I just want to float." Ramona focused

on the clouds above them. This was bliss. Surrounded by water, weightless.

Bobby's tub was nice, but it had nothing on this. Of course with the tub she could have bubbles.

Someone bumped into her. She lost her balance and went under. She resurfaced, sputtering.

Strong arms held her up.

"Oh hey, I'm sorry," a voice in her ear said.

She twisted as she wiped water from her eyes. Her gaze was met by dark eyes belonging to a handsome young man with tousled black hair.

"Y'all okay?" His arms still held on to her.

"I'm good. Not a problem." She smiled, not minding being in his embrace.

He smiled back, and she realized he wasn't as young as she'd first expected.

"I'm Ethan. What's your name?"

"Ramona."

"You here with anyone, Ramona?"

"Yeah." She caught herself as he released her. "Just a friend." A friend she shouldn't be thinking about the way she was. Maybe another male distraction would be what she needed.

"I'll see you around." He winked and then swam off.

He was cute. Maybe she should keep an eye on him. Maybe she should check in on her student. She stood when the water was shallow enough. Bobby lounged and seemed to be doing a fine job of observing everyone, but not her.

"How should I categorize your friend? Opportunistic flirter or player?" His voice sounded a bit gruffer than normal.

"What's that supposed to mean?" Ramona asked as she twisted the top off a hard cider. She took a sip—it was cool and a dry sweet, perfect for this location, and a million times better than the light beer practically everyone else seemed to prefer.

"That guy you were flirting with. That wasn't an accidental crash, you know."

Had Bobby been watching? Ramona tried to hide behind her bottle. She felt a flush burn her cheeks.

A scream caught her focus. Instantly Bobby stood and scanned the area to see what everyone was looking at. Before Ramona could focus on where everyone was pointing, Bobby was running toward the cliff face.

Several people were climbing the cliff wall toward a small figure. How had they climbed up that high? Hanging more than half-way up was a little kid. Ramona thought it was a little boy based on their clothes—bright primary colors, T-shirt and shorts. He had his hands on an outcropping, and his toes were barely keeping up against the cliff.

Ramona watched as Bobby scaled the wall and angled to the left, probably taking the quickest path he could find. Her comparison to a mountain goat earlier hadn't been far off. Clearly he had climbed the wall a time or two. He had arm reach and strength on other climbers as he hauled himself up by his fingertips.

She continued to scan the cliff and along the top of the cliff wall. The child was maybe twenty feet from the top. And only a few feet from a narrow ledge that looked as if it would fit a kid. No one could get close enough. A collective gasp let out as one of the rescuers fell away from the wall and plunged into the water. Several people swam over to check on him. She didn't move. She lost sight of Bobby.

If the child could just get to the ledge, everything would be fine.

Another scream. Arms shot up and were pointing again,

this time not at the kid but at a large animal along the cliff. It looked like a big dog from where she was. It blended into the cliff face. The animal was a golden color underneath with sides of redder fur. It looked like it had a black patch along its back. She blinked a few times and realized that animal was more wolf than dog. It creeped carefully along the narrow ledge toward the child.

Ramona heard someone mention getting a gun, and someone else yelling they might shoot the kid.

Everything happened at once. Ramona knew the actions her brain registered took only a few seconds, but it all happened in slow motion. The child began struggling to hold on, his little feet kept losing purchase on the rocks beneath. The wolf jumped. The kid was falling, and then he wasn't. The wolf had a firm grasp of the red T-shirt in its jaws and was dragging the kid up and back along the cliff ledge. And then it was gone. Leaving the child perched, safe for now, on the ledge.

Ramona could hear the wails as the child's panic took over and he began crying.

Bobby climbed along the cliff just below where the wolf had deposited his rescue. He reached the crying figure at the same time as two other men. They carefully handed the kid to each other, allowing one person to climb while the others took care of the kid. They all disappeared behind branches as they continued to move toward the side.

Less than five minutes later, there was a cheer as one of the rescuers arrived from the trail carrying the child, a little boy. He was younger than Ramona had at first thought. His mother ran over to the rescuer and grabbed her son into a fierce hug.

Bobby emerged a few seconds later with the other man who had helped. She watched as they approached the mom and kid. They said a few words. Bobby shook the other guy's hand, got a hug from the mom, and returned to where Ramona was standing.

She threw her arms around him, relieved that he was safe, that the kid was safe. She dropped her arms awkwardly as soon as she realized what she was doing.

"That was intense. You okay?" Ramona asked.

Bobby had dirt smeared across his chest and up the side of his face.

She wanted to reach up and brush the dirt from him. Bobby stood in front of her, breathing heavily. Their eyes locked and everything stopped. Ramona shifted her gaze to Bobby's lips. She felt his fingers skim along the back of her arm.

Bobby took a step back and shook his hands at his sides. "Whoo, what a rush. I can still feel the adrenaline pumping."

"Did you see that wolf? It totally pulled the kid to safety," Ramona said, trying to keep her tone conversational. Ramona's heart pounded at the base of her throat, and she had only been an observer. Or was it pounding because of Bobby?

"Yeah, that was something. I thought it was going after him. Easy prey, but damned if it didn't just drop the kid and take off. I need to cool off." Bobby turned from her and jumped back into the water.

She sat back down with a heavy sigh and watched as everyone at the swimming hole slowly returned to cavorting in the water as if nothing had happened to put all their lives temporarily on hold.

"Hey, Ramona, right?"

Ramona looked up. Ethan was gingerly walking over the rocks, approaching her. He really was cute and nicely built, on the thinner side, but he had nice shoulders and good pecs. He sat down next to her, resting his arm across his knees.

"That was something. Wasn't it?" he asked.

"Yeah, a real rush. I'm glad everything turned out okay. That could have turned nasty. Really nasty."

"Did you see the wolf? I never believed the stories before, but damn if that wasn't Haven's own rescue wolf."

She turned a glare on Ethan. "Really? The rescue wolf?"

He pointed up the cliff to the ledge where the action had taken place. "You saw it. That wolf rescued that kid. There have been stories all over town: Some lady gets her purse snatched, but the wolf chases the thugs down and gets her purse back. Some kid starts to run into traffic, but a stray dog stops them somehow. Never really believed them, but damn."

"Someone gets stuck on the side of the road with a flat, they see the wolf, and somehow within an hour a tow truck magically shows up? I can see how you wouldn't exactly believe it until you witnessed it yourself." If she hadn't seen it, there was no way she would have believed it either.

"Exactly. What are you doing later?"

She hadn't expected him to ask her out. She paused longer than she'd intended, having forgotten how to answer when someone asked her out. It had been a very long time.

"She's having pizza." Bobby loomed over both of them.

She hadn't noticed him getting out of the water.

"Hey, sorry, thought she said she was here with friends." Ethan left before Ramona had a chance to respond to him.

She huffed and looked up at Bobby. "Now what part of being my friend includes chasing off potential dates?"

"The part of being your friend that protects you from assholes like him. He wasn't interested in a get-to-know-you date. He was looking for a hookup." Bobby sat in the space Ethan had vacated.

"And you know this precisely how?" Ramona didn't bother to hide her annoyance.

"It takes one to know one. I know my kind when I see them in action."

10

————

Bobby felt like he was going to come out of his skin when he saw Ramona in that bikini. Good thing he had already been in the water. His bathing suit would not have been able to hide his body's reaction. His gut got tight. His groin throbbed.

Her skin was creamy gold, and in that white bikini, she radiated more than her normal glow. He needed to give up on thinking she was some angel sent to save him. While her body was heavenly, he only had sinful thoughts about it.

Maybe tricking her into being his friend wasn't the brightest thing he had ever done. He needed her to see him as something other than a penis for hire. Actually he was pretty sure she already did, but did she even realize he had one?

He let out a bark of a laugh. His stupid penis was the cause of all his problems. He didn't want the women who wanted him for it, and the one woman in town he wanted— no, needed—wasn't interested.

No, she was interested in Ethan.

Ethan could have any other woman in town. Hell, Bobby

was already aware the Roadhouse was starting to take away some of his female patronage. Ethan could have them, but he could not have Ramona. Especially not after she had hugged Bobby and he knew what her soft body felt like pressed against his.

The glass in his hand shattered as his claws sprang forth. Just like on Saturday, the thought of Ramona being interested in Ethan had pulled Bobby's wolf forward. He shook his claws back into hand form and cursed.

The dogs went crazy with barking as Bobby heard the crunch of tires on the drive. Two cars. He finished picking up the broken glass in the kitchen and walked out the side door. He barked back at the dogs to get them to shut up.

Brad stepped out of his truck. Behind him a couple emerged from a rental car. He noticed the man first. He was tall and well-built. There weren't too many guys in town with a stature like his or his brother's. The woman was pretty, with long, straight black hair and Rubenesque curves.

"Hey, Bobby, I want you to meet the Palatines." Brad stepped to the side and indicated the couple. "This is Dante and Geena."

Bobby reached forward and shook their hands.

"They are the genetic relatives I got that letter about. You remember that letter?"

"Oh right, the genetics thing you share with Petey."

"And we think most likely with you," Dante added.

"Come on in. Can I get you a drink?" Bobby led the way inside.

Geena and Dante took a seat on the couch while Bobby grabbed a couple of beers from the fridge and a Coke for Geena.

He pulled over kitchen chairs so that he and Brad could

sit. He really was going to need more furniture if people were going to start coming over.

Dante leaned forward, resting his elbows on his knees. "We recently discovered that a rare genetic anomaly our family has had for generations is trackable in those ancestry DNA tests." He gestured at Brad. "That's actually how we were able to find your brother. His results came through our labs and—"

"Your labs?" Brad asked.

Dante nodded. "Yes, the family realized we need to protect this information. Along with another family that shares this rare gene combination, we took controlling interest in a few labs. When the gene sequence shows up in tests, it gets forwarded to us for research purposes, and we run the tests again, and then reach out."

Brad crossed his arms. "Is this why my test needed to be redone?"

"Precisely," Geena said. "As we mentioned to you earlier, we're here to help if we can. I know you are very concerned with how this will impact your son when he gets older, but unfortunately we can't tell if it will or not. Not until he hits puberty. We don't know yet the extent of where in the genetics these genes are hiding."

"And what will or will not happen when Petey hits puberty?" Bobby asked.

Dante squirmed in his seat, almost as if he were uncomfortable. "He'll get bigger and stronger than his friends." He gestured with his palm up toward Brad and Bobby. "He'll develop a sporadic body hair issue. His ability to heal will be exponentially greater. He'll have better audial and olfactory capabilities."

"It sounds like things you do, that I can't," Brad cut in, staring straight at Bobby. "So I brought them over to meet you. Apparently I only have half of the gene set. And Petey also only has half the gene set."

Geena sat up and placed her soda can on the coffee table. "But that doesn't preclude the anomaly from manifesting. We have plenty of relatives with half the gene pair with the manifestations."

"What exactly are you trying to ask?" Bobby stood up. It sounded like they were talking about his special skill of shifting, but they weren't coming out with the words. It made sense; after all, how does one approach a stranger and ask if they are a werewolf, when those things only exist in the movies?

Geena smiled at him and then looked back at Dante. "I've got this. Bobby, you've got a girl?"

Did he have a girl? Good question. There was one he wanted. He smiled just thinking about Ramona.

Geena smacked Dante on the front of his shoulder with the back of her hand. "What's her name? Tell me something about her."

Bobby creased his brow. Why was this woman interested in his relationship with Ramona? He shifted his gaze to Brad. Brad nodded.

Bobby sighed. "Ramona. She's out of my league." Bobby paused. What could he say about Ramona? A vision of her in the bikini crossed his inner eye. He could just make out her peaked nipples through the fabric. Full breasts, narrow through her ribs, with hint of feminine soft belly bellow her navel, round hips, strong thighs; she was perfection.

"He's a shifter," Geena announced.

"How do you know?" The words were out of Bobby's mouth before he even thought to not say them.

"Yeah, how did you figure that out so fast?" Dante asked.

She giggled. "Seriously? Same reason I knew Bradley

here wasn't one. The eyes." She turned to Dante. "Sweetie, what do your eyes do when you have intense emotion?"

Dante grabbed the woman and pulled her into his chest. "You mean like when I want to...?" He waggled his eyebrows at her.

"Or you're really angry." She pushed on him to let her go.

"Wolf eyes, they glow," Dante said.

"Bobby's eyes glow when he's really mad," Brad confirmed.

"Or when he's talking about his sweetheart. Does she glow?"

Bobby staggered back. How did this woman know that Ramona glowed? "She's not my sweetheart. Not yet. And yeah, she glows. She has a halo of white light that surrounds her." Bobby sat with a thud.

Dante chuckled. "That's the mate glow, buddy. It means you found the perfect woman."

"I don't think she needs to glow for me to know she's perfect."

"Good, now that we can all acknowledge the elephant in the room—" Geena started.

"You mean wolf," Brad cut in.

"Exactly. We don't have DNA results on you, Bobby, so we don't know if you have half or the full set of the genes." Dante turned his attention to Brad. "We aren't there yet with the science to explain why he can shift and you can't. Or to even be able to predict if Petey has enough of the genes to be a shifter. Or which genes exactly indicate the ability to shift.

"What we do know is your girls don't have it, so they won't pass it on to their children. However, we will provide genetic testing to their families as they grow. It's up to you to share this information with them or not. And you can wait to share that until you know if your son is a shifter."

"However, Petey will need to know he can pass this along. Of course his children will have access to full genetic testing as well," Geena continued.

It was almost too much to take in. Bobby had been alone in this most of his life. His mother had run away because he started shifting into a wolf, his dad's life had been destroyed because of it. Only Brad had stuck with him. He wasn't the only shifter out there.

Bobby let out a long, slow breath. "If Petey does shift, how does Brad tell Melissa so that the kid can grow up with his mother around?"

"Bobby," Brad started.

"No, this is important. We lost our parents because of me. You've already said if Melissa leaves, you'd die. I don't think anyone here wants Petey to have to go through what we did. Melissa is going to need to know."

"I can help with that. Any of the human mates would be willing to help out," Geena said. "Look Brad, you have half the DNA. You probably have some of the traits, just not fully expressed. I mean you are bigger than average, you're probably stronger than average as well. You're incredibly good-looking—"

Dante made a grumbling noise.

"Shut up, Dante. You know that's one of the traits. Show me a Palatine or an Aventine who is even remotely average looking." She returned her attention to Brad. "When you met your wife, did you basically stop looking at other women completely?"

Brad's forehead crinkled up. "Yeah, I did. I only wanted to be around her, just to be near her."

"And to this day, she is…" Geena paused. She twitched her face into an expression of concentration.

Dante picked up her hand. "Perfection?"

Brad nodded. He wiped his hand over his mouth and grabbed his beard. "Yeah, Melissa is still perfect, maybe more so than when I first met her."

"I'm going to hazard a guess that you somehow read her as a mate, even if you can't see the glow." She turned to Bobby. "Does your Ramona know about you?"

Bobby shook his head.

"You're gonna need to tell her," Geena said.

"Yeah, sooner than later," Dante added.

"Easier said than done," Bobby said. "I have a bit of a reputation, and I'm still working on getting her to see that's not me anymore."

Geena shook her head. "The shifting part is easy. What she'll have the problem with is understanding that you have completely changed. And I bet you did the second you saw her glowing."

"What Geena is getting at is that our mates tend to not freak out when they learn of our true nature. Maybe Melissa is Brad's mate and she'll accept it all in stride. That last part… well, I was a bit of a libertine until I met Geena."

Bobby let out a sharp laugh. "Libertine. That sounds so much more sophisticated than fuck boy, or man ho."

"Don't forget my favorite, horndog," Brad added.

"Geena asked if I'd take her for a ride on my motorcycle." Dante sounded thoughtful.

"Melissa asked me if I wanted a slice of cherry pie." Brad definitely sounded thoughtful.

Bobby knew those were the defining moments for these men. The moment they knew there was something different, special about their wives.

Had the defining moment for Bobby been when Ramona was surrounded by glowing angels' wings? Or had he known before that? Before he saw the glow.

"I really think it's when she described the perfect bacon sandwich and asked if I could make her one."

Khendra gave Ramona a hug, and then she hugged Debbie.

"Feels like I haven't seen y'all in forever," Khendra said. She began playing with Ramona's hair. "Girl, you need to come in. This heat is not your friend."

Ramona laughed and smoothed her hair down. "No kidding, the humidity this year has been horrible. Were you waiting long?"

Ramona had met the two in the parking lot in front of the Roadhouse, Vanessa's new favorite hangout spot. Supposedly the bartender here was a contender for Bobby's position as the most sought-after piece of man-meat in town.

"Nope, just got here. Vanessa said to get a table," Khendra said as she pulled open the doors.

"This place used to be a Pizza Hut, didn't it?" Ramona asked. "It's got that roof shape."

"It was Chinese takeout after that. And then it was a bar called Road Stop," Debbie said.

"It hasn't been the Roadhouse for very long. I mean, wasn't it just called Das Road Haus last year?" Khendra asked.

Debbie rolled her eyes. "Yeah, they dropped the German real fast when some neo-Nazis tried to take over."

The interior looked like a hand-me-down diner with teal vinyl-covered chairs and neon lights in the corners. The floor was covered in black and white checked tiles. The place was packed.

"Vanessa said it would be crowded," Khendra said.

"Are the drinks that good?" Ramona asked. She realized she preferred the darker wood and stainless steel, no-fuss interior at Ray's. Maybe it was because she knew Bobby was there. And honestly, no matter how good-looking this guy was, he couldn't be as charming and attractive as Bobby.

They found a table and slid into the seats.

"You look happy today. Glad to be out of work?" Ramona asked Debbie, noticing her big smile and ready laugh.

"I didn't go in to work. Spent the day in bed," she said.

"Then you must be feeling better. You certainly don't look sick," Ramona commented.

"Oh honey, I was feeling good all day long. Derrick was in bed with me," Debbie announced.

"I knew you two would get back together. But why the hell are you out with us, if he is at home in your bed?" Khendra asked.

"Poor man needed to recover, so I left him sleeping." Debbie laughed. "Besides I need to see who I'm lining up for the next time he breaks up with me."

Most of the clientele were women. It was like some bad joke. All the single women in town here for one guy. It was worse than the first night she'd walked into Ray's, and there had been a lot of women there that night.

Vanessa approached the table, and everyone stood and gave her a hug. "Have you seen him yet?" she asked as she sat down. "What are y'all drinking? I feel like margaritas."

"Oh, a margarita sounds good. We could get a pitcher. Do they do food here?" Debbie asked.

"Just nachos and giant pretzels," Vanessa answered.

"I'm good with a pitcher. Let's get some nachos too,"

Ramona added. "So who are we looking for?" She swiveled around and didn't see anyone who stood out from the crowd. A few men sat at the long bar, and a few guys were at tables with some of the women. There had been no doubt who Bobby was when she first saw him. But there was no one here like that tonight.

Ramona tapped Debbie on the arm and pointed to one of the men at the bar. "Is that Coach Shumer? I thought Ray's was his hangout of choice."

Debbie craned her neck to look. "Oh yeah, that's him. Bobby probably kicked him out one time too many, so he's drinking over here."

"I always figured him for a more traditional bar drinker, you know, like going to the King's Arms or a place like that."

Debbie laughed. "Well, there is only one place like the King's Arms in town, and if he went there, he would be an alcoholic. If he were an alcoholic, he might lose his job. At Ray's he's hanging out with the football heroes of the town, and this place is the closest thing we have to a sports bar. He can say he's studying the competition. I mean, look at all the TVs."

"You're right. Ray's doesn't have any TVs." Ramona nodded.

"No, but Bobby gets in a big projector screen for the Super Bowl and the playoffs," Khendra added.

A waitress came and took their order. Within a few minutes she returned with a large pitcher full of neon-green blended margarita. "Your nachos should be ready in a few minutes—"

Loud music reverberated through the bar. "Maybe later; looks like Ethan is going to do his thing," she said.

The music continued, and a chorus of whoops and yells followed. Debbie hit Ramona on her arm a couple of times and pointed. Standing on top of the bar, playing air guitar, was the cute man from the lower dam. He had the same messy black hair, only now he wore a tight shirt and tighter leather pants. She laughed. That was Ethan. He was cute, but he looked ridiculous dancing on the bar, pretending to be some rock star.

"You've got to be kidding me? That's why all these women are here?" She leaned over and yelled in Debbie's ear.

"Admit it, Ramona, he's kind of hot. And this is brilliant!" Debbie yelled back.

The screams from the audience grew louder when he ripped the front of his shirt off. Ramona burst out laughing some more. His chest was oiled.

"Does he do this every night?" she asked Vanessa.

"No, he doesn't. That's the fun part. You never know when he's going to get up there and put on a show. Last time he didn't take his shirt off. Apparently one night he actually stripped down to his shorts."

"Are you serious? Oh, we so need to be coming here more," Khendra added.

The song ended, and the crowd screamed and hollered as he left the bar. Ramona couldn't help but keep laughing. Ethan was good-looking, but he needed to put on a surprise striptease to get all these women in here. Bobby never had to do that.

She needed to stop it with the comparisons.

"So is he as easy to hook up with?" Of course Debbie would ask that. Even if she was back with Derrick, she kept her options open.

"Apparently, he has a waiting list. And he doesn't have as many rules as Bobby did." Vanessa huffed.

"What do you mean 'did'?" Bobby still had hookup rules.

Even if Ramona hadn't actually seen him arranging one lately, not that she had been watching out for them. She found it to be in her best interest if she avoided paying attention.

"Apparently Bobby has been saying no a lot lately," Khendra said.

"Oh really?" Vanessa quirked a perfect eyebrow. Ramona figured Vanessa would be interested in knowing that she wasn't the only one Bobby turned down.

"You would be surprised what I learn in my shop. And I don't have some Hippocratic oath preventing me from sharing what I've learned."

Debbie leaned in. "Spill what you've got, Khendra."

"Ladies." Ethan announced his arrival with their nachos.

Debbie pulled back from leaning across the table so that he could set the hot plate down.

"I enjoyed your show tonight," Vanessa purred.

"That's why I do it, so that you can enjoy me. Vanessa, right? I recognize you"—he twisted around, pointing at everyone else at the table—"but I don't recognize the rest of you. Except you. Almost didn't recognize you with your clothes on, Ramona. How've you been?"

Ramona chuckled. She did not miss the glare Vanessa shot her from across the table. "Been back up to the dam?" she asked.

"Not this week. I'll probably go up next week."

"Oh, I love the lower dam. It's so relaxing up there. Swimming just makes me feel so good." Vanessa was definitely purring. She rubbed her arms in a way that suggested she wanted Ethan to rub her.

"Maybe I'll see you there." He winked at Vanessa and left.

"Wait, you ran into him at the dam and didn't say anything?" Debbie asked.

"I didn't realize he was some kind of minor celebrity around here. Bobby said he was a major player and kind of warned him off." Ramona shrugged.

"Wait, wait, wait, wait, wait, hold up. Did you just say you were at the lower dam with Bobby Cray, ran into hottie Ethan, and that Bobby warned him off? What the hell have you been up to, girl?" Khendra's hands whipped around and her head bobbed in a circle.

"I'm more interested in what you have been learning in your shop," Ramona deflected.

"Me too," said Debbie, "but I also want to know what the hell you were doing with Bobby at the dam."

"Khendra first." Ramona pointed across the table.

"Uh-uh." Vanessa pointed at Ramona. "You first."

Ramona slumped. "Okay, I was just hanging out with Bobby. I mentioned I had never been to the dam, and everyone was talking about it, so he let me tag along last weekend. No biggie. Apparently Ethan tried to hit on me. I still think he was just being nice after he crashed into me in the water. Anyway, Bobby came over and growled at him. Told me the man was a serious player, and when I asked how he knew, he said, 'it takes one to know one.'" Ramona shrugged at her friends. "It wasn't a big deal, really."

"Well, the chatter in my chair is that Bobby might have a girlfriend, and that's why he is off the market."

Everyone's eyes turned to Ramona.

She shook her head. "Oh, it's not me. Trust me, it's not me." While she also didn't have a Hippocratic oath, she wasn't about to tell everyone she was training Bobby on how to be a better man, even though he didn't really seem to need it.

Vanessa leaned back in her chair. "So you're telling us that you aren't at all interested in Ethan, and you aren't a little interested in Bobby."

Ramona put her head on the table. She knew she was blushing. "I have zero interest in Ethan. He's fun to watch, but he's all yours." She inhaled sharply and let it out slowly. "I might have a little crush on Bobby. But he isn't interested in me, and I don't do the casual-sex thing. So there's that. And like you heard in your shop, I think he has a girlfriend. Or at least he seriously has his eye on someone. And it ain't me." Ramona took a long drink of her margarita. She was going to need a few drinks to get through the night after the confession she'd just made.

"I knew you'd like him," Debbie cooed.

11

Ramona leaned back in the tub. What was she going to do? Bobby clearly had succeeded in considering her a friend, and she was letting herself fall in love with him. Was it letting, or was it happening and she didn't have any control over it?

She shouldn't be here. She shouldn't keep coming and using the tub, putting herself into a position where Bobby might see her naked. Would that be so bad? Could she handle how he would react? So far he had been very considerate and made sure there would never be a chance for him to catch a peek at her. She almost wanted to accidentally let the robe slip, exposing her skin to him. Almost.

Deep in her belly she knew that would be ego shattering, especially if he got embarrassed and simply covered her up with an apology. No, Bobby was a friend, and she knew better than to hijack a situation and turn it awkward.

Besides, she would have to give up letting him brush her hair. Something she loved possibly more than the giant bathtub. She closed her eyes and let the water soothe her.

She knew she shouldn't be here, but she needed to see

Bobby before she left for two weeks. Needed to burn his face into her mind so she could see him when she closed her eyes. Needed to sense his warmth and masculinity one last time before heading back to her parents' house for the baby watch.

Her sister, Lorena, had passed the point of being uncomfortable and super cranky with baby number two. Ramona had only mild pity for her. After all, at one point she too had thought her life was going to be wedded bliss, spending years barefoot and pregnant, married to the youngest high school principal in the district. Well, none of that was working out for her, and frankly, she never wanted to date another school administrator again.

One thing she'd garnered from Lorena's time pregnant, it was never as cute or as entertaining as anyone ever tried to make it out to be. Those maternity photo shoots were tiring, uncomfortable, and then depressing. Lorena had had a beautiful portrait taken, and now every time she looked at it, she complained about how unbelievably fat she was. She wasn't fat, but she did have one huge pregnant belly. Not one of those cute little fashion accessory bellies that the maternity models let hang out. No, she looked like she had swallowed a barge, and the skin on her belly was angry about it.

With this pregnancy she'd shown Ramona the bright red road map of stretch marks, plus the dark band down the center of her belly. Lorena wasn't cute-pregnant, and she resented it. Of course her husband didn't care. He looked at her like she was the most amazing creature on the planet. Ramona would catch glimpses of him when he didn't think anyone was looking.

Ramona never would have gotten a look like that from Devon if she had turned into a walking planet with his offspring. He was too vain. He would have been too concerned with what people thought about his wife getting so big. Ramona knew there was no way she wouldn't look like she'd swallowed a barge. It was in her genetics.

The low rumble of Bobby's car caught her ear, followed by the sound of tires crunching on the gravel drive. *I wonder how Bobby would look at his pregnant wife.* Would the woman he got pregnant even be his wife? He didn't seem to be the kind of man to have a string of baby mamas, but she still didn't know if Tyler was his or not. He may sleep around, but he said he was responsible about it.

At least that's what he'd told her. His exact words had been, "Condoms are a wonderful invention." And fool that she was, she believed him.

She fluffed up the bubbles so that there would be no accidental exposure, no matter how much she thought about it.

The car engine stopped, and she could hear the dogs bark.

"Hey, Bobby. You're home earlier than I thought," she lied. She knew exactly when he would be back.

"Hey there, Angel. I thought you were heading up to Dallas as soon as school got out." He stood on the opposite side of the bamboo wall, his hands full of grocery bags.

"I wanted to relax after school. Hitting the road was not appealing in any way. Lorena isn't going to have the baby today or tomorrow, so I'm not going to miss anything by heading up in a day or two. Besides I have some stuff to take care of around the apartment." *I wanted to see you, and you weren't going to be at Ray's.*

"You have dinner plans?" he called out as he headed into the house.

She waited until he came back out before answering.

"Not really. I'll probably hit a drive-through on the way home. Or nuke a frozen dinner."

"I bought a bunch of frozen burritos. You want one? I can toss them in the oven. They should be ready by the time you're done."

"Sounds great."

"You want a beer or a Cherry Coke?" he asked.

"Nothing. I'm good."

She wasn't good and she knew it. She needed to get distance from the situation. Maybe even distance from Bobby. These next two weeks would be good for her. She would come back to Haven full of family and ready to start the new school year. She would ditch the little annoying crush while she was home.

But not until one last hair brushing.

She looked around. She didn't see Bobby. Maybe she could risk getting out of the tub and into her robe before he came back. That didn't mean he couldn't step out of the house at any second and catch her. No, best not to risk it. "Hey, Bobby?"

"Yeah, what's up?"

She could hear his boots stop just at the door.

"You mind hiding for a bit, or taking the dogs up the drive?"

He chuckled. "You ready to get out? Sure thing."

His footsteps crossed the patio behind her. He whistled for the dogs. She listened as he continued to talk to the dogs about having to take a walk so the lady could get out of the tub.

She waited a few moments longer before sitting up and climbing out. Gravity always felt so much heavier after a nice long soak. She grabbed a towel and rested back on the rim of the tub, wiping her face. The heat and the water on her skin felt wonderful. She didn't want to wrap up in the robe. It would be too warm this evening. She reached for a second towel, and with luck, it was larger.

She wrapped the towel around her with extra to spare for tucking in sarong style. Her shoulders were bare, and for some reason she felt more exposed than if she had put on the robe. Of course the robe could fall open just as easily as the towel might come undone, but there was an added sense of security with sleeves and a belt.

Bobby chased the dogs up the drive. This was becoming a habit, one he didn't mind at all. When he got back, there would be a glistening-wet Ramona waiting for him. Her long, dark hair starting to curl up into waves. Her soft moans of pleasure as he brushed and braided her hair pulled at places in his body.

What he wouldn't give to be able to watch her climb out of that tub. A Venus emerging from the waves. Graceful limbs and beautiful curves, he could imagine water coalescing into drops on her breasts. He felt a tightening in his groin. He needed to relax. He never had accidentally caught sight of her, as much as he wanted to. Seeing her beautiful and nude wasn't in the cards tonight, but in time...

She called out, letting him know that she was as dressed as she needed to be. The dogs tore off back to the house. They sensed a treat. A smile played across his mouth. Ramona was his treat. She was adorable in that robe. Blue was not her color, but it had been the only robe he could find. He needed to get her a new one, a rose-colored one, like the color of the dress she'd worn the other day. That would make her skin absolutely glow.

He huffed a laugh. She didn't need special colors to glow. She just did. It seemed the more he thought about her, the more she actually glowed the next time he saw her. Now that he knew what it meant, a sign that so far hadn't been wrong, he needed to tell her. She was absolutely worth spending every second of time he could with her, and he wanted her to know.

The sight of her stopped him in his tracks. She wasn't all cute bundled up in her robe as usual. She looked like a dream. Her shoulders were bare, her figure highlighted by the tight wrap of the towel she wore. This evening her glow pulsed with his heartbeat, as if she were sending out a beacon calling him in. He was a moth, and she was his flame.

He cleared his throat a few times and continued onto the porch. "Too warm for the robe?" Had his voice just cracked? He cleared his throat again. "I'm gonna toss those burritos in the oven. You want that beer now?" He knew he needed one.

Brushing her hair and not touching her was going to be a test tonight. A test that he would not pass up for anything. She was leaving him for two weeks. It wasn't that long, but he had gotten used to having her here at least once a week, and in Ray's or at the movies. They hadn't gone more than a few days apart since the beginning of June.

He slid onto the chair behind her. Her hair hung heavy with water. He wrung out the excess and began picking the comb through the ends. Water sprayed the front of his shirt. It was neither cooling nor refreshing. He was wound too tight.

Soon he was sinking the teeth of the comb into the thick hair at the back of her head, dragging it down through the dark mass. Ramona didn't squeak or protest when the comb caught and yanked. She moaned softly, a sound that made his cock stand at attention. Thank God for tight jeans.

She sighed with satisfied sounds as the comb slid effortlessly through the already combed tresses.

Using the comb, he divided her damp hair into three thick sections. Tendrils reached out as if her hair had consciousness, and captured his fingers as he worked. Slowly, not wanting to rush the process, Bobby plaited her hair. He didn't care, and maybe did so on purpose, but his hands seemed to graze the skin of her shoulders and back more than they'd ever made contact with the robe when she wore it. He took extra time smoothing her hair into contained sections. When he finally reached the middle of her back, he didn't want to let go.

The fine strands at her hairline coiled into tight springs. Bobby clenched his teeth to keep himself from playing with the loops. Water pearled on her skin under her ear. His finger trailed above the drop as it fell down the side of her neck and along her shoulder. His finger skimmed over her soft skin. He froze, realizing that he was touching her. He had no right to be, not like this. He let his hand fall heavily onto her shoulder.

The oven timer buzzed.

He squeezed. "Why don't you get dressed while I get dinner set up?"

12

Ramona looked at the pile of dirty laundry in the corner of her bedroom. She had two thoughts simultaneously: she needed a hamper, and it had been forever since she had taken dirty clothes home with her when visiting her parents. She picked the pile up and stuffed it into the duffel bag. With an extra pair of shorts and a T-shirt or two, she had enough clothes to last for her visit. Even if it did mean she was doing laundry as soon as she arrived tomorrow.

Her doorbell rang.

It was late, really late. She hoped Mrs. C was all right. She never came over this late, but that was the only person she could think of who it could possibly be.

The breath caught in her throat when she saw Bobby standing there.

"What are you doing here?" No hi, no come in, just surprise. She opened the door, but Bobby didn't step in.

He ran his hand over his brow and pulled his long hair behind him. The ends had really become sun bleached this summer. She was going to miss that about him, the way he moved, the way his hair framed his whole being.

"I wanted to show you something." He reached forward and grabbed her hand and led her outside.

"Let me get my keys."

He let go, and she scrambled back inside. She shoved her keys into the front pocket of her shorts and locked the door behind her.

"Where are we going?" She followed him to his car and got in the passenger seat. He still hadn't said anything else. It made her nervous. Her stomach was trying not to flip-flop out of control, but it was one in the morning and Bobby had just shown up on her doorstep. Was she stupid for having just left with him, not knowing where they were headed?

He drove for a bit. It was too dark for her to tell where they were headed. At first she thought it was the lower dam, but he turned north, so that wasn't it.

He parked alongside the road, got out, and opened her door. "Come on." He offered her his hand.

"Bobby, are you going to tell me where we are going?" she asked as she stepped out of the car. The night was warm, and crickets were making a riotous noise.

"You'll understand when we get there. Watch your step."

Watch your step? How? She couldn't see anything. "It's pitch-black out here."

Her hand was engulfed in his, and he gently guided her down a path.

He climbed a boulder and turned to help her up. "Here, sit."

She did as instructed. It was still dark, but now she could hear water moving. Maybe they were back at the dam. "Is this the upper dam?"

"Not quite, but we are close to the water. Lay back and look up."

She gazed at Bobby. He was already lying back, his head supported by his hands. He reached up and pulled her shoulder back. He put his arm out, and her head rested against the crook of his shoulder. The rock was warm against her back. Bobby felt firm and comfortable under her head.

"Oh wow, look at all the stars," she said with a small gasp. The sky was black and dotted with a billion points of light. She could even see the pale swath of the Milky Way cut across the sky.

Her heart pounded so loudly in her ears she was certain Bobby could hear how nervous she was. She loved the feel of him and his warmth. He was past warm and into hot.

"Hey, you're really warm. You feeling all right?" she asked.

"I'm fine. I tend to run a little hot."

She reached over and felt his forehead. "You should get checked out. You might be fighting something if you have a fever."

She tried so hard not to touch more of him, not to cross that line of friendship, not to allow herself to get carried away. This was platonic, right? Leaning on his shoulder stargazing wasn't crossing the line into romantic territory, was it? The warring feelings in her head said this was romantic as hell. Her pounding heart and somersaulting stomach agreed.

"I wanted you to see this before you left. You have to come back to see this again. You don't get the stars like this in Dallas." His voice was a low rumble. The timbre of it did things low in her abdomen.

She tried not to giggle nervously. "No, you don't. You can

barely see the stars, too much light. Don't you get a view like this out at your place?"

"Yeah, but you've been to my place, and I didn't think dragging you out of your house in the middle of the night back to my place was the smartest move."

Why not? What was wrong with his place in the middle of the night? Unless he was also thinking there was a bed there, and she probably wouldn't say no to him right now. Yeah, that's why he didn't take her back to his place. He didn't want her to think he was going to seduce her. But they weren't at his place, there wasn't a bed in sight: seduction not expected.

She let out a sigh. Seduction was never going to happen, he was a friend, and that was all he had interest in. After all, she reminded herself for the millionth time this summer, she was training him on how to have a platonic-level relationship with the opposite sex so that one day he could have a successful long-term relationship with some woman he loved.

"I'm going to miss you, Angel. Two whole weeks?"

"Thirteen days. I'll be back. I have to be for orientation."

"What am I going to do for thirteen days?" he asked.

Did she detect a wistful sound in his voice? "Your poker game is on Thursday. You have end-of-month books to take care of. You have your fan club to entertain you."

"My fan club, as you call it, is boring. I've become a bit of a town joke, don't you think?"

She sat up and gazed at him. He looked sad, his mouth pulled down into a frown. His focus was up high in the sky on the stars.

"As your friend, I once said I would judge you, but I would never hold certain things against you. Remember that?"

"Oh yeah, and I remember that when I proclaimed myself as the self-aware man slut of Haven, you about ran for the hills."

She huffed. "Yeah, so I'm finally comfortable enough as your friend to lay it out for you. Sure, it's just sex, but for a lot of people there is no such thing as *just sex*, there is a railcar of emotional baggage that comes with it."

"You have a baggage car?" he asked.

"A whole freaking train of them. So while I may never understand the no-attachment, recreational use of sex, I get that you do. If that's something you want to separate yourself from, then you have to be the one that says no. As long as someone can crash into you for a hookup in the IGA, you're gonna have a reputation you call a joke." She didn't think he was a joke. She wished that her baggage cars of emotional attachment weren't leaning so heavily in his direction. "As long as you hookup at random, low-grade fevers are something you should get looked at. One of your dates may have shared something with you, that you don't want to go passing on to the next one. Get my drift?"

She felt a soft rubbing on the back of her hand. His thumb ran back and forth across her skin. Bobby probably didn't even realize he was doing that. But that little motion, that little bit of being comfortable with her... she fell in love with him a little more. And realized she was going to have to leave Haven with a broken heart after next spring. It figured that as soon as she thought she'd found the space she got to be herself in, she would have to leave.

Dr. G had finally come through with a signed contract for another school year. She was employed. But Haven was too small of a town for her to be able to be around when Bobby finally began courting whichever woman he was doing all of this for. She had it narrowed down, it was either Abby or Chareese.

"You could always do something with Chareese," she suggested. Might as well get the ball rolling so she could start to get some distance before her heart became even more invested.

"Why would I want to do that?"

"I thought she was a favorite from the fan club."

Bobby laughed sharply. "No. She thinks she is, but no."

"Oh really? Then what about doing something with Tyler and his mom, Abby?"

"That's not a bad idea. I could take the kids and hit the lower dam. Melissa and Abby would probably appreciate that. Get some time away, and I could earn some serious Uncle Bobby points."

"Uncle Bobby? Wait, Melissa is your sister-in-law, right?"

Bobby made an affirmative *uh-huh* sound.

"But you only have a brother, I thought. Who exactly is Abby then?"

"It's complicated," he said.

"Bobby, I'm sitting with you on a rock in the middle of the night, out in the middle of nowhere. This seems to be the right place for complicated."

"Then you had better get comfortable. It's a long story."

He pulled her back down so that she rested against him. Damn him, this was comfortable.

"Essentially Abby is my adopted sister. Back when she was nine or ten, Brad dated her mother for a bit. She was a good kid, and even after her mom and Brad broke up, she would come around. We had a pool. I went to OU and hadn't moved out of the house completely. Melissa wasn't around yet. I went away, and—"

"What do you mean, you went away. That's not the first time I've heard that."

Ramona tried to look up at him, she would need to move for it to work, and she didn't want to move.

Bobby draped his arm over her shoulder. Yeah, she wasn't going to want to move anytime soon.

"That's another story for another time. I'll tell you, I promise."

"Okay, but next question, where were your parents?"

"You just want to know everything tonight, don't you? By then my parents were long gone. Mom took off when I was eleven or twelve. It destroyed Dad. He started drinking. He wasn't exactly there anymore, even though he was, if you know what I mean."

"Oh Bobby, I'm sorry." His arm tightened around her.

"It is what it is. Dad took off a few years later. Brad moved back in and pretty much had the job of making sure I finished school and didn't get myself killed from the time I was fifteen."

"How much older than you is he?"

"He's five years older than me. He had to quit college to make sure I was taken care of."

"Brad's a good man, isn't he?" she asked.

He sounded like he was. Maybe that was why she was convinced Bobby was also a good man. He had a positive influence when he really needed one.

"He is. It's why Abby is in our lives. She knew he would help her out when she really needed it. So, let's see, I was back and living with Bobby and Melissa. One day Abby shows up a teary mess on our doorstep. She was fifteen, maybe sixteen. I didn't find out until later what was going on. Abby got knocked up, and her mom kicked her out of the house. She wasn't going to have a teenaged pregnant daughter, and she sure as hell wasn't going to help her figure out what her options were. Abby was out on her own, so she went where she knew someone would take care of her.

"Melissa stepped in and took over. I know they were deep in things for a few weeks. Like I said, I didn't really know what was going on, but I had my suspicions. There were loud fights. There were lots of tears. She and Melissa talked about taking a little vacation for a few weeks. Maxfield came over looking for her, and man did Brad give that kid the once-over. I've never seen my brother come so close to pounding someone without ever touching them.

"In the end Abby ended up having a miscarriage. She and Melissa bonded, Brad went into hyper-protective mode, and she lived with them until she and Maxfield ended up getting married when she was nineteen. Our relationship is different depending on who you ask. To Brad, she is his daughter; Melissa would say some combination of sister and best friend. To me she is definitely a kid sister. I still see her as that freckle-faced nine-year-old."

"And Tyler?"

"Maxfield's pride and joy. He's deployed right now, but we expect him home in September or October. I can't remember."

"Your sister? Ya know, I thought at one point..." She paused. She felt like an idiot now, but in the dark, under the stars seemed like as good a time as any to confess her foolishness. "I thought that Tyler was possibly your kid."

Her head bounced against his chest as he laughed. "Definitely not. That would be like me dating Melissa. Never going to happen. You know that's something in movies I never understand, when one brother hooks up with the other brother's ex. I can't imagine thinking of Melissa like that, and I know she sure as hell would never see me as anything other than her brother."

Ramona yawned.

"It's late. I should get you home."

No. She wanted to stay out here all night leaning against him. "Not until you tell me what you meant when you say you went away."

Bobby sighed. "Can you promise you won't hate me?"

"C'mon, Bobby, you've gone from 'it's complicated' to 'please don't hate me' in one night. I'm not exactly going to storm off on you. I don't even know where we are exactly, or how to get back." She sat up and looked at him. His eyes locked with hers. They seemed to have picked up some ambient light. They glowed gold from within.

"Did you hurt someone?"

"No, I did not hurt someone, but I did do something exceptionally stupid."

Ramona sat back on her haunches. "Uh-huh?"

"It's late, Ramona. How about I tell you on the drive back?" She watched as he stood up and stretched. He held a hand out to her. She felt a new tingle this time when she placed her hand in his.

"Before I forget. There is a monster truck show coming to the fairgrounds. I've never seen one of those. Would you be interested?" he asked.

"Hell yeah, they are crazy fun. You get to yell and cheer for trucks rolling over other trucks. You've never been to one?" Ramona said as she followed him back down the path to the car.

"I've never had anyone to take before. I'll get tickets."

Ramona buckled in and waited for Bobby to start the car. "Okay, spill. What did you do that was so incredibly stupid?"

"I let my life fall apart because of sex."

"Oh yeah?"

"I made it to OU on a football scholarship. Everything was going great. I was passing my classes thanks to my girlfriend. I was in line for a future as a pro ball player. I expected to get drafted within a year, so I just needed to keep passing classes until then. Everything was sailing along smoothly until Taylor dumped me."

"Is that the same Taylor you dated in high school?"

"Yep, I thought I was going to marry her, but I wasn't smart enough for her. Dating a high school football player was one thing, college and possibly pro, something completely different. I was having problems keeping my grades up without her tutoring, so Coach got me a tutor. Janey, a pretty girl who was jumping my bones by the end of our second tutoring session. Of course I thought I was in love with her. She was smart, completely crazy, wild. She partied. She did drugs."

"You got into drugs?"

Ramona watched as Bobby guided the car through a deserted Haven. Everyone else in the little town was asleep.

"No, we had regular drug testing on the team, so I avoided that. But I went with her wherever she went. I drove her car when she was high, which was most of the time. I followed that girl like a love-sick puppy dog."

"Because of sex?"

"Right, because of sex. Taylor and I never slept together. So when this girl was all sex all the time, I got stupid. I was like some kind of sex junky. Janey started sharing me with some of her friends, and can I tell you that fried my brain. I had a girlfriend who didn't care that I was banging her friends. Turns out she was banging other guys, and I wasn't her boyfriend. I was a twenty-year-old liberated ex-virgin having all the sex. There wasn't much blood left for my brain to function on."

"I agree. That was pretty stupid. But how exactly did that make you go away?"

Bobby pulled into her drive and shut off the car. He twisted in his seat to look at her.

"I got arrested. So those drugs she was into, she wasn't paying for them with the tutoring money the team was paying her. She was hitting gas stations and convenience stores. And guess who was driving?"

"You were." Ramona didn't know how to feel about all of this.

"Exactly. To be fair, I was a clueless idiot and believed her when she said she was just running in to grab an energy drink, but they didn't have the one she wanted so we had to go to the next convenience store to get what she wanted. She was arrested for armed robbery, and I was arrested for being the getaway driver."

Ramona felt her jaw drop open. She didn't know what to say.

"Look, Ramona. I didn't know what was happening. My coach got me a good lawyer, but because I ended up having to serve some time, I lost my scholarship and lost my chances at going pro. When I got out of jail, I needed to separate myself from sex so that I couldn't be manipulated like that again."

"And it worked, didn't it?" Any hopes she'd ever had of Bobby becoming emotionally invested in her were now dead. He had been used, and made sure he became the user. Why had she let herself develop these feelings? She felt tears sting her eyes. She faked a yawn and hoped that if he saw her cry, he would chalk it up to being overly tired.

"I don't hate you, Bobby. You've had a tough ride, but you

seem to be on top of things now." She opened the car door. "I'll stop by Ray's to let you know when I'm back in town."

"Have a good break. We'll go to the monster truck show when you get back."

"Yeah, sounds good." She waved at him as she opened her front door.

How was it possible to fall in deeper over the man while he was breaking her heart at the same time?

13

Ramona missed Bobby more than she wanted to admit. Being away from him for two weeks had been hard. Especially since all she did all day was sit around and watch her sister be pregnant. That wasn't exactly true. She and Mami had cooked plenty of casseroles for Lorena to put in the freezer so that they had meals prepared for after the baby was born.

Daddy played with Todd, Lorena's three-year-old, who was spending most of his time at their house considering Lorena was due any day. Ryan went to work, dropped Lorena off in the morning, and picked her up in the evenings on his way home. Most nights Todd slept over. It was easier that way, in case Lorena went into labor in the middle of the night.

Between the cooking, the babysitting, and the pregnancy watch, Ramona kept thinking about how Bobby would be as a father. She already knew he liked kids. Well, he liked his nieces and nephews. She really needed to not go there. But he had asked her to the monster truck rally, and she could swear those were date words, not let's-go-do-this-thing words.

She didn't know. She wouldn't know until she saw him again. She halfway hoped he would find out where her parents lived and come find her, take her out in the middle of the night, and find a place to go look at the stars. She wanted him to take her back to that rock and make love to her under the stars.

She knew that wasn't going to happen. Out of curiosity she looked through the job openings in a few of the Dallas-Fort Worth area school districts. There were so many she probably could have stayed and never had to worry about running into Devon in a professional capacity again. But she couldn't stomach being in the same city as him. Now that she had some distance from the situation, she knew she'd made the right choice, but thought maybe she could come back after Bobby claimed his girlfriend. For now Haven was home, and as long as Bobby didn't actually break her heart, she loved living there.

The websites listed enough job openings this close to the start of school, Ramona felt confident that she could get a job at any time. That was one thing about being a math teacher: job security. Too bad there wasn't such a thing as relationship security. No, that wasn't true, there was. It was called marriage. But since that didn't look like it was going to happen anytime soon for her, it might as well not exist.

She'd barely slept the night before she was going to drive back to Haven. She needed to be at school the day after for orientation, but that wasn't it. She wanted to see Bobby again.

She felt her body finally relax as she pulled into the gravel lot at Ray's and saw Bobby's Charger. It was dark and cool inside, just as she'd remembered. Two weeks and she'd thought she was going to forget all the little details. There was a couple in her favorite booth, so she found another one on the other side of the pool tables. She hadn't seen Bobby yet. He was probably in the back or in the kitchen. It was quiet, and there weren't many customers, but she knew he was keeping an eye on things.

She had tossed her bag onto the bench when a roar came up behind her. She was surrounded by arms as thick as trees and pulled in for a fierce hug. She squeaked in surprise as he lifted her off her feet. Bobby's hair got everywhere, and she sputtered to get it out of her mouth. She was still wiping his hair from her face when he set her down.

"Welcome back, Angel. I missed you."

She sighed when she could finally see his smile. His eyes picked up the light from the neon over the bar and glowed. She couldn't help but laugh and return his smile. "I missed you too."

"What time did you get back? You want a BLT, no L, no T?"

"I came straight here." She felt a twinge of panic. Would Bobby realize why she'd come straight here and not stopped at home? Could she be any more obvious? "Yeah, I'm starving. That sounds perfect."

He gave her a squeeze and left to head into the kitchen.

He came back with a tall iced Cherry Coke. His hair was pulled up into a messy top knot. She realized he put it up when he cooked. He probably wore a hairnet back there too.

She sighed. She didn't want to go back to Dallas. She didn't want Bobby to find a girlfriend. She wanted him to figure out she was in love with him and that he was falling for her.

He delivered the sandwich and slid into the booth. "I got

the tickets for the monster trucks for the day after tomorrow. It starts at six. You want me to pick you up?"

Ramona groaned. "I'll have to meet you there. Orientation goes until five thirty. I'm afraid I'll be showing up in work clothes."

"I can pick you up from the school. You'll probably be better dressed than anyone else there. You'll look just fine." He paused, and she felt like he was staring into her soul. "But if you're more comfortable, I'll meet you there. Text me so I can meet you at the gate with your ticket."

"I can do that," she acquiesced.

He held her gaze for a bit longer than normal. Her eyes darted to his mouth as his tongue licked his lower lip. She thought for a second that he had been staring at her mouth, but no, there was no reason for him to be doing that.

He tapped the table, and she knew he was going to get up and head back to work.

It was annoying, but necessary, to strip the classrooms down every summer so they could be disinfected and polished. Like most teachers, she removed everything at the end of the year in June, but because she had taken on summer school classes, she'd had time to move back in. Expecting Dr. G to play classroom roulette, she hadn't put everything back up on the walls. He didn't, and she got to keep the same classroom. She used the quiet times between students on the first afternoon of orientation to get her classroom situated back the way she liked it.

Her students came in. Some of them even had their parents in tow. She handed out packets and explained carefully that they needed to fill out the forms right now, and if that wasn't possible, their parents had to come in and fill out the forms before classes started in a week. They could not take the forms home. Half of the forms left her classroom anyway, with the parents.

If she was lucky, she would see some of them returned before the three days of orientation was over. If she was lucky.

She checked off names, gave directions to the next classroom on their schedules, and watched the clock. Yesterday afternoon's orientation with the seniors hadn't seemed to take up nearly as much time. This afternoon was a very long day, very long. Maybe it was because today was freshman orientation. Maybe it was longer because Bobby waited at the other end of it.

Her stomach clenched when Dr. G knocked on her door. He had nothing on her. She had been out of town for two weeks. She gave him a brittle smile.

"Ms. Campbell, how is orientation going for you this afternoon?"

"Everything is going well. I've had about two-thirds of my freshman check in already, and a smattering of the other students have checked in as well." There were always students who came to orientation when they could, it didn't matter what grade they were in.

"You have quite a few repeating this semester. Is that going to be a problem?" he asked.

She didn't have as many repeating as she could have. That algebra one class had been pretty rough.

"It shouldn't be. I'll be able to monitor what everyone is actually learning all semester. Last year was a challenge coming in when I did. I had to repeat some instruction they should have mastered early on in the semester, but testing showed they hadn't."

Repeat students didn't faze her. They tended to have more focus than the first-time student. They knew her; she knew them. Also, she had confidence that she wouldn't have nearly as many repeats at the end of this semester as she did from taking over Mr. Hagen's classes.

"I shouldn't need to tell you that we at RavenCroft don't like to hold back students unnecessarily."

"No, Dr. G, you don't need to tell me." No one liked to hold back a student unnecessarily, but teachers hated passing students just to meet some standards foisted upon them by non-educators. "I understand RavenCroft is establishing a certain reputation for educational excellence. I would like to think that promoting students with sound demonstrable knowledge fits that reputation." If he wanted to converse in educational jargon, she could handle that. It was more appropriate than for him to discuss her shopping habits or what nonsense her pizza delivery boy spewed from his mouth. She was actually smiling when he left her classroom. She could work with this version of Dr. G.

Her bags were packed and hanging from her shoulder while she leaned on the edge of her desk, watching the clock. Students hadn't been in her room for over twenty minutes, but she couldn't leave until five thirty. She prayed as she watched the hands tick closer to the time she could leave, that no one would walk through her door at the last second. The minute hand moved; the bell rang. She was out the door.

She tried not to run to the entrance gate when she finally found a place to park at the fairgrounds. As she walked, she texted Bobby that she had arrived. She described the gate she approached and hoped it was the right one for him.

She smiled when she saw him. Her muscles relaxed, and

everything was immediately better. He stood out, a good head taller than anyone else around. Well, except for... She sighed, his brother, Brad, was there. That meant that his sister-in-law or even their kids would be there. Her smile quavered. This wasn't the date she had let herself think it was going to be.

Bobby had plenty of people to come to a monster truck show with. She had let her emotions translate the words into what she wanted to hear, not what he was saying.

Bobby handed her ticket over, and she pushed her way through the turnstile. The hug she had planned on giving him stayed tucked away. She plastered her first-day-of-school smile on and let her professionalism guide her. Bobby introduced her to his brother first. She shook his hand. It was big and warm like Bobby's. Melissa was enthusiastic and had a natural smile. Ramona liked her. Maybe it was the way Melissa called her *sweetie*. Maybe it was the way she linked her arm through Ramona's as they make their way up into the stands.

"Hey, Bobby, there you are." Chareese's voice felt like fingernails on a chalkboard. She teetered like she walked on her tiptoes, her heels were so high. Her arms were full of popcorn and drinks. She began unloading onto Bobby. He took everything from her without saying anything. He gaped at her like a goldfish, mouth opening and closing without a word.

"I didn't know if you liked Raisinettes or Junior Mints, so I got both."

Hijo de puta, no. Ramona's stomach sank, she had a hard time catching her breath. The muscles in her shoulders clenched.

Damn, words had meaning. *Like*, that word indicated a certain level of affection. If he had a deep level of affection for Chareese, maybe he wouldn't have said *like*. Ramona was fairly certain he had said he didn't like her. Maybe he had meant something more?

Chareese leaned against Bobby's arm, and he didn't move. Maybe he had intended on introducing Chareese as his girlfriend all along tonight. He was acting nervous enough. He looked a little flushed, a blushing boyfriend. Her stomach roiled.

Ramona bit the inside of her cheek. She was not going to be sick; she refused to be sick over this. She would fake her way through the evening; she would yell too loud at the trucks, and picture Bobby's head under the wheels. She would sit next to Melissa and make a new friend. She would go home and start applying for those jobs she'd found last week in the greater Dallas-Fort Worth area. Daddy would help her get out of the lease situation. Dr. G could run amok with any rumor he wanted about her.

Ramona followed Melissa into the stands. Chareese followed right behind her. Bobby brought up the end. Why was Chareese sitting next to her? Why was she even here?

Ramona tried to ignore Chareese as she yammered on at Bobby. That was easy enough. The sound system was so loud she had to keep her focus on Melissa in order to hear anything she said anyway.

"Bobby tells me you have twins?" Ramona asked.

"Sure do. Sophie and Sadie, they are a handful, seven goin' on seventeen most days. Plus a toddler, they keep me busy. Now you're a teacher, right?" Melissa was practically yelling over the noise.

"Yeah, I teach math over at RavenCroft."

"You know I think we're now zoned for RavenCroft. That means in eight years you could be teachin' my girls." Melissa patted Ramona on the arm.

"Oh, you don't want that. I teach the remedial math classes. I can tell from what Bobby told me, you have some smart kids on your hands. They won't be in my classes."

Chareese cut in. "I'm so excited to meet y'all. When Bobby mentioned monster trucks, I couldn't wait to get my ticket."

Ramona followed Melissa's gaze as she looked over at Chareese.

"What did you say? I can't hardly hear you," Melissa yelled across Ramona.

Ramona felt her smile crack. Chareese was the antithesis to her own darker complexion and black hair that absorbed the humidity to become a cloud around her head. Chareese was dressed for a date at the fairgrounds—tight short shorts, a cute little floral blouse low cut to show off cleavage, and knotted to show off her midriff. Ramona wore a basic cotton dress that was limp and wrinkled from a long day at school. Chareese was tanned and bleached and straightened, and if Ramona didn't hate her before for being shrill and demanding, she hated her now for being shiny and bright and with Bobby. The hate and disappointment felt like a hard lump in her stomach.

"So Bobby told you about the monster trucks?" Melissa asked.

"Yeah, he's such a good friend, isn't he?"

Friend. Damn it.

The hard lump in Ramona's stomach started to slither, she felt nauseated. It didn't matter that she'd known this day was coming, the day Bobby would have a girlfriend. She hadn't expected it so soon. She really hoped it wasn't going to be Chareese.

"I've never seen one of these before, have y'all?" Chareese asked.

Melissa shook her head.

"Oh goodie, we can all be monster truck virgins together." Chareese squealed.

Ramona tried to chuckle. It sounded like the death throes of a crow. "I don't think monster trucks are something to claim virginal status over. They're fun but not life altering."

"Oh, so you've seen them before?" Chareese asked.

"Yeah, two or three times." Chareese didn't need to know that Lorena had been a driver groupie, and they had followed one guy around Texas one summer. Ramona had to have seen close to a hundred shows.

"So if we're virgins,"—the song over the sound system ended—"that makes you like a monster truck whore, right?" Chareese was still yelling into the silence the end of the song left. Everyone heard her call Ramona a whore.

Ramona had tunnel vision. The slithering in her stomach rose, and she felt bile burn the back of her throat. No one had ever called her a whore, not even over chocolate. She couldn't do this. She stood and started to crawl over Chareese and Bobby to get out. "I don't feel good. I need out."

"Chareese, that was uncalled for," Melissa said loud enough for Ramona to hear as she ran.

Bobby caught her arm as she passed him. Her eyes locked with his. She didn't even try to hide the tears as they formed. She waited for what felt like an eternity for him to say something, anything. He didn't.

"Let go of me." She wrenched her arm away from him and ran.

Getting out of the fairgrounds like swimming upstream during salmon season. She was buffeted by the crowd as she tried to move in the opposite direction.

14

Bobby couldn't find Ramona. She wasn't at her apartment. Mrs. C hadn't seen her, and she wasn't at the school. He knew he should be at Ray's, but Jenna could take care of things tonight.

The look on Ramona's face when Chareese had popped up out of nowhere at the monster truck show had felt like a knife twisting in his gut. He'd been too stunned to say anything when Chareese started dumping all that food into his arms. He hadn't even remembered mentioning the monster truck rally in her presence. Everything that could go wrong had gone wrong.

He'd tried to go after Ramona, but Melissa had caught up to him. She was not afraid to give him a piece of her mind. Chareese had been exceptionally rude, and Ramona was a sweet girl. Ramona was clearly upset by what Chareese said. Now either he needed to go talk to Ramona, or get his butt back into the show and accompany Chareese.

He left to chase after Ramona, but by then it was too late. She was gone.

He pulled into the tire shop. Brad was in the middle of

balancing the tires on a minivan. Bobby paced back and forth in the lobby until his brother was available.

"What's the matter with you? I swear you come in here growling and scaring off my customers," Brad chastised him immediately.

"I've lost her, Brad. I've lost her and I can't find her and I don't know what to do." He felt so empty, scared.

"Lost who?"

Bobby sat down and looked at his empty hands.

"Are you talking about Ramona or Chareese? Why the hell did you invite two women to the truck show? What kind of an idiot are you?"

Brad was right, he was an idiot.

"I hadn't invited Chareese. She was just there. I saw her at concessions. I didn't even say anything like 'come sit with us.' She just showed up."

"Well, you should know if you are planning on dating that one, Melissa wasn't impressed with her. I think her exact words were 'what the hell is Bobby doing with a bimbo like that?'" Brad's words weren't helping.

Bobby kept staring at his hands. "I had an angel and let her slip through my fingers before she even knew what she meant to me."

"Why don't you send her some flowers, a card, show up on her doorstep and beg her forgiveness." Brad stood impatiently by the office door.

After leaving the fairgrounds Bobby had driven straight to her apartment. Her car was in the driveway.

"She wouldn't answer the door yesterday. She won't answer her phone and now I can't find her." Bobby felt helpless. He was hollow for the two weeks Ramona had gone home, but this was different. This felt as if a hole had been ripped through his chest.

"I fucked up. I love her. What am I supposed to do?"

"Well unfuck it. Figure it out. Tell her who you are. I need to get back to work."

Bobby stared at the door after Brad left.

Unfuck it? How in the hell was he supposed to do that? Brad was right. It was time to show Ramona his secret.

Maybe she had talked to her friends. He drove to the police station.

Debbie sat behind the reception desk. "Hey, Bobby, what brings you into the precinct? Having problems down at Ray's?"

"I'm looking for Ramona. Have you seen her?" Words were hard to form.

"Oh, she went back to Dallas. Her sister finally popped, so she went home to see the baby."

He turned and left. He managed to remember to give Debbie a little wave and to say thanks.

She'd gone back to Dallas.

She'd left him.

He never should have mentioned the monster trucks to anyone. He'd been excited like a kid in a candy shop. He'd found something that would be a good first date to take Ramona on.

She would recognize that he was acting as if they were on a date. She would say something like, "That's what you do on a date."

He would respond with, "That's because we are on a date."

And she would smile and maybe blush. He would kiss her on the cheek, and they would share a giant pretzel. And afterward he would take her home and rock her world.

But no, he had to blab and mention the stupid show to Brad and again while at work, and that stupid bitch

Chareese had to overhear and show up and act like he had invited her.

He hadn't even known how to tell her to get lost without Melissa coming down on him. He panicked. He was a big stupid coward. And it didn't matter, Melissa came down on him anyway because he hadn't told Chareese to take a hike.

Road signs indicated Dallas exits were coming up. What was he doing? Had he really been driving for hours? He didn't know where Ramona's family lived. She wasn't returning his calls. He couldn't show up on the doorstep to every Campbell in Dallas looking for her. Or could he?

No. He shook his head. He couldn't.

He exited the freeway and got back on heading home. He would wait for her. She would have to come back for school in a week on Monday.

She had to come back. He wouldn't play games anymore. He would confess everything. Everything.

The bell rang. Finally. Ramona could not wait to get out of this place. How dare Bobby send her flowers? How dare the office interrupt her class to call her down to pick them up, and how dare Dr. G find it appropriate to comment on the state of her love life?

She was glad for the excuse to get out of town for the week before classes started. Baby Noah was a happy distraction. The flower delivery to her apartment had been embarrassing enough to come back to. Her stoop was covered in vases of flowers; some had clearly been sitting there all week and were dead, or dying. Somehow this was worse, getting flowers at school where everyone could see them. But they were pretty. And no matter how much she felt like hurling the stupid yellow flowers into the trash, they were nice and she hated to waste them. Mrs. C would like them.

She just wanted to go home and climb into that big bathtub that wasn't hers. That stupid tub that she had no right to miss. And that stupid man who owned it. Her heart hurt.

It was bad enough she hadn't been able to find a principal willing to hire her last week. Now that she was back in Haven, starting the first day of school with the flowers had felt like rubbing salt in a wound.

She focused on getting to her car without dropping anything. With a heavy bag on one shoulder, arm wrapped around the vase of flowers, and another tote bag in the other hand, she didn't even see Bobby, had no idea he was waiting for her until she felt the tote being lifted from her grasp.

"Hey!" she cried out before realizing what was happening. She glared at Bobby. She didn't want to talk to him.

"Let me take that," he said.

She narrowed her eyes, hoping that lasers would shoot from them. Chin lifted, she continued to her car. She looked at the locked vehicle and then at Bobby. He made an "uff" sound as she shoved the flowers at him. She wrenched the tote away from him and dug out her keys.

The car lock beeped, and she unloaded her burden into the front seat floorboard. Bobby hovered behind her. She pulled the flowers out of his grasp and leaned into the car, buckling them in so they wouldn't spill.

"Ramona, I get it. You aren't talking to me. Will you at least listen?" He sounded tired. He looked tired. His coloring was off. She told herself she didn't care.

She was tired too. Tired of crying because she had set herself up. Tired of having some hidden expectation when she'd known what the rules were going in. Tired of letting herself get hurt. And tired of putting in an effort when someone said they wanted change, but they didn't really and they weren't willing to do the damned work.

What did it matter if she had helped Bobby figure out how to be a friend first? He didn't care, all he was interested in was easy sex and no commitment.

"Look." He shoved a piece of paper at her, folded and molded to the shape of his butt from having been in his back pocket for too long. "I wanted to show you I'm clean. I got tested. I just seem to have some low-grade fever. But it's nothing. My body temperature has always been high. It's important to me that you see this."

Ramona stared at him, her arms crossed over her chest. She held still, played it cool, but her brain and her gut were riots of emotion. Why did it matter to him that she see this now? He had made it pretty damned clear that he had defined boundaries when it came to her.

She was an idiot. But that night under the stars. It really had sounded like he was leaning toward letting her know there was something between them. It hadn't been her imagination. They were going to step it up from friends to dating. That hadn't simply been a gut feeling.

The muscle in her jaw started twitching. She was holding her mouth too tight and clenching her teeth. She forced herself to open her jaw just a little, stop the clench, relax the muscle spasm.

It was harder to fend off the tears without that tension, but she didn't need to go back to the doctor for TMJ treatments. Been there, done that. Thanks, Devon. Anything Bobby said right now was lip-service. Talking to make himself feel better.

"You really aren't going to say anything, are you?" He

raised his eyebrows and held up his hands. He leaned past her and tossed the test results onto the passenger seat.

"I want to explain a few things to you, and I can't do that in a school parking lot. Will you come over? You can soak in the tub. Please, Ramona, let me explain."

And with those empty words, she pushed off from leaning on the car, slammed the passenger door, and walked around. She got in and started the car.

Bobby leaned over and braced his hands on the hood. "Ramona, please."

She looked at him, looked over her shoulder, threw the car into reverse, and pulled out. He could have held her car in place, it was so small and he was so big in contrast.

She saw him stumble as she drove out from under his hands. It was exactly how she had been feeling, like the ground had been ripped right out from underneath her.

The next day, another flower delivery. And another one the next day. She left them all in the teachers' lounge.

She was careful leaving the building after the bell rang. She didn't want to confront Bobby again. Or run away from Bobby, which was what had really happened.

She was going to go home and see if there were any schools that started later in the year that were still hiring. As long as they were within an hour's drive of her parents' house, she could do it. Would she spend her life running away from romances gone wrong? The real question was, could she stay in Haven, where she would run into Bobby at the IGA?

There were too many questions she didn't have answers for, and coming up with the what-ifs and the if-that-then-thises was too much.

She needed to get back into her regular routine. She wanted to run away. If she went home, it would be in defeat, and then she would have to face Devon and her cousin, Joanne. Could she go back? Jo really would have won then.

She had moved here on a wing and a prayer and the ego of being an effective math teacher. Math teachers could always find a job. Math teachers should never have affairs with their principals, no matter how long they had been dating, and no matter if they were secretly engaged or not. Working in Devon's school had seemed like such an ideal situation. They would have the same schedule, not conflicting district break schedules. He knew she was an excellent teacher, and he would let her do her job. She thought she could trust him with her career.

Now she was stuck with Dr. G, who kept sticking his nose in where it was not welcome. At least he hadn't commented on today's flowers.

She started the car and eased it out of the parking lot. A Tire World red tow truck screeched to a stop on the road in front of her. She stopped and waited for it to move. She beeped.

Brad, easily as large as Bobby approached her side of the car. Now that she saw him climbing out of the tow truck in the daylight, she could see how much alike he and Bobby looked. But he wasn't Bobby. She would talk to him.

"You got a minute, Ramona?" he asked.

She rolled down her window and nodded. "Yeah, why?"

Brad leaned into her window, resting his arms across the door. "I need to talk to you about my brother."

She squinted at him, not certain where this was going.

"Can we go somewhere to sit? Can we go talk at the Dairy Queen and I buy you an ice cream cone?"

He looked really worried. And maybe this was some kind of ploy Bobby had arranged. But that ice cream cone sounded like a good idea, and hanging around in this dusty parking lot was not going to be an easy place to have a conversation.

She nodded. "Sure."

Brad pushed off her car, returned to his truck, and finally pulled forward, clearing her pathway. She followed him the few short blocks to the ice cream shop. He suggested she find a table, and he went and bought two large soft serve cones.

Brad was already licking at his when he handed her the cone. She said thanks and began licking the cool, smooth treat. She picked up a napkin and wiped at her mouth.

"So what is it you wanted to talk to me about?" she asked.

"I think my brother is dying."

Ramona choked. Brad reached forward and took her cone while she coughed into a napkin. Her eyes watered, and she finally cleared her windpipe of the ice cream that had gone down the wrong way. "What's wrong? Why do you say that?"

Brad handed her cone back. "I've never seen him like this. I don't think he's eaten in a few days. He didn't go in to work last week at all, left Jenna scrambling with how to run things.

"I went out to check on him yesterday. He was sitting in the same damned chair on his deck, surrounded by beer bottles, that I had left him in the day before."

Brad sighed. "From what I can get him to tell me, he's done gone and messed up something terrible with you. I'm pretty sure it has to do with whatever happened at that monster truck rally. But he won't tell me what exactly is going on."

"How is that dying? Sounds like maybe he has some

remorse." Ramona caught a drip of ice cream before it could run across her knuckles.

"That bar is his life, and he hasn't gone in to work. When I was out at his place the other day, he hadn't fed those animals. He's just stopped. Says he had an angel in his grasp and he let her slip away. Something tells me he means you." Brad took a few licks of his cone to keep ahead of the melting.

She couldn't just let Bobby stop being, or could she? He had called her Angel before, so what did it mean that she got away?

"Will you agree to talk to him? I can make him take a shower and meet you someplace, or are you willing to drive up there with me? I can show you—"

"I know the way to his place," Ramona interrupted.

"What? How? Bobby doesn't tell anybody where he lives. Never has anyone over, which is a shame, 'cause his place is perfect for a big barbecue and party."

His place was pretty perfect, but too small to host something like a big party. She shrugged. "He let me use that tub since I don't have one."

"Then you are special to him. Please, Ramona. Honestly, I have never seen him like this before." Brad looked genuinely concerned. She remembered Bobby saying he was a good man, so here he was looking out for his little brother.

"I don't want Bobby to go and die or to stop functioning. He did look pretty rough when I saw him on Monday." She took a mouthful of her ice cream. "Okay, fine. Tell him I'll come over for dinner tomorrow at seven. But he has got to stop sending me flowers. People are asking questions, and my principal is being nosy. So tell him to cut that out."

15

The dogs ran around the front of her car in greeting as they typically did, excited to see a visitor. She called them by name as she got out of her car, and they settled. Swarming around her legs like a bunch of bodyguards, they followed—or was it herded?—her onto the deck.

She stopped when she saw how Bobby had set up the table back here. There were flowers in the center, and an actual tablecloth.

The door slammed open. He still hadn't fixed that hinge. He looked a little gray around the edges, but he had cleaned up for her. And he looked nice in a loose short-sleeve button-down and linen drawstring pants. She looked over him and realized he was dressed like he was going out. Crap, Bobby was dressed for a date, and she had come over in the same wrinkled dress she had worn all day long.

She couldn't help it. He looked good. Her eyes froze on his feet. He wasn't wearing shoes. She almost expected his legs to biologically end in cowboy boots. Long, tapered toes curled under her scrutiny. She glanced up. Bobby stood just outside of the door, a towel-covered plate in his hands. They stared at each other in silence.

Bobby regained his composure first. He continued over to the grill. "How do you like your steak?"

Ramona sighed. "More medium than rare, more rare than medium." She held up her bag. "May I put this inside?"

Bobby nodded. "Of course."

They were uncomfortable with each other, tiptoeing around whatever it was Bobby was going to say. What Ramona wasn't sure she wanted to hear, or did she hope for him to say something she wanted to hear?

He whistled for the dogs, and their noises moved from the side porch to the front of the house. From the sounds the dogs were making, Bobby had given them new bones. That would keep them busy and away while she and Bobby ate dinner. Once those dogs got their teeth on those bones, nothing would budge them.

She unceremoniously dropped her bag onto the couch. The cat twined between her legs. She reached down and scratched the big tabby behind the ears. She scanned everything that was out on the counter. It looked like the makings of a salad. The oven timer binged.

She reached over and clicked it off. "Want me to get this out of the oven?" She called out.

"Please," Bobby called back.

The warmth wafted into her face and blurred her vision for a second. She peeked in, then glanced around for some pot holders. Finding what she needed, she pulled the low pan with sweet potato fries out and set it on top of the stove.

Bobby stepped back into the kitchen. "Thanks." He handed her a serving basket. "Put them in this. Would you prefer the salad be pre-dressed, or do you want to control your own dressing?"

"In control, I guess." Salad dressing, probably the only thing in her life she could control. She used a spatula to transfer the fries.

"Great, grab what you want from the fridge. Steaks are probably already overdone," he said as he carried the salad and serving utensils out.

Ramona followed him with the fries and a few dressing options. The steaks smelled divine. The table looked nice. This was a date. She knew a date when she saw one. That or she was clueless as to his intentions. That seemed to be a running theme in her life these past few months.

She sat and watched as Bobby plated the steaks and something else from the grill. She couldn't take her eyes from him as he placed her meal in front of her. "Thank you."

She didn't look down at her plate to see grilled asparagus next to the steak until Bobby returned to the grill to get his own dinner. She waited until he sat before she served herself some fries and spinach salad.

"We should eat first," Bobby mumbled.

Ramona cut into her steak. It melted in her mouth. Her whole body relaxed as she chewed. She sneaked a look at Bobby through her lashes. He was focused on his eating.

"This is really good. I'm surprised you cooked for me."

"Why? I cook for you all the time, Ramona."

"No, you don't." She laughed in admonition.

Bobby held her gaze before he dropped his eyes back to his meal. "I think I've made every hamburger and BLT you've ever ordered at Ray's."

"Really? I guess I didn't realize... I was ordering from the bar and..."

"Well, who do you think does most of the cooking during the off hours? Me. And even if you come in at night, you never order straight from the menu. So there I am making you some special concoction."

She swallowed, embarrassed. "That must be why the food there is always so good."

Bobby set his fork down. "Ramona." His voice was low, barely above a whisper. He had only eaten about half of his steak.

She stared at her plate. Her eyes lost focus, and she blinked as she felt tears trying to form. She sucked in a deep breath and looked up, focusing out on the clear blue sky that had that not-quite-sunset intensity to it. "I know I was out of line. You had every right to bring a date." The words were hard to force out of her throat. They caught along the dry edges and wanted to stay deep inside. "I just didn't think..."

"Angel, stop. You aren't the one who needs to apologize. I am. I had made it pretty damned clear that I was going to take you out. And not to some group event, and not with me showing up with another woman. I messed up. I was telling Brad I had gotten tickets, and then he went and got tickets, and it all got away from me. Then somehow I thought I could prove to you I could be friends with women when Chareese showed up. But that was the wrong example. And then she went and opened her mouth, and... I don't even like Chareese. I ran into her at concessions."

Each word felt like a stab wound; some were worse, some were little scrapes. Ramona felt a lick at her fingers, and her hand found comfort in the fur behind Una's ears. The dog seemed to know she needed emotional support. When she looked at Bobby, his face mirrored hers with the amount of pain in his eyes and around his mouth.

"We are friends." She spoke slowly. "I reacted as if I could stake some claim to your company. We never made a rule that said during my coaching that you could or shouldn't date. I guess I—" Ramona bit her lip and returned to look out to the sky. Una pressed into her thigh. A trickle of sweat tickled her lower back. Her heart felt like it had stopped beating, and she could not take a deep enough breath.

"You had told me you didn't date. I made assumptions." She looked back at him. His eyes held her, almost like an embrace, but she knew better. There were no embraces from Bobby, only occasional hugs and, if she wanted, a no-strings-attached really good fuck, but no embraces.

She pulled the cloth napkin Bobby had set out from her lap and placed it with some finality on the table next to her plate.

"You look like you want to leave. Please don't go." Bobby stood and was next to her. He reached out and picked up her hand. "I didn't date. That wasn't a date. That was a mistake. I should never have let her come sit with us. Everything went sideways, and I mistakenly tried to show you that I could be a friend and not just some fuck boy."

He clicked at the dog, and she scampered off. He crouched down next to Ramona and swiveled her chair so she faced him. "Please, Ramona, I am begging. Will you give me a second chance? I want to show you something, show you how important you are to me."

She wrung her hands together in her lap. He had messed up, but her expectations were what had sent her over the deep end. She could have been mad at him and tried to enjoy the event. But she had made a fool of herself. Her stomach was a nervous mess. No wonder Bobby had suggested they eat first.

"I overreacted, Bobby. I think we both had different expectations for what was supposed to happen. You're right,

I did think it was going to be the two of us, and when it wasn't—"

"You were fine until Chareese came up. I didn't give you a chance to adjust at all. I had just dumped Brad and Melissa on you. And I sure as hell was caught off guard with Chareese. I can't apologize enough."

"Sure you can. I accept your apology. Can you accept mine?" She blinked a few times, tamping down her emotions.

"Look, Ramona, Brad was talking to me. And he's right. If I want to be serious with you, I need to tell you everything. I have to show you everything." He started to unbutton his shirt.

"Whoa, stop." Ramona started to scoot farther back into her chair. "I'm not gonna sleep with you. So, I don't know what you think..."

His shirt came off, and Ramona was caught up in the glory of his physique. Sure she wanted to see him, he was gorgeous, but not like this. She wanted a romance, love, not some I-messed-up-let-me-repay-you-with-my-body payment. When his hands went to the drawstring on his pants, she knew she blushed. She blocked the view with her hand. She dropped her gaze and focused intently on his feet. "You should probably stop now."

His feet disappeared under a pool of fabric.

"Really, Bobby. Please put your clothes back on."

She closed her eyes, and then Una was nosing her in the face.

Ramona grabbed the dog's ruff and pressed her face into the thick fur. "Una, tell your human to get dressed please."

A second dog nosed into her face. Ramona started back and opened her eyes. She wasn't holding on to Una. This was a new animal, bigger, redder. Wolfier.

Ramona scrambled back, and the chair tipped. She rolled and pushed away, then sat on her hip, leaning on her hands.

Una was joined by the other two dogs. They yipped and bowed and wagged their tails at their newest member, the wolf. The wolf stayed in place but pranced and wagged and panted at Ramona.

She called out weakly, "Bobby?" She didn't see him anywhere.

The animal yipped. And his front paws danced. His coloring looked familiar: tan underbelly, red sides, black spot by his tail.

Una made a play dive for him. He bit the air and then ran off. The other dogs followed.

Ramona watched as they wrestled in the dirt and grass off the porch. They ran back and forth and then went far out into the yard. She could hear their yips and playful barks fading into the distance.

"Bobby?" she called out again. Why had he left her alone with a wolf out here?

She pushed into a slightly more upright position.

The wolf was back. His tail wagging, his jaws open in a doggy grin.

Oh Jesus H, he's going to eat me. She looked around frantically. Where was Bobby? He had taken his clothes off, and now there was this wolf.

She stopped.

No. It was too far-fetched.

"Bobby?" She looked at the wolf.

The wolf sat and stood, and sat again, and then bobbed his head. His huge head nodded.

No, there was no way. "This isn't possible."

The wolf nodded again.

"Let's say I'm not going crazy, and you aren't going to eat me. Where is Bobby?"

The wolf stepped over to where Bobby had left his clothes in a pile. He nosed at the clothes and returned to sitting in front of her. Ramona swiped at her face. Sweat had formed in her panic, and so had tears.

"You can understand me?"

He yipped and danced a little.

"What's one plus two? Smarty-pants."

The wolf yipped three times.

"No." It was barely a whisper.

"I like tomatoes on my hamburgers."

The wolf growled slightly and shook his head furiously.

She sobbed out his name. And the wolf pressed against her.

Ramona turned into the furry chest and gasped for air. She laced her fingers into the thick coat and held on. Reality was slipping, but the beast was warm and strong, and she held on so she didn't slip further away.

Una nosed in under Ramona's arm and rested against Ramona's lap. "Are you one too, or are you just a dog?" Neither animal bothered to answer her. Maybe she would know she was completely insane if one of them had bothered to start talking.

"Why did you do this to me? I didn't mean to fall in love with you. I didn't want to. I know you won't ever feel the same, but why did you show me this? Why did you give me this burden?"

She pounded a few times against the solid animal. He never flinched or moved. She felt him nuzzle at her hair, but that was all.

16

Ramona's head throbbed. But that's not what woke her. She thought she had heard her name.

"Ramona, Angel, time to get you up and ready for school," Bobby's voice crooned in her ear.

She wriggled back into the warmth of his embrace. The pressure of his nose rubbing against her hair actually helped to ease the headache.

Her eyes flew open. She froze. She was in Bobby Cray's arms. In Bobby Cray's bed.

She vaulted out of the bed and pressed against the wall. She stared at him. Her heart was going a mile a minute. He smiled up at her, his wide, naked chest all exposed like it was meant to be on display. Blankets were a rumpled, piled mess. *Oh Jesus H, is he naked?*

She closed her eyes and took a deep breath.

"Good morning, beautiful." She felt his warmth and his nearness a second before his arms wrapped around her and he placed a kiss on her forehead.

Why had he kissed her? She tried to swallow.

He ran a hand up and down her arm. "You cold? You're shivering. Do you want some coffee?"

He left her; she heard him pad into the kitchen.

She opened her eyes and peeked out the door, afraid she was going to see his naked ass. She sighed in relief when she saw that he wore knit shorts. But the rest of him was naked, and she could see all his skin. His hair was piled up in a super messy, bed-head top knot. That reminded her that her own hair must be a complete disaster.

She tiptoed into the bathroom, trying not to call attention to herself. She rummaged through the under-counter baskets looking for a brush. A man with hair like his owned at least one brush. She knew he did. Now where did he keep it?

Jesus H, there aren't any brushes in here. She found a hair band and pulled her hair into a quick ponytail.

Her face looked puffy. She had definitely cried herself to sleep last night. She splashed cold water on her face and wondered what had happened. She was still in all her clothes. All of them. Including her bra. She wouldn't have put her bra back on if they had done anything, would she?

She finished her ablutions and stepped out. Maybe she could sneak past him and go out the door and leave. She didn't know if she could face him this morning, not knowing.

"Coffee's made. You want some?"

She froze in her tracks and stared wide-eyed as Bobby approached her. He wrapped an arm around her and pulled her in close. The breath caught in her throat. *What is going on?*

"It's not too late to call in for a substitute, is it? We could spend the day together."

Damn it, it was a school day. She swung her head side to side. "No, I don't think so. What time is it?"

Bobby swiveled and looked behind him. "Ten to six. I had set the alarm for five thirty. Is that okay? You still have time for breakfast, right?"

She looked down at her dress. Panic still surged through her veins.

Bobby was half-naked and smiling like a fool.

"I've got to go. I have to take a shower and, no, sorry." She eyed her purse and dived out of his arms. She grabbed the bag and rushed out the door. "I'll see you later." She called out in a hurry as she made her escape.

She didn't breathe again until her car turned onto the road and sped back toward her little apartment.

In record time she was in her classroom prepping for the day. She could not focus. Every time she relaxed for a second, her mind's eye went back to that broad chest and all those muscles. And sweet baby Jesus, his nipples. She didn't know what it was about that man's nipples that did her in, but his certainly called out to her. And they demanded to be licked.

She slammed the stack of books in her hands down on the desk.

"You okay, Miss Campbell?" Kayla asked as she entered the room seconds before the first bell.

"Uh? Oh, yeah, I'm fine. Just dropped these." Ramona continued to organize the books as the rest of her students filed in. She didn't have a clue what she was supposed to be teaching today. Thank goodness for planning calendars, standards, and having taught this same material for the past six years.

A quick review of what she was supposed to be doing, and she managed to conduct class without being too distracted by the memory of Bobby's backside in those shorts this morning.

By the time the bell rang for lunch, Ramona felt like one of the zombies she had her students prepping to fight. She hadn't eaten any breakfast, and she'd forgotten to pack a lunch. She rummaged in her purse and found enough change to bravely venture into the school cafeteria. It wasn't as bad as from when she was in high school, and it wasn't as good as the school she'd left in Dallas. It reminded her of gas station quick-mart food. Not the best, then again not the worst.

"Ms. Campbell, report to the front office. Ms. Campbell, please report to the front office."

A chorus of oohs came from the students as her name crackled over the loudspeaker.

She sighed and carried her lunch tray with her down the hall toward the office.

"You in trouble, Miss Campbell?" a student teased as she passed a small group in the hall.

She used her hip to push open the office door.

Her grip tightened on the tray, which saved her lunch since her other reaction would have resulted in chicken sandwich and fries all over the floor.

The back counter looked like a florist. Maybe it wasn't that bad, but her initial reaction was flower overkill.

"Hey, Ms. Campbell. You got a few more flowers delivered." Marge swept her hand back, showing off the display.

"Oh, he's got to stop. This is too much," Ramona said under her breath.

"Well, apparently whomever it is, the driver wouldn't tell me, said they were supposed to be delivered one an hour, every hour until two, but he didn't have time for that nonsense, so he brought them all in at once."

Ramona took a deep breath. The flowers smelled wonderful. She set her tray on the counter and stared at them. In the middle was one single red rose in a bud vase. "Is there a card?"

"Sure is." Marge handed over an envelope.

Ramona opened the envelope. Her gaze kept going back to that single rose. Nerves in her lower abdomen did a flip, and she was more nervous than she should have been reading a little note card.

She read it, and read it again.

Thank you.

She flipped the card over. *That was it? Thank you?*

She shook her head. She didn't understand Bobby, not in the least.

She froze and felt a flush creep up her neck. Oh Jesus H, maybe they had done something and she really could not remember it at all. Was that why he was thanking her?

"What do you want me to do with all of them?" Marge asked.

Ramona pointed to a mixed bouquet with yellow and blue flowers. "Have one of the students run that one down to the teacher's lounge." She pointed to the rose, and another arrangement. "I'll take those back to my room. Is it okay if I leave the rest and pick them up at the last bell? I don't have a place for them in my room, and they'll die if I try to keep them in my car for the rest of the day. You want to take some home with you?"

"Sure thing, honey. I think they are pretty. Your boyfriend certainly must be in love with you to have had all of these sent. He's been sending them all week. Is he in the doghouse or something?"

Ramona laughed. "You could say or something, but

doghouse is pretty close. Has Dr. G commented on these yet?"

"He's not in today."

Good, Ramona really didn't need him calling her into his office to discuss the intentions of whoever was sending all of these. And he would. No matter how often she told him to please not.

Ramona carried the last of the flower arrangements into her apartment. They overwhelmed the place. But now that she was talking to Bobby, they didn't make her angry. Nervous, uncertain, but not angry.

A soft tapping sounded on her front door.

"Hello?" she asked as she swung the door open.

"Hi, Angel."

She closed her eyes. He was too handsome to look at—his smile was dazzling, and sparks flew from those golden eyes of his. His hair was a mane of golden brown. And his voice ran over her like warm water.

"Why are you here?" She backed up to let him in. He never visited her at home. It made her nervous.

The more she remembered last night, the more her nerves twisted in her gut.

"I wanted to see you before I head in for work." He stepped toward her, an arm reaching out.

She danced away from him. She hid behind a flower arrangement and fussed at the flowers.

"I see you got them."

"They are lovely, Bobby, but you have got to stop sending me flowers at school. It gets kind of embarrassing."

"The students being little jerks?" His brow creased.

"I can handle the students. It's the other teachers and the principal." She bit her lower lip.

Bobby walked around the table to her and slid his hand over her shoulder.

She twisted and ended up against the back of her couch, the table between them.

"Ramona, what's the matter? Why won't you let me touch you?"

"About that." She paused and searched for the words that would make this somehow less embarrassing, less nerve-racking. "Last night."

Bobby's smile broadened, and he looked even more happy than when she had opened the front door. *He wouldn't be grinning like that if they hadn't. Oh Jesus H.* She whimpered and ducked her head, trying to hide behind her hand.

"Hey, what about last night?" he asked.

She could feel him standing right in front of her, could see his belt buckle when she opened her eyes.

"I don't remember much about last night."

"Oh." He sounded defeated and took a step back. "So you don't remember the wolf?"

"Do you?"

He nodded. "I remember everything from when I'm in that form, like how you asked me if you liked tomatoes. Clever test."

"I remember the wolf. So that wasn't my imagination. I had long dog fur on my dress this morning. It wasn't Una's. I remember crying, a lot. But the next thing after that, I woke up. And we were in bed, and you were half-naked and—"

"And you don't remember anything in between?" He was back, close. His hands ran over her arms.

She still didn't look up. "I'm pretty sure we didn't do it,

but then your note just said thank you, and"—she spun away from him; she couldn't even face his belt buckle— "then I thought maybe we did. And I don't know what to think." She completely covered her face.

Bobby rested his hands on her shoulders. His thumbs began rubbing in small circles. It felt so good she wanted to melt.

"We did not make love last night. You fell asleep crying on me. I said thank you for listening; thank you for letting me show you my secret."

She turned and looked up at him. He was very close, close enough to kiss. She could feel his breath on her face. She placed her hand in the center of his chest and pushed him back. He took two steps before she lowered her hand.

"Are you okay? You're shaking like a leaf."

"I'm nervous. I'm scared. I'm not sure what's going on."

"Are you scared of me?" Bobby's voice was somber.

She couldn't talk. The words stuck in her throat. She was terrified of him. She nodded.

He took a big step back. "You don't need to be. I would never hurt you. My wolf would never hurt you."

She pressed her fist into her lips, willing the tears to not start. She unclenched her fist and placed her fingers over her mouth. She breathed in with a shudder.

"I'm actually not afraid of your wolf. I'm afraid of you."

Bobby staggered as if he had been slapped. "Why me? What did I do?"

"Nothing." She was crying now. She couldn't help it. She'd had her heart broken before, and she was terrified Bobby would crush hers. "It's what you know, and how you'll use it against me."

Devon had taken all her love and fears and twisted them

against her. Bobby could hurt her with a casual flirt and never know how he destroyed her.

"Use what I know against you?" He raised his voice. His tone was confused. "I told you that I can shape-shift. What on earth do I have to use against you? If anyone should be nervous here, it's me."

Ramona gulped. "I know, it's all backward. I'm sorry. I told you that I'm in love with you, and I'm scared that you will turn that against me, humiliate me. Break my heart." She hid behind her hand again.

"Hey, hey, hey, Ramona." Bobby's voice was so soft. His arms came around her, and he cradled her into his chest. "Is that what happened? Is that why you moved to Haven in the middle of the school year?"

She nodded, letting the tears fall.

"I would never use your love against you. You made me the happiest man on earth when you said that last night. Angel, I showed you my wolf because I'm in love with you. You showed me how to be your best friend, not anyone's friend but yours. And I think I froze and let things get fucked up on purpose because I was scared. I felt like dying once I realized I had hurt you. I honestly would rather die than ever do something like that to you again." He tucked his finger under her chin and lifted her face.

His eyes seemed to glow from within. He lowered his head to her. His hair cascaded around her like a curtain. She was surrounded by him, his hair, his scent, his arms. Ramona's head swam with colors and lights as he slid his mouth across hers. His lips were soft and warm. He tasted sweeter than she had imagined. He pressed into her. She twisted in his embrace and wrapped her arms around his neck.

Cupping her face, he kissed her more deeply. Her lips

parted with a soft moan, and his tongue tip tickled her lower lip before seeking out her tongue. Bobby lowered his hand. The one around her back pulled her in tighter. The other brushed down the side of her neck, grazed cross her shoulder, palmed her breast. She moaned into his mouth.

The nerves in her stomach coalesced into a hard knot. Ramona's hands were up and shoving him away. "Whoa there, mister. What do you think you're doing?"

Bobby chuckled. "I was kissing you and touching you."

"What makes you think I'm okay with that?" She pushed the nervous panic back down into her gut.

He slid his eyes from side to side. He pointed to the center of his chest. "I'm in love with you." He placed the same finger on her breastbone below the divot at the base of her neck. "And you're in love with me. I thought that meant I could touch you and make love to you a little before I had to go to work."

Her baggage cars of emotional attachment screamed at her. They wanted his hands on her. Ramona shook her head. "Not so fast. What do you mean, 'make love a little?' We just went from friends to realizing we have feelings for each other. We haven't even been dating."

Bobby gestured, opening his arms wide. "What was all of that then? What have we been doing for the past ten weeks?"

"Becoming friends. Getting to know each other. But that wasn't dating. I don't know if I can date you if other women think they can be with you."

"I'm not interested in other women, Ramona. I'm in love with you. I want to hold you. I want to pet you and whisper in your ear."

"How many women have you said that to? Huh, Bobby? And you sleep with a different woman practically every night. Ya know, how am I supposed to deal with all that? I need to build some reassurance on the romance side of this now."

Bobby ran his hand through his hair, gathering it at his forehead and brushing it back. He sighed. "That's all reputation, not reality. Dating rules?"

Ramona bit her lip and nodded.

"Let me have them." He dropped his hands.

"You aren't mad?" Ramona squinted up at him.

He snorted. "I'm not mad. Maybe a little frustrated, but I am in love with you. That means I follow your rules, do what I have to do for you to know that you can trust me. I go at your speed. I have never, wait... No. I have only ever told one girl that I loved her and that was Taylor, and we never had sex. I don't toss that word around lightly. So if I tell someone I love them, I really do. It's not something I say to get a woman into bed."

Ramona slumped back. Relief rolled over her body. "What about the other thing?"

Bobby sighed heavily. "There is only you. I honestly have not been interested in anyone but you for a few months now. The last time I had a hookup was back before Memorial Day. It's been a long summer."

The breath stopped in her lungs. "That's before you asked me to be your friend coach. Before all of this."

Bobby nodded. "Yeah. I knew I would have to be your friend before I could ever hope for you to have feelings for me."

"So you did all of this so I would sleep with you?"

"Well." Bobby scrunched up his face. "Yes and no, it's kind of hard to explain."

Ramona crossed her arms over her chest. "You showed

me you can turn into a wolf. I think you'll manage this one just fine."

Bobby ran both hands over his face and paused, so it looked like he was trying to hold his head together.

"You walked into Ray's one day. I could probably tell you the exact date if I thought hard enough. I made you a brownie sundae, and I saw my future in your eyes." He looked around the room, his eyes focused on anything but her. His gaze finally settled and locked with hers.

Ramona felt the intensity of his stare in her chest.

"You were an angel. You had this halo and wings of light. I knew I had to change everything. I think I fell in love with you that very second. Or maybe I had been falling ever since we first met. I don't know. But what I did know was something Brad had told me. I had to be a friend first before I could expect a woman to love me."

"Oh." Ramona couldn't think. Bobby had done all of that, for her.

His phone rang. He grabbed it and looked at the caller ID before turning the ringer off.

"I'm late. Will you come by for dinner?"

Ramona nodded.

"Can I kiss you again?"

17

"Y ou'll be fine, and I'll be back in a few hours." Bobby
looked over at her.

She shook with nerves. She had already met Brad and
Melissa, but not as Bobby's girlfriend. Today she was girlfriend, and not just friend. Today was officially meeting the
family. The nerves in her stomach rioted.

She took a deep breath and relaxed back into the seat. "I
know, I know, but now it's... well, now I'm meeting the
family, and they will be judging me differently. They're
gonna be thinking if I'm only your girlfriend now because
we slept together."

Bobby began to grumble.

"I know, I know. I'm being uno cabeza estúpida. It's none
of their business, but it's still going to be there in the back of
their minds."

"You want me to say something to Brad about it?" Bobby
asked, his eyes so full of compassion Ramona wanted to
kiss him.

She laughed. "Hell no! They'll wonder what's wrong
with me because I haven't."

"Or maybe they'll realize this is serious. Look, Angel, Brad and Melissa like you. I mean, Melissa ripped me up good over the monster trucks. I think they already like you more than they like me. C'mon." Bobby opened his door and climbed out of the car.

Ramona stared straight ahead. Bobby had a small family, nothing like the crazy madness of hers with all the cousins. Their opinions pulled more weight because it was such a small group. She breathed and focused. They loved Bobby despite his reputation, despite his faults. Maybe they would like her a little simply because Bobby did. She let out a breath and opened her door. She peered up at Bobby, who stood waiting for her.

"You ready?"

Ramona nodded. Bobby pushed two cases of Coke into her arms. He picked up another case of drinks and two bags of ice. He led the way into the house.

She lagged behind him and stared at the modest house. It wasn't large, but it was well cared for. Bobby and Brad had grown up in this home, and for years it had been the two of them. Letting people into their lives had to take trust. Somehow this was reflected in the care they had taken of the place. How easy would it have been for two young men, barely adults, to let things fall apart around them? They hadn't, and they more than survived, they'd succeeded. They'd thrived.

Coming in from the hot, the air inside was cool against her skin. Small plastic toys announced kids lived here. From what Bobby had told her, one toddler lived here, and Tyler, Abby's son, was over here a lot. So that made two toddlers and two seven-year-old twins making use of those toys.

Squeals and giggles from farther back in the house let

her know that, at least for the moment, they were happy kids.

The cacophony of noise grew as Bobby led her farther back into the house and through the kitchen. Following Bobby's lead, Ramona deposited her cases of Coke on the counter.

He turned to her and held out his hand. Ramona slipped her hand into his larger warm one and took a deep breath. This really shouldn't be this hard.

Bobby slid open the sliding glass doors, and they stepped back out into the heat. The warmth engulfed Ramona, and she felt her nerves subside.

"Uncle Bobby!" a small voice called out, and seconds later Bobby was tackled with the *thud thud thud* of small bodies wrapping themselves around his legs.

He bent over and picked up the toddler, a small, practically bald, blond creature with large round eyes, wearing an olive-drab tutu. Bobby turned to face Ramona. The smile on his face combined with the messy child in his arms gave her cramps. Damn ovaries exploding into overdrive.

"This is Princess Pete," Bobby introduced. "Petey, this is Ramona. I need you to be extra nice to her today. She is kind of nervous. You watch out for her while I'm at work?"

Ramona shot Bobby a questioning look. He winked in reply and mouthed *boy*.

The toddler said, "Uh-huh," and stuck out a sticky hand to shake like a trained puppy. Ramona dutifully shook it.

Then she looked down into the faces of the twins who still hung on to Bobby's legs.

He twisted so that one little girl was closer to Ramona, and then the other one was. "Sophie, and Sadie."

Ramona said hi, and then the two pigtailed girls ran away in a fit of giggles.

"Don't put him down," Melissa announced as she climbed up the ladder from the pool. She wore cutoffs and a T-shirt that had more patches of plaster and paint on it than it had of its original color. She reached for Petey. "Hey, Ramona, welcome to our home." Melissa leaned in as Bobby bent down and gave her a quick kiss on the cheek. "I need to put this one down for a nap. Brad should be back in a few. He ran out to get charcoal for the grill."

"I'll be back later," Bobby announced.

"Abby said she was going to stop by after she got out of brunch with Max's family. Oh, and I should warn you, Lindsey and Mama might head over too." Melissa said. She leaned toward Ramona. "Bobby and my sister sometimes don't always get along."

Melissa disappeared into the cool dark of the house.

"I get along fine with Lindsey. She's just overly opinionated." Bobby slid an arm around Ramona's waist and pulled her to his chest. "You gonna be okay?"

Ramona raised her eyebrows and stared up into his face. "I love you, and I've got Princess Pete watching my back when he gets up from his nap. And I don't know what I was all nervous about."

"See, that's my girl." He leaned over and captured her lips in a kiss.

Ramona would have loved for there to have been more kiss, but this was neither the time nor the place to make out, no matter how much she enjoyed it.

"I'll be back by the time Brad is grilling burgers for dinner." Bobby dropped his arms from her waist and stepped through the sliding glass door, leaving Ramona standing awkwardly alone on the back patio.

A noise from the other side of the pool preceded a gate

swinging open. Brad stepped through carrying a large bag of charcoal and some mesquite sticks.

"Hey, Ramona. I saw Bobby pull out as I got here."

Ramona lifted her hand in a little wave.

Brad dropped the goods in his arms with a huff.

She looked at the size of his arms, almost as impressive as Bobby's, and wondered if carrying that bag had really been an effort at all. He dusted his hands off on the back of his jeans before extending one to her.

She took it.

"Thank you for talking to him that day. I didn't exactly expect this, but..." Brad paused. "I'm glad you two... ya know..."

"You care for him a lot, I could tell. You were worried, and—"

"I love my brother," Brad cut her off. "He looked like he was dying inside. I've never seen him like that. Never. And now look at him. He said you didn't even know?"

Ramona looked down at her feet. "No, I didn't know he felt that way."

Brad pulled her in to a tight hug and then let her go. "He's a tough one to love, but he's worth it."

"No, Brad, he's easy to love, and that's what's scary. But yeah, he's worth it."

"What y'all talking about?" Melissa asked as she stepped back onto the deck.

"Just welcoming Ramona to the family," Brad said as he placed an arm around Ramona's shoulder. "Giving her some pointers and tips on how to keep a Cray man in line."

"That's easy—love him and keep him stocked in beer." Melissa laughed as she handed Brad a chilled bottle of the aforementioned beer. "You want one?"

Ramona shook her head. "No, I'm good."

"You ready to work? Bobby told you what we were doing, right?" Melissa asked.

Ramona spread her arms, presenting her work clothes. "Yup, I am all set to work."

Melissa yelled at her twins, "You let me know when that boy wakes up, okay?"

They scampered across the deck full of giggles.

She turned to Ramona and clapped her hands. "Well, let's get to it. You and me are on the pool, and Brad is finishing the grill."

Ramona nodded and followed Melissa's lead. She climbed down into the dry pool, where she was handed one of the scrapers.

"So what are we doing exactly? Bobby said it was a big push to get the deck finished."

"That's it exactly," Melissa confirmed. "We used the pool one last time in its miserable condition. I want a nice pool for next year. Hopefully Brad will be able to finish bricking in the grill today. And maybe by Christmas I'll have a full-blown outdoor counter with a grill top and a smoker and maybe even a sink." She raised her voice. "Right, Bradley Cray? I'm getting a sink on that counter?"

"Yes, ma'am," Brad called back.

"So what I need you to do," Melissa continued speaking to Ramona, "is remove the surface plaster off. You can see where it's already peeling. We need to scrape all that. And then I'm gonna tile it with concrete and little glass pebbles."

"Ooo, that sounds like it will be nice."

"I hope so. I've been looking at this pit for years. I want a descent pool that me and my babies can swim in."

"Amen to that. How long has this pool been out of commission?" Ramona asked. She poked the flat blade of scraper against the side of the pool and watched as a thin layer of plaster crumbled away from a cement backing.

"We use it, but it's not in good shape, and it leaks. I don't think they took proper care of it since, well"—she dropped her voice and leaned closer to Ramona—"since their daddy took off. It's needed to be replaced for a long time."

Ramona's eyes widened, and her lips shaped an O. That had been a very long time.

"Bradley got the parts he needed to make it one of those saltwater pools, so my babies don't have to swim in chlorine. It turns their hair green."

Ramona pushed the scraper along the pool between the concrete wall and plaster coating. Chips of plaster flaked off. More stubborn areas required a bit more effort and elbow grease to get the coating to budge. A shard of the rock-hard coating flew off and stabbed Ramona in the cheek. "Hijo de puta." She clapped her fingers to the sting, and they came away red with blood.

"Melissa, you have any bandages?"

"Sure in the bathroom."

Ramona climbed from the pool and headed inside. When she returned, she had a bandage on her cheek and a cold Coke in her hand. She sat on the rim of the pool as if she were dangling her feet into water. She tapped her heels against the side of the pool.

"Mama, Mama, Mama, Petey is awake." One of the identical girls came bounding through the open sliding glass door.

"I'll get him," Ramona volunteered, pushing up to her feet. She paused inside to let her eyes readjust. She poked into one small bedroom—nope, this was clearly the twins' room. The next room assaulted her senses. "Whoa, someone needs a diaper change."

The whining grunt she was answered with indicated she had said something wrong. "Princess Pete, you ready for clean pants?" She lifted the sleepy tot from his crib. "Okay, buddy, where do you keep diapers?"

"Oh, hi," a voice from behind Ramona said.

Ramona turned to see the newcomer. She recognized the young woman Bobby had called his adopted sister.

Abby extended her arms and reached for the little boy. "I'll take him." She scooped Petey from Ramona's arms and placed him onto a changing table.

"You're Ramona," she declared. "I'm Abby. I take care of Princess Pete and the girls when Melissa works."

"So you know who I am?" Ramona asked nervously.

"Yeah. Bobby told me. I think he wants to tell everybody, but he also wants to be cool, ya know?" She laughed. "He's a good guy."

Ramona sighed. "He is. He is."

After a quick diaper change, Abby set Petey on the floor and he scampered out to the front of the house. They followed him out and caught up with him and another small boy already playing with one of the copious plastic toys Ramona saw when she'd first entered the house.

Ramona squinted when she stepped back out onto the deck.

"Was that Abby I heard come in?" Melissa's voice asked somewhere from the depths of the pool.

Bobby picked up the half-empty glasses in one hand and wiped the table down with the other. The day was moving slow, and he didn't expect to see Ramona for a few more hours. It was quiet in here with most people out at end of summer barbecues. After all, that's where Ramona was.

She made time speed up and his heart race.

He would much rather have any part of her warm, supple body under his hands right now than this dirty towel. He let a smile take over his entire face as he thought about her.

She had been so cute and nervous when he dropped her off at Brad's this afternoon. Melissa already liked her, and Brad did too. So she had nothing to worry about.

But he wanted to be there with her, have her and those luscious legs sit on his lap. He would be able to touch her skin, and until she was comfortable with him touching more skin than just her leg, he would take as much leg petting as he could.

She was such an anomaly to him. Sweet and feminine in her school dresses, but she wore shorts all the time, and God help him, a bikini to the lower dam. She let cussing slip all the time. Was she even aware that she cussed in Spanish?

He was beginning to have a hard time, literally, in his pants. He needed to stop thinking about how soft the skin on her thighs was, or how her round ass felt as he cupped it through the fabric of her shorts.

Last night had been wonderful. He had totally forgotten the joy and anticipation of getting to the next level of intimacy with a woman. Something Ramona was slowly reintroducing him to.

Damn, it was almost too slow for his body. He could wait. She was worth it.

If she did everything with the enthusiasm of her kisses, he knew he had a lifetime of ecstasy ahead of him. And the woman could kiss. He suppressed a groan remembering the feel of her T-shirt and the warm breast underneath filling his palm.

He owed his brother a beer or ten. He had been so right when he said the right woman would not be offering for a hookup.

"Bobby Cray!" He winced as the wrong woman walked into the bar and screeched his name. "Why did you go and leave me by myself at the monster trucks. That was embarrassing."

"I had to leave," Bobby said with as even a tone as he could keep.

"I was sitting with you."

"Nobody invited you, Chareese. You were there on your own to begin with." Bobby groaned, his pleasant thoughts replaced by this harpy.

"Well, it's not like I was interrupting anything. You were just there with your brother and his wife and her friend. It's not like it was a date." She stood in front of him, hands on hips.

"Actually it was a date—"

"You don't date. Bobby Cray doesn't date. Doesn't do nooners, doesn't stay the night, won't touch you if you're married, in a serious relationship, or drunk."

"No, Chareese, Bobby Cray doesn't do hookups of any kind anymore. I have a girlfriend with whom I go on dates," Bobby corrected her.

"Bullshit. You're just saying that to avoid me," Chareese sneered.

"You don't believe me? How 'bout this?" Bobby stood up to his full height and opened his arms wide. He raised his voice. "Excuse me, everyone." He looked around to be sure he had the attention of the few people who were in Ray's this afternoon. "I am no longer available. I have a girlfriend and am in a monogamous relationship. Thank you; go about your business."

He leaned in close to Chareese and sneered. "Was that clear enough for you?"

She pursed her face. It looked exceptionally pointy.

She squealed, shook, and then turned. "Fuck you, Bobby!"

She stormed out past a tall blonde with a sleek haircut, slow clapping. "Oh, honey, I think you missed the point. He won't be fucking anyone anymore. Will you, Bobby?"

Bobby chuckled. "No, I won't. How you doing, Lindsey?"

Ramona grunted as she hit a stubborn patch of plaster.

Melissa sat above her finishing a late afternoon snack of grapes. Her twin girls sat on either side of her. The girls ate more from their mother's plate than their own. The boys—Brad, Tyler, and Petey—had all retreated into the house for some male bonding time. In other words, they were watching an animated car and truck movie.

Abby worked next to her on the same stubborn section of the pool. "Tell me again, why are we doing all this free labor?"

"'Cause pool?" Ramona asked.

"Right. 'Cause pool," Abby repeated.

"Go inside and watch the movie," Melissa directed the twins. "And tell your daddy, Mama said he has work to do and get his butt back out here. You mind your brother and your cousin."

The glass door slid open and then closed again as the girls went inside.

Melissa stood and made her way to the opposite side of

the pool to grab the scraper she had been using earlier.

"Hey, y'all," a sharp voice called out as the sliding glass door slid open again.

"Hey, Lindsey—" Melissa began.

"So, you're not gonna believe this," the voice continued. Lindsey stood far enough away from the edge of the pool that Ramona couldn't look up and see her. That also meant that she and Abby were not visible from where Lindsey stood.

"I just came from Ray's, thought I'd swing by and say hey to Bobby first and grab some ice before heading over here. Chareese was in there giving him the what for."

Ramona shot a wide-eyed look at Melissa. Melissa's jaw hung open, and she tried to make a noise to interrupt her sister.

But Lindsey continued. "Get this: he tells her to get out of his bar, that he's not interested in a hookup."

Ramona leaned her back against the wall of the pool and bit her lip. Bobby didn't like Chareese, but she didn't seem to get it. Ramona knew about their past. It was history, over, done. She had to admit hearing he had slept with Chareese, no matter how far in the past, stung. Insecurity attacked Ramona. Would Bobby be able to be loyal to her? Why did Ramona even think she had a chance with him? She closed her eyes and tried to breathe. The air suddenly felt too hot, to heavy.

Abby walked to the far side of the pool, where Lindsey should be able to see her. "Bobby has a girlfriend now. A serious girlfriend."

"I know. He told me. And when I made some comment how that never mattered to him before, he threatened to kick me out of the bar too."

Ramona smirked when she heard that. This was why

she could trust Bobby.

"All I can say is the girl's hoo-ha must be made of gold for Bobby to be so aggressive about wanting Chareese to back off."

She couldn't listen anymore. She needed to stop Lindsey from saying anything about her hoo-ha and Bobby. Ramona jumped and then pulled herself up the side of the pool, so she hung over the edge by her arms. "Hi."

A very glamorous woman with a chic blonde haircut, designer resort palazzo pants, and a bikini top removed expensive-looking sunglasses and glared down at her.

"Lindsey, this is Ramona," Melissa introduced them. "She's Bobby's girlfriend."

"Oh shit." Lindsey twisted side to side in what looked like embarrassed annoyance. "So you and Bobby, huh? Well, I guess if he's getting it someplace—"

Ramona pulled herself up to sit on the side of the pool. "Actually, we haven't slept together yet."

"What?"

"No way."

"Well fuck me." The other women all spoke at once.

Lindsey pointed at Ramona. "He's not sleeping with you, and he's turning other women down?" She flopped her arms at her sides in an exasperated movement. "That's it. It's a sign of end times. Stop the presses."

Melissa sat heavily on a plastic chair.

Abby giggled. "He really is in love with you, isn't he?"

Ramona shrugged. "I guess so. If all y'all's reactions don't confirm it, I'm not sure what would."

Lindsey shook her head. "Well, I never thought I'd see the day Bobby settled down. Good for you." She redirected her attention to Melissa. "I thought you said this was a pool party. What happened to the pool?"

18

Ramona spun the taps and left the tub filling. Inside the house she tossed her change of clothes onto Bobby's unmade bed and took her fluffy blue robe into the bathroom to strip down for the tub.

It was weird. She still wasn't used to it. She had been a guest in the house for several months, but now, knowing Bobby was in love with her, it somehow felt different. Almost like this was home, not her apartment.

Cat twisted between her ankles and followed her outside. The dogs dozed in the dirt just off the deck.

She twirled her fingers through the water, checking to see if it was warm enough. Evenings still held on to the heat of the day, so she didn't want the tub to be too hot, but if it wasn't hot enough now, the water would get too cold too fast. And Ramona wanted to be able to lounge for a while. She spilled in a hefty portion of bubble bath.

She made sure the little inflated pillow was blown up all the way, and suction cupped it to the side of the tub. Even though she was alone, out in the middle of the country, she still felt a twinge of panic that someone might see her for the few seconds between the time she took off the robe and stepped into the tub.

She sighed and settled into the deep, warm water. Bubbles spilled up and over, covering her completely. The uncertainty of how and when to let Bobby take their relationship to the next level bothered her. They had successfully traversed the terrain of making out and were getting into petting, but something in her stopped it before she would allow skin-on-skin contact. She ran her hands over her breasts, slicking the water around. Hmm, Bobby touching her skin would be magical.

She needed to stop comparing the progression of this relationship to how she and Devon finally got together. Having a crush on the boy next door, and finally getting him to notice her, and then finally have him take her out and kiss her—yeah, that situation did not apply here. She had been in love with Devon for a very long time before he even noticed she was a girl. She didn't have that lifelong slow burn with Bobby. No, she'd met Bobby less than five months ago, and she was an adult. Adults entered relationships differently than kids did, and she needed to stop applying first-time kid logic to how she and Bobby grew into their relationship.

He was right. What had they been doing over the summer? Getting to know one another. She already knew him enough to know she wanted him; she knew she would have sex with him in that bed inside the house. So why was she dragging her feet?

Right. Somewhere not so deep down, she still had all those romantic notions about true love and monogamous relationships and sex being worth the wait.

The rumble of Bobby's car announced that he had

returned home. One of the dogs huffed a low complaint of a bark, but none of them moved.

"Hey, Angel," he called out as he passed into the house behind her.

If he accidentally saw her today, because she wasn't being hyper-cautious, that would not be a bad thing. He had already seen her in a bikini, and she'd felt pretty damned exposed in that. It wasn't a small bathing suit, but it did not leave much to the imagination. No, she wanted flesh. Next time they made out—well, tonight—she wanted his hands on her skin.

She closed her eyes and relaxed deeper into the water. It felt good, and it made her realize how much she needed Bobby to touch her.

The gentle sounds of the country around her lulled her into a near-dozing state. Bobby moved about in the house. The dogs moved around and made soft woofing complaints. An overwhelming smell of grass and farm animal assaulted her senses. The wind must have shifted from the neighboring ranch. It did that from time to time. She ignored it, knowing it would pass.

A soft lapping by her toes brought her back up to the surface of almost being awake. She kicked at the lapping. A spray of water would get the dogs to stop drinking her tub.

A loud snort and bovine complaint brought her completely awake. Her eyes flew open.

The dogs were not drinking from the tub. The biggest longhorn steer she had ever encountered—okay, the only steer she had ever encountered; those little cows at the petting zoo did not count, and neither did a steak—stared back at her. It shook its head. Ramona tried to press herself back through the wall of the tub. She watched the ends of the horns and tried to figure out how it wasn't knocking the porch down.

"Bobby," she called out softly.

The steer returned to drinking from the tub by her feet. She was afraid to splash water at it again. What if it tried to run at her? She would never survive those horns, and hell, its head was practically half her height.

"Bobby!" she called out again, a little bit louder.

"What's up—Oh, that's what's up." He let the screen door slam behind him as he stepped onto the porch. "Okay, big guy, stop drinking my lady's tub. All those bubbles are gonna give you one helluva tummy ache. And you have five of them. It won't be good."

Bobby ducked under the horns and approached the side of the beast.

Ramona was terrified it was going to turn on him and attack.

She gasped when he wrapped a hand over one of the horns and started pulling the head around. "Come on, buddy. This isn't your backyard."

The steer lowed and finally backed up and turned. Ramona ducked as the beast swung its head around. How it didn't crash into everything with those horns, she didn't know. How Bobby managed to not get impaled, she didn't know; she was happy it didn't happen.

Bobby shoved the steer on its shoulder, and as it walked away, he slapped its rump.

"I'm going to follow this guy back to the hole in the fence he came in from." The dogs were up and following along with him and the beast.

"Be careful," she called after him.

He waved as he followed the beast loping away from the house.

Ramona anxiously waited for Bobby to return. His property stretched away from the road for a good distance. She heard the dogs first, barking happily, having enjoyed the trek to the edge of the property and back. Sweat stained Bobby's shirt.

"Where did that monster come from?" she asked as he stepped up onto the porch.

Bobby gestured, indicating the direction. "There's a break in the northeast section of fencing. I leaned it back up, so it at least looks like a functional fence. I'm going to have to do a full fence ride and see if there any other sections that need fixing." He wiped his face with the hem of his shirt.

"Does that happen very often?" she asked.

Bobby shrugged. He stepped closer to the tub. "Every so often one or two steer find their way onto my property. That's the first time one has ever made it up to the house."

"You don't sound worried."

"Why are you? They're just big cows, docile. You have more to worry about from Cat." He chuckled.

"But those horns."

"Mostly for show, Angel." He stepped toward the tub.

She looked up at him. His expression made her nervous, made her skin tingle. His eyes glowed, and his lips curved into a wicked half smile.

Ramona sank a little farther into the tub. "What are you doing?" So far he had been conscious of giving her space when in the tub. He either stayed on the far side of the bamboo wall or turned his back or closed his eyes.

She sucked in a breath as he pulled his shirt off and began toeing off his boots. "I'm getting in that tub with you, Angel. You get to decide if the jeans stay on or are coming off, but I'm getting in." He began emptying his pockets.

Ramona stared at him. His chest was broad and strong,

and she loved snuggling up to him. Skin on skin with that chest was going to be new. The nerves in her body zinged with an electric charge.

Her breath stuttered in her chest. "On, they stay on." She wasn't sure if she was ready yet. All the little rumors she had been hearing about Bobby turning women down and flat out announcing he was done with it, he was in a relationship made her heart skip. He made her heart throb, but was it too soon?

She scooted forward in the tub and gathered bubbles around her. She couldn't help being shy around him. The fact that he wanted her seemed to make it worse.

The water splashed and Ramona giggled. Bobby adjusted and wiggled into position behind her. He wrapped his arms around her middle and dragged her sliding back against him.

She sighed as she rested her head against his shoulder. *Jesus H, I'm an adult.* She could let him touch her and nothing bad would happen.

He spoke softly. "This is what I always imagined this tub for. Me and my lady soaking in the sunset." He wiped a few stray hairs back from her brow. "I never realized how perfect it would be."

"Is this what you were thinking about when you climbed in with me a few months ago?"

He kept his arm tight around her middle. Her breasts brushed against his arm when she moved. She held her breath and bit her lower lip.

"I was probably thinking more along the lines of this." He started to nuzzle her ear.

She leaned into the movement and didn't bother to suppress a soft moan.

Bobby clenched and released a fist several times. The

movement of his fingers brushing her middle tickled. She squirmed.

"It's a good thing I kept the jeans on. You keep that up and I don't think I'll be admiring the sunset."

"Then stop tickling me." She giggled.

"I don't know where to put my hand, okay. You are all skin underneath these bubbles, and I want to touch you."

She grabbed his hand and caressed his fingers out flat against her belly. "There. Better?"

He hummed a positive sound into her hair. He splayed his other hand farther down, closer to her hip.

His hands felt warm, the pressure something she wanted more of.

She slipped her back across his chest, the water removing all friction between them. The motion was slick. The feeling cranked her desire past level ten.

Bobby's fingers grabbed into her soft skin.

"You feel so nice." His voice was thick with want.

Ramona felt it right in her core. She tilted her head to the side and swept her hair over her shoulder, exposing her neck.

Bobby didn't need a second hint. His lips began nibbling behind her ear and trailing down the exposed skin to her shoulder. The hand that was low on Ramona's belly, near her hip, slipped lower.

She picked up his other hand. "This needs to be here." She placed his large hand over her breast.

Bobby clenched his hand, grabbing onto her, kneading her flesh.

He growled. Ramona felt it reverberate through her back.

She made a mewing sound when his grip changed and he rolled her nipple between a finger and thumb.

Bobby's other hand stopped. His fingers raked through the thatch of hair above her sex.

"I'm going to keep touching you, and I am going to make love to you right now unless you tell me to stop." His voice sounded as if he could hardly contain his emotions.

Ramona knew exactly how he felt.

"But you can't make love to me if you keep your jeans on," she pointed out.

"I don't need a penis to make love to you, woman. I've got two hands and a mouth."

Ramona tried to suck in a breath, but she stuttered with nerves. He already made her body need to be touched, and he hadn't done anything.

She closed her eyes and bent her knees. "Then don't stop."

She bit her lip in anticipation as Bobby's fingers slid farther down. He caressed the soft flesh between her legs, and as he petted back up, his fingers found their way between her folds.

Ramona bit her lip harder and stifled another mewing sound.

"Angel, you don't have to stop yourself from making noises. We have all this space; go ahead, fill it with your screams."

Her head rolled back on his shoulder, and she let out a moan. His hot breath caressed her ear. Fingers kneaded her breast and tugged at her nipple. His other hand expertly stroked around her bundle of nerves.

Ramona squirmed. Her hips began a matching counter thrust to the movement of his fingers. He dipped one into her depths, and then a second finger.

"Doesn't that feel good?"

Ramona practically cried, "Oh yes."

Ramona's cries could not express the way her body sang under his touch. He played her like a fine instrument. Strumming, stroking, and pressing, each movement of his hand elicited another vocal response. All the nerves in her skin rioted and cried for their turn to be caressed. He needed more hands. Her breasts demanded attention, yet there was no way she wanted him to stop the rhythmic stroking of her sex.

Her inner muscles quickened their pulling/sucking motion. She arched her back. "Oh God, Bobby!"

The orgasm took over, and Ramona couldn't move.

He growled, and his motions grew more intense, more demanding, driving her orgasm harder, faster.

She couldn't take anymore. She collapsed against his chest. Bobby continued to stroke her, but with long breaks between each movement of his hand.

She twitched and let out little cries of surprise with each motion. Finally she clenched her legs together, trying to still his hand with her thighs.

"I can't... You need to stop." She could barely speak as her body shuddered again.

"I don't want to stop."

She could hear the smile in his voice.

"I want to do that to you all night long."

Ramona reached down and removed his hand.

"I don't think I would survive all night long." She laughed.

She slid back and forth, trying to snuggle back against his chest. She gave up and turned around. She pressed into him, the sensation of crushing her bare breasts against his naked skin made her rethink her claim of not being able to keep that up all night long. She reached up and wrapped her hands around his neck.

She felt the hard bulge in his pants press against her belly. If he could do that to her with his hands, why was she stalling on letting him make love to her the way he wanted, no clothes at all, penis included?

She nipped at his chin, scraping her teeth over the stubble.

"I love you, woman."

"Yes, you do. Jesus H, you are amazing."

His hands grazed down her sides and slid over her hips. His hands scooped over her ass and held on. He pulled her closer, up his chest.

"You feel better than I imagined. And trust me, I have imagined touching you for so long."

She giggled. "It's the water. It makes everything all slippy slidey."

"Hmm, yes it does. Thank you."

"Thank you for what?" she asked, looking into his eyes. They caught the reflection of the sunset and glowed.

"For letting me touch you. For falling in love with me. For letting me love you as much as I do."

Ramona pressed her lips to his.

Bobby returned her kiss with as much attention as he had to making her scream. He cupped her head and held her to him as he licked and caressed her lips with his.

He was right. He was completely capable of making love to her while keeping his jeans on.

19

Ramona focused on wiping the rims of the jars off. Mrs. C stood slightly behind her, watching every action she took. So far today they'd stewed and prepped what felt like gallons of apples for the apple pie jam.

"There." Ramona stood back and admired her work; every rim was spotlessly clean.

Mrs. C stepped forward and inspected the work. "Looks good, Ramona."

"This is somehow easier and yet more precise than I thought it would be." Ramona laughed.

"If it was difficult, I'm sure our ancestors would have used a different method of preserving food," Mrs. C replied. "Now, sugar, take the lids from the hot water bath."

Ramona followed the instructions. The water was still hotter than comfortable, and the heat traveled up the handles of the metal tongs. She didn't mind, especially if the hotter the water, the less likely botulism was to form. She dropped the lid onto the first jar.

"Try to shake off some of that excess water," Mrs. C corrected.

For her first canning lesson, Mrs. C had shown her how to can stewed tomatoes. This time they made jam. Ramona wasn't an expert and enjoyed the lessons. She thought she might be able to do this on her own next time. The idea of canning fresh salsa appealed to her.

She shook the water off and placed the sealing lid down. All those apples and they only had a dozen half-pint jars of jam.

She walked over and adjusted the temperature under the Dutch oven Mrs. C had brought over. She used this for her final water bath. The jar tongs looked as if they should do more than just lift jars in and out of the water bath. They looked like canning jaws of doom.

Ramona picked up the tongs and grabbed the first jar.

"I think you're missing something there, sugar," Mrs. C admonished.

The front door to her apartment banged open. "Angel, I thought I'd swing by before work," Bobby called out.

Ramona put down the jar lifter and smiled.

Mrs. C stepped out of the kitchen. "Bobby Cray, where are your manners? You don't barge into someone's home without knocking. And you certainly make sure you know whose home you are entering. I think you owe Ramona an apology for being so rude."

Ramona wiped her hands off on a kitchen towel and followed Mrs. C out of the kitchen. She rested her hand against the older woman's shoulder. "It's okay."

"Hey, Mrs. C." Bobby leaned in and gave the older woman a kiss on the cheek as he walked in to the living room. "What are you two up to?"

"We are canning. What are you doing here, young man?" Mrs. C huffed at him.

He gave her a dazzling smile and then focused his gaze

on Ramona. "Ramona is my angel, my sweetheart. I came by to see her. I have a long night at the bar tonight and am going to miss her."

"Really now?" Mrs. C turned her gaze to Ramona.

Ramona stepped forward and gave Bobby a quick hug. "It's true. And he's allowed to come on in. So it's okay." She grabbed his hand and pulled him toward the kitchen. "Come see. Mrs. C is teaching me canning. We're making jam."

Bobby looked at the row of jars waiting to go into the water bath. "Did you can those tomatoes you gave me?"

Ramona nodded.

"I thought those came from Mrs. C."

"Nope, she taught me how to do it." Ramona was excited to show off her new skill. She quickly washed her hands before picking up a metal screw band and twisting it onto the first jar. "This is what I was forgetting, isn't it?" she asked.

"That's right, dear. Don't screw it down too tightly. You don't want to break the seal when you remove it tomorrow."

After twisting the bands onto the jars, Ramona picked up the tongs. One by one she placed the jars of apple pie jam into the water bath. She covered the large pot.

"Tah-dah! And now we let it boil for fifteen minutes." Ramona held her arms out, presenting her accomplishment.

"Now set a timer, sugar. And remember to take those collars off tomorrow. I'm gonna skedaddle on home and let you two visit before Bobby has to get into work."

"Thanks, Mrs. C. And thanks for the canning lessons. This is fun." Ramona gave the older woman a quick hug.

Bobby walked Mrs. C to the door. "It was good to see you, Mrs. C. Next time are you going to share your secret peanut butter cookie recipe with Ramona?"

"Why would I do that? It's a secret." Mrs. C said.

"Well, you won't share it with me. I thought maybe it was a secret female thing."

Mrs. C laughed and patted Bobby on the cheek before leaving.

Ramona began moving the dirty dishes to the sink and rinsing out the pan they'd cooked the jam in.

She let out a giggling squeal when Bobby grabbed her around the middle and picked her up.

He set her back on her feet and looked deep into her eyes. Her breath caught as he swept a stray hair away from her face.

"Am I going to have to put in a garden for you?" he asked.

"I don't know. I'm learning how to do this. Who knows if it actually works for me?"

"Well, you let me know if you want a garden. I'll put one in for you at the house." He picked up both of her hands and led her out of the kitchen.

His breathing was a little faster than normal.

"You feeling okay?" Ramona asked.

Bobby nodded. He bit his lip and then removed something from his front pocket.

"Look, Angel, I know you aren't the kind of girl who would sleep with someone without knowing there is a commitment there."

Ramona's stomach did a flip. Her pulse sped up.

Bobby pulled her down onto the couch, so she sat across his lap. He lifted her left hand, turning it so the palm was up. "I hope you know there is a commitment here from me. I would like to think that you know this."

He showed her what had been in his pocket, a ring. It was a hefty block of silver with the shape of Texas outlined in tiny blue stones. Raised letters along the edge of the surface declared *State Champions* and the year of the award.

"This was my championship ring. I want you to know that I am committed to you. I want everyone else to know this too." He placed the ring in her hand.

Ramona wasn't sure how to respond. She was delighted, but this wasn't an engagement. At least she didn't think it was. They hadn't ever talked about getting engaged or married, but every now and then Bobby would say something that made her think he was in this for the long haul. She knew she was.

He fished something else out from his pocket. He placed a thin plastic bar next to the ring. "Melissa gave me a spacer that should adjust it to fit. Look, Ramona, I want to be with you for a very long time. Until we decide exactly what that means, will you wear my ring?"

Bobby wanted to go steady. It made her want to laugh. It wasn't an engagement, but she still flung her arms around his neck and kissed him. For a guy like him, this was a pretty big deal.

An annoying buzzer pulled her from the bliss of having Bobby's lips on hers.

"My jam!"

20

"I like this." Bobby sat across from her and watched as she graded.

She smiled. She liked it too, being near him. But were they talking about the same thing? "What do you like?"

"You here, working."

"I've been coming in to do grading for months."

"I know, and I like it. I've always liked it." He grinned.

"You know, Dr. G is going to get wind of this and he's going to call me down to his office and scold me."

"No, he's not."

"I wouldn't put it past him." She shuffled the stack of completed grading.

Bobby continued grinning at her.

"Okay, what's up?" she asked. He acted as if he was plotting something.

"I love you, and I was thinking no one is going to come out tonight, not with the storm rolling in. I should send Rob home and close up early." His voice dropped, his grin changed to a half smirk, and his eyes narrowed a little. A golden light flashed from their depths. "And then I could make love to you on the pool table and on the bar, and in this booth. And then I'd like to take you home, and try that in the tub again, and—"

Ramona felt the blush burning her cheeks. "How about we start with a bed?" she asked.

"I will make love to you anywhere you let me."

Ramona huffed out a half laugh. "You're a tease."

"Sweetheart, I'm anticipating, planning."

There was a loud crash, the music stopped, and the lights went out.

"Storm's here," Ramona announced.

"Hey, the lights are out!" Rob called from the kitchen.

"You got a flashlight back there?" Bobby yelled. "You stay put," he told Ramona.

Ramona could hear him shuffling around; suddenly there was a bit of light barely illuminating the bar. Bobby held his phone with a flashlight over his head.

She followed his movements. The back door cracked open as Bobby pushed on it. A dim gray light spilled into the bar. It wasn't much, but enough she could see to gather her papers into some semblance of order and packed back into her bag.

She walked over to the kitchen. The two men were moving things about and appeared to be generally cleaning up. "Is there anything I can do?" she asked.

Bobby stopped wiping down the grill and put an arm around her waist. "Could you go out to my place and make sure the dogs are in. And then call me when you get home, so I know you're safe."

"Do you want me to stay with the dogs?"

"No, Angel, you don't have to do that. You're more likely to have power in town at your place. I don't want you stuck out there."

"How late are you planning on staying here?" she asked.

"Not long, but cleanup takes time and I'd rather get it done now."

"Okay." She acquiesced and leaned up on her toes to give him a quick kiss. "I'll call to let you know what it's like out there."

Lightning flashed, and the entire sky was as bright as daylight. Of course, it should have been light outside, but the thick black clouds had turned the afternoon dark as night. The clouds weren't so bad. Ramona didn't mind a good storm; it was the wind that unnerved her.

Tropical Storm Hector was supposed to dissipate once it hit the coast. Apparently no one told the storm, and right before landfall it had become an officially named hurricane. Hector had dumped a lot of water and caused some major flooding. It wasn't letting up, and it was moving inland slowly.

The tops of the trees whipped around, but nothing near the ground was moving with the same velocity. Haven was in for a long night.

Bobby was right. There was still power on in town. Ramona made a mental note as she headed out to his place.

The animals were more than ready to be inside. Cat slinked in through the door before Ramona managed to have it all the way open. She freshened their food and water bowls and gave each of the dogs a new chew treat. She ruffled ears, and since they seemed content and none of them flinched during a particular stunning show of lightning and thunder, she headed home.

Ramona stopped in front of Mrs. C's house and ran up the front steps. The wind had picked up. Things at ground level were starting to move around.

"Ramona," Mrs. C said as she opened the door. "Whatever are you doing out in this?"

"I was about to pull in and thought I had better check to make sure everything was okay with you."

"Thank you, how kind. I'm perfectly fine. Are you going to be okay in that cottage of yours?" she asked.

"I should be. There aren't any big trees, and my unit is in the middle," Ramona explained.

"Well, if you feel like you need to come over here to be safe, don't you hesitate."

"Will do, Mrs. C. You stay safe." Ramona dashed back to her car. Big fat raindrops started pelting her from the sky. They were so far apart she literally could have dodged them.

She swung her car into her drive and ran inside.

She called Bobby.

"Dogs are safe and sound. How much longer do you have?" She expected that he would almost be done by now.

"I sent Rob home, so all I need to do now is finish the mopping."

"Bobby, are you mopping the entire bar?" she asked.

"Of course. I'm taking advantage of no one being here and doing all the cleaning while I can."

"In the dark," she added.

"Yeah, well, the lights are out. What am I supposed to do?" he asked.

"Okay, be that way. Call me in a bit, will you?"

"I'll call when I'm finished. I love you. Are you okay with this storm?" he asked.

"I'm good with storms, but this wind is kind of freaky. Just call me later, okay?"

Ramona wrung out the pile of delicates she'd washed. She was too distracted to focus on grading, and the pile of hand-washing had been growing. Now seemed liked a perfectly reasonable time to tackle this particular chore.

Lighting and thunder crashed. Ramona jumped with a small *eep* of surprise.

She wrestled with the wooden folding drying rack until it stayed up. Every time she used it, she forgot the secret on how to latch it. And every time she told herself not to forget. She was draping a camisole over the bar when her phone rang.

"Hey, Bobby, you finally finish up there?"

"Yeah, but now I'm stuck. The lower lot is half flooded. My car is going to need days to dry out before it can run again. I had to block the front door with those water absorbing sand bags to keep the water out."

"Damn, I didn't realize it had gotten so bad." Ramona walked over and looked out her front door. Once the rain started, it had not let up. Branches were down. Water rushed through the gutters of the street, but there was no flooding at her apartment.

"I don't like you being stuck there. I want to know you are safe," Ramona said.

"I'm safe as houses, okay. You know exactly where I am."

"Yeah, but you're not here." Ramona's voice was wistful.

"I know, Angel. I'd rather be there too. We could make out," Bobby laughed.

All noise except the storm stopped. Ramona sat in darkness. "Well, my power just went out. You know, I was thinking..." She paused and took a deep breath. "I was thinking we could see how well the bed worked."

"Ramona." Bobby's voice was low. "You aren't toying with me because I'm stuck here?"

"No, I've been thinking about it, and I can't see any—" All the lights and TV came roaring back on, only to crash back into silence and darkness. There was a *pop* and a booming explosion outside. She screamed.

"Jesus H, Bobby... Bobby?" Her cell phone went dead.

The rain pounded on the roof.

Ramona placed lit candles on various surfaces throughout her small apartment. She didn't need many, just enough to provide light for watching her laundry dry. There wasn't much else she could do.

She heard a faint scrabbling at her door.

She tried to focus on the sound, but it was gone. The storm must have picked up and the trees were making noises. She thought she heard the sound again. She moved quietly to the front door. Listening. She definitely heard the noise again. Without her outside light she couldn't see if someone was there through the peephole.

The scratching again, this time Ramona was standing right behind the door, there was also a whining noise with the scratching. It sounded like a dog. She opened the door.

A crash of lightning illuminated a large, very wet, red wolf with glowing gold eyes pawing at the screen.

Another crash of lightning and Bobby transformed. Before he took two steps in, he had Ramona pinned against the wall, his mouth on hers. His kiss was needy and demanding, giving her his desire, wanting her passion. Rain followed him in. He kicked the door closed behind him. Even after the shift his skin and hair were still wet.

Ramona wrapped her arms around his shoulders, pulling him close. His hands found her hips. Ramona backed up toward her bedroom, pulling Bobby with her. She tripped, falling backward onto the bed. Bobby's mouth never left hers.

His kisses pushed Ramona back into the pillows. Her

hands twined into his wet hair. His hands ran down her sides and hooked into the waistband of her shorts.

She smoothed her hands across the top of his chest, feeling his thick, hard muscles under her fingers. Her heart beat loud in her ears, competing with the sound of thunder from the storm.

"Condom," she breathed. "I don't have any, and you didn't bring any with you."

"Hold on." He pushed up and away from her. His gaze lingered on her face before he left the room.

Ramona licked her lips as she watched his large, shadowy form leave the room. In the dark, she couldn't make out any details. Lightning flashed just enough to outline wide, strong shoulders tapering to thin hips and long, well-formed thighs. His physique was powerful and glorious. She was ready to touch all of him, to be consumed by him.

Seconds later he returned, holding up a box of what she assumed were condoms.

"Where were those?" she asked, not even mad he had hidden a box of condoms in her apartment.

"In the top of the hall closet. I put them up there after you told me you loved me. I knew we would need them at some point."

Bobby paused in the door. She could see his glowing amber eyes in the dark. He was outlined by another flash of lightning.

"Angel." His voice was rough with desire, but he didn't move. He stood frozen in place.

"What's the matter, Bobby? What's wrong?"

Bobby lingered in the doorway for a few moments, looking at her, the glow in his eyes fading. He filled the door. She should have been intimidated by the sheer size of the man, but she wasn't. She loved his strength; she loved how he towered over her and surrounded her when he held her.

He moved slowly. He sat on the edge of the bed. "I've wanted to touch you for so long and now that you want me to, now that I can, I am almost paralyzed by the profound importance of it. I should be worshipping the altar of you, not thinking about desecrating you with touch."

Ramona sat up and rested her hand on his shoulder. She could feel him shaking. He was staring at the box in his quaking hands. He turned his gaze to her. "I think I get why you had us wait. This is important; this is going to be life changing. It's not just sex anymore, is it?"

She shook her head. "It never has been for me."

"I finally understand the concept of sacred and profane love. Agape and Eros. I want, I need them to be both for you."

Ramona sat back. "Bobby." With his attention on her she pulled the tank top off over her head and removed her bra. She hoped her movements were fluid, sensual. "Shut up and make love to me."

A growl escaped his lips as he lunged for her, dropping the box in his haste to claim her. Their lips crushed together as tongues tangled. Bobby's hands found the button to her shorts and hurriedly undid the zipper. Her shorts and panties followed the rest of her clothes to the floor.

Bobby pulled away again, turning to locate the box of condoms he'd dropped. He tore the box open and grabbed a foil packet, ripping it open with his teeth. "I can't do this right, not properly, not the way you deserve. I need you too much." He rolled the condom down his length and looked at Ramona. Her eyes never left his face.

"First you're paralyzed, now you're in a hurry. What's

taking you so long—ah." Her last word dissolved into a gasp as he thrust into her.

The storm crashed louder above them as they collided together. Everything stopped; all time, all motion, stopped. Ramona stared into Bobby's eyes. They glowed fiercely. He filled her. She understood what he meant. This was the perfect combination of sacred and profane. This was emotion made physical. They didn't move at first, reveling in the sensation of being joined.

Ramona reached up and caressed the side of his face. She tangled her fingers into his hair.

Bobby closed his eyes and leaned into her touch. Time and space rushed in. They began moving in rhythm, a smooth, unhurried motion. Bobby kissed her face, her chin, trailing down her neck to her collarbone. Ramona dug her fingernails into his shoulders as he left a scorching trail across her chest before claiming one of her breasts with his mouth.

Her hips rocked, matching him thrust for thrust, in time with the steady drumbeat of rain on the roof. Her body felt as if he was the lover she had waited for her entire life, the lover her body had been made for. Everything fit—he filled her with erotic pressure; his hands cupped her breasts perfectly, his lips, his tongue, everything felt beyond perfect. Her skin burned where he touched her. Her nerves sang a heavenly chorus with every thrust.

She locked her feet behind his hips, intensifying their intimate contact. Bobby cupped her butt and thrust even faster, matching the frenzy of the raging storm.

Ramona couldn't focus on anything beyond his touch. She forgot how to use her hands to touch him. She gripped his upper arms, holding on, digging her nails into his flesh. Ramona threw her head back and cried out as waves of orgasm slammed through her body. Lightning flashed simultaneously with a loud crash of thunder as nature joined her in an explosive release of energy.

Bobby growled at her response and began moving faster. His body seized up in an orgasmic spasm as he grasped Ramona to him. Bobby's roar of release as he spilled into her was drowned by the booming of the storm above them.

They fell limp together, spent. Bobby rolled onto his back, pulling Ramona with him so she lay draped across his chest.

"Thank you." His voice was thick with emotion.

"You keep saying that," Ramona panted, her face resting against his chest. "Why are you thanking me this time?" She trailed her fingers over the contours of his arm, stroking down to the back of his capable hands.

"For teaching me patience. For showing me how different sex can be when it really matters."

Light and noise blared through her apartment. She jumped. Ramona grabbed a robe and rushed into the front room. He followed her out with the sheet wrapped around his hips.

"I think I liked it better with the power out." He leaned against the wall where the hall opened into the living room, watching Ramona as she moved about turning off the TV and blowing out candles.

"I did too." She paused, smiling at him. "Help me make sure I got all the candles, then do that to me again."

"Make love to you?" He cocked an eyebrow at her.

"Yeah." She smiled coyly at him and bit her lower lip.

Bobby leaned over and blew out the candle that sat on her entry table. He visually checked that all other candles he could see were out. Nodding toward her kitchen, he asked, "Did you get the one in there?"

"Got it." Ramona stepped back in front of Bobby. All the lights in her apartment were turned off except the soft night-light she always left on in her hallway. It provided enough of a warm glow to see by.

He reached forward and unfastened the tie to her robe. Keeping his eyes locked on hers, he slipped the robe from her shoulders so that she was exposed to him. Ramona didn't flinch. She didn't feel the sudden urge to hide. She was his now; all shyness was gone. She reached forward and pulled the sheet from his hips. She swallowed a hard lump in her throat. This beautiful man was hers.

He was gorgeous, marble-statue perfect. His sex was proportional to the rest of him. His manhood pulsed and grew under her scrutiny. She didn't need to ask if he was ready so soon.

His hand cupped the back of her head, and he pulled her into his embrace. His lips captured hers, tenderly licking and biting her lower lip.

Ramona could feel all of his skin against hers. He was warm and smooth. He made her tingle. Lightning and thunder crashed overhead, and Ramona flinched.

Bobby's warm hand soothed down her back.

"This time"—he bent slightly, scooping her up into his arms—"I will make love to you properly."

"That wasn't properly done before? It seemed pretty properly done to me."

Bobby set her on the bed. "No, that was too rushed. This time I will worship you the way you deserve."

21

Ramona picked up the stack of handouts. Today was going to be a distracted day for the students; she needed to get as much information into them as she could before the bell rang.

"You comin' to the game, Miss Campbell?" Kayla asked as she walked into the classroom.

"Of course I am." Of all the games this season, this was the one she wouldn't miss. RavenCroft Ravens were going up against the Central Tigers. If the Tigers won, they would be headed to the playoffs. If the Ravens won, they would officially become one of the top-ranked teams in the state, even if they didn't make it to the playoffs.

Darius Michaels entered, surrounded by a gaggle of other students who did not belong in her classroom. His popularity and local school celebrity status was rising higher and higher each week. It was her job to keep him passing this class. He and his posse stopped inside the door.

"Oh no you don't, Miss Campbell, uh-uh." Darius wagged an admonishing finger at her.

She stopped what she was doing to face him. "What are you going on about, Darius?"

The young man lifted his arm and pointed at her hand. "That." The expression on his face was deep disappointment.

There was a collective "ooh," and "uh-uh" from his hangers-on. The masses clearly did not approve.

Ramona lifted her hands and looked down the front of her dress. It was one of her favorites, dark blue back ground with tiny bunnies and carrots and small yellow flowers. "What?"

"You've been wearing that blue and silver ring. It's got to go. Those are Central's colors. You're wearing a Central ring. How could you?" Darius sounded so disappointed. "I thought you would be on our side."

Ramona looked at the ring on the middle finger of her left hand. It had been on her hand for weeks. She flipped her hand around to show the ring to the crowd with Darius. "This has nothing to do with football."

"Bullshit," someone in the back of class coughed.

She rolled her eyes. "I know it's a championship ring, so yes, it has to do with football. But I'm not wearing it in support of Central. My boyfriend played for Central. It's his ring. He gave it to me."

"Miss Campbell, did you get engaged?"

What little of her class that had been in their seats were now up and crowding around her with Darius and his group. Someone held her hand out, and everyone admired her ring.

"Not quite. Nothing official. It's more of a promise ring. For now this says he's my guy and I'm his girl," Ramona explained.

"Oh that's so sweet."

"Is it that big guy we saw you with?"

"So you're definitely not pulling for Central?"

Ramona hadn't realized wearing Bobby's ring would have opened her up to so much scrutiny and so many questions from her students. She had been pretty sure that they never paid much attention to her, and if directly questioned wouldn't have even been able to answer correctly what color her black hair was.

"No, I will be in the stands rooting for RavenCroft."

The bell rang, announcing the beginning of class.

Ramona pointed to half the kids crowded around her. "You lot aren't in my class. Get to where you need to be. My class, time to take your seats."

Unfortunately, the distraction of the ring set the tone for the rest of the entire class. No one could concentrate or focus on the task at hand. Everyone was too concerned over the game tomorrow night. This meant that Ramona was losing two classes this week to the football game, since tomorrow would be replaced with what amounted to an all-day pep rally.

She collected the papers. She would try again on Monday. For the last few minutes of class she let the students talk football. Game play, stats, odds, these were all based in mathematics. She needed to spend some time working her algebra assignments into football-related questions. Zombies would only hold their interest for so long. These kids already knew the math; they just didn't realize it. And they didn't know how to apply what they knew to the questions on the test. Knowledge transference, that's what she needed to leverage. Get something they were interested in, get them to apply what they already knew, and then pull the curtain back and show them how much they actually understand. And then get them to do that on their own.

≈

Ramona drove into the parking lot at the Roadhouse. She wished that her friends wanted to hang out at Ray's more. Of course she wanted to be near Bobby, but honestly, the food was better. There was food. Nachos and giant pretzels did not make up a menu. The Roadhouse had a blended margarita machine, and that was something Ray's did not have.

Debbie stood inside the door waiting for everyone to arrive.

"Don't they have any tables?" Ramona asked.

"They do, but they have some new policy about waiting to be seated, and most of your party must be ready for a table. I guess Ethan and his surprise strip shows are getting popular," Debbie replied.

"Well I'm here now, so that's half of us, right?"

"Khendra said something that made me think Vanessa might not be coming." Debbie shrugged.

The hostess arrived and escorted them to a table. She placed down single-page laminated menus.

Ramona picked it up and flipped the menu back and forth. "They finally got some food in here. What do you want to bet these are gas-station burritos?" She laughed.

"Yeah, this is menu a la microwave." Debbie quirked her lips to the side as she studied the menu. "I miss Ray's, they have a real grill."

"Okay, I wasn't going to say anything 'cause I didn't want everyone to get on my case because of Bobby, but yes please, can we go back?"

Khendra arrived and pulled out her chair, announcing, "No Vanessa tonight."

"She'll miss her favorite show," Debbie pointed out.

Khendra shrugged. "Girlfriend said she wasn't coming out tonight because she has to start cooking for Thanksgiving. But I think it has something to do with Ethan."

"I'm helping my mama cook. She wants me at her place at the crack of dawn on Thursday. I might spend the night," Debbie said.

"I'll be at my sister's. What are you doing?" Khendra asked.

"I'm taking Bobby home to meet the parents," Ramona confessed.

Debbie reached across and grabbed Ramona's hand. "That would explain this. When were you planning on filling us in?" She waved Ramona's hand with Bobby's ring around.

Ramona felt her cheeks tighten with a blush and smile. "It's Bobby's."

"Obviously, girl, unless you played high school football. What we want to know is why have you been acting like it's no big deal?" Khendra pointed out.

"Yeah, 'cause I'm pretty damned sure that not even Taylor wore his championship ring back in the day. You aren't engaged and holding out on us, are you?" Debbie asked, still holding Ramona's hand.

Someone staggered into their table, jostling everything. The man mumbled something and grabbed for Ramona's hand.

Debbie slapped at him. "You need to sober up, Coach, or I'm gonna have Derrick out here to take you home," Debbie announced.

Coach Shumer grunted before pushing away from the table.

Debbie shook Ramona's hand, returning them to their conversation.

"Not engaged, but committed. It's a promise ring," Ramona explained. She extricated her hand from Debbie and gazed fondly on the ring. It was big and chunky, and her most favorite piece of jewelry. Devon had given her diamond earrings for their engagement. That way she could wear them, and they would both know, while it was still under wraps to the rest of the world.

This ring, without an engagement attached to it, meant so much more. She knew Bobby loved her, and he wasn't trying to hide their relationship. He had marked his territory. She knew she shouldn't have felt a flutter at that, being claimed like a piece of property. But damn if her insides didn't turn to mush knowing he wanted her as much as she wanted him. More importantly, he wanted everyone to know it.

The waitress approached their table and announced that the kitchen was effectively closed until after Ethan did his thing tonight, but she could go ahead and take their order and hopefully get their drinks. Ramona had already eaten dinner; so had Khendra. Debbie was going to brave one of the burritos, and they all decided to split a giant nachos whenever Ethan reopened the kitchen.

"How did he convince the owners to let him do this?" Ramona gestured to Ethan's bad karaoke and dancing on the bar.

"I think his uncle owns the place. I mean, he is helping them to bring in a crowd, and he can pretend to be a rock star." Debbie seemed to have the scoop on everyone in town.

Ramona watched Ethan gyrate for a bit before she melted into a fit of giggles. "He really needs to take some dance lessons."

"Oh you're just saying that because you are not swayed by those magical hips of his." Khendra laughed with her.

"And you are?" Debbie looked at Khendra.

"Oh, I don't know. I've looked a time or two."

Both Debbie and Ramona "oohed" at Khendra.

"How does Vanessa feel about that?" Ramona asked.

"Ain't nobody gonna tell her. Ethan is all hers if she can bag him. But I'm still planning on looking." Khendra laughed.

Ethan finished his two-song set and left the bar with most of his clothes still on.

"I wish that boy would learn to lip-synch and not try to actually sing."

The waitress returned a few minutes later with the nachos and Debbie's burrito.

Debbie eyed the long food item with consternation. "I think I'd be better off with an actual gas-station burrito." She poked at it.

Ramona picked up a fork and poked at it. "Well, it's definitely dead."

A commotion at the far end of the bar pulled their attention. Three obviously drunk men were shouting.

"I never can quite figure out why guys come here to drink," Ramona said. "I would think that the Ethan Show would be a deterrent."

"I think getting kicked out of the other bars in town are really why they are here."

There was more shouting, and then one of the drunks was on the floor.

"Drunk man down," Khendra announced.

"That's Coach Shumer," Ramona said, recognizing his oversize cowboy hat.

"He's been sloshed since the game. That game was a mess," Debbie said.

"Mess? That game was a slaughter. Central didn't crash

and burn. They were down and whimpering the entire game." Ramona described the final game of the season. Not only had RavenCroft prevented Central from making it into the playoffs, they'd massacred the other team on the field.

"If they haven't let him go already, they certainly will soon," Debbie added.

"It must really suck to have your career riding on the skills of a bunch of kids."

"Tell me about it," Ramona sighed.

The lights went down, and Ethan climbed back up on the bar. He really did take himself too seriously. She may have been mad at Bobby over the summer for interfering when Ethan had been hitting on her, but looking back, Ramona smiled. Bobby had been jealous. Her insides buzzed knowing he had liked her back then, even if she had been completely clueless.

The show ended, and they ordered another round. The waitress delivered little black folders with their checks. The Roadhouse was trying to go upscale: menus, a floor show, and check folders. Ramona slid her card in and set the folder down on top of the other two.

"I think I'm gonna tell Derrick next time he goes over to play poker that he needs to take a few lessons from Bobby," Debbie announced.

"In what?" Khendra asked.

They all stood; Ramona hitched her purse onto her shoulder and followed her friends outside.

"Derrick needs to learn about expressions of commitment," Debbie said.

"You want an engagement ring or a promise?" Ramona asked.

"Right now, I'd be good with a promise," Debbie admitted.

"Start dropping hints. Christmas is in a month," Khendra said.

Ramona groaned. "Don't mention that. I'm not ready."

"Well, y'all have a good Thanksgiving." Debbie gave Ramona a hug and then hugged Khendra.

Ramona hugged her friends one more time and went to get in her car. Crap, she forgot her credit card. She waved at Khendra as she pulled out of the lot. She ran back inside.

The waitress handed her the card. "I'm glad you came back for that. I was about to run outside looking for you."

Ramona was fairly certain the waitress had not been about to go look for her. She was busy wiping down tables, not getting ready to run outside.

"You have a good Thanksgiving," the waitress called out as Ramona left.

She fished her keys out of her bag and headed toward her car. Coach Shumer staggered over toward his GMC. She ignored him. That was a mistake.

Tires squealed to a stop too close for comfort. He was too drunk to be driving. If he had gone to Ray's, Bobby would have taken his keys. The idiot almost hit her. Coach surged out of his truck. She could smell the fumes rolling from him before he took two steps.

Expecting him to apologize, she was completely caught off guard when he hit her. His fist glanced off the side of her head by her ear and then plowed into her shoulder.

Ramona cried out in pain, stumbled, and reached for her head.

Coach pulled her hair, yanking her head back.

"Get off me!" Ramona yelled and tried to shove at the man. He was bigger than her, and solid.

With her keys in her hand, she reached out and tried to scratch him. A vise-like fist closed on her wrist. The pressure was too intense. Ramona let go of the keys in her hand.

Coach snatched them and hurled them away.

Ramona's gaze frantically searched the parking lot; no one else was out.

"Gimme that hand." His speech was slurred.

She could understand the words but not their meaning. She slapped at him as his arms tried grabbing for her. Thinking that Coach was trying to rob her, Ramona dropped her purse and kicked it under the car.

Coach punched her again. This time his fist hit her shoulder.

She staggered back.

He grasped her left arm and yanked hard.

Ramona fell. The pavement stung, and scraped the skin from her knees. She tried to twist away from him.

He trapped her arm between his arm and body. He turned away from her. It felt like he was pulling her finger off.

"This ain't your ring. You didn't earn this ring." He twisted and pulled on Bobby's championship ring.

She cried out again. "Stop it. That's mine. No!" Her struggles did not stop him.

Ramona fought to make a fist, but Coach dug his thumb into the tendons of her wrist.

The ring finally came off. Coach released Ramona, and she collapsed to the ground, crying. "Give me back my ring."

Coach yelled into her face, "You don't get to wear this, RavenCroft scum." He got into his SUV and drove off.

Ramona sat back on her heels in total shock. Her finger hurt, her wrists hurt, her knees stung, and her chest felt like it was collapsing in on itself. That man had just taken her ring. The ring Bobby had given her as a token of his love.

She cried. She felt stupid. If she had paid better attention, he wouldn't have been able to surprise her like that. She should have fought back harder. This was her fault. She shouldn't have been showing it off knowing he had just had one of the worst games of his career.

Wincing with each movement, she crawled under her car to get her purse. She needed to find her phone so she could use the flashlight to find her keys. After only a few minutes she located them.

Though drunk, Coach hadn't been particularly forceful with his throw. But his punches had hurt.

Her shoulder hurt. It was going to be bruised.

Ramona climbed into her car and cried some more. She was going to have to tell Bobby. She didn't know what to say. He was going to be so mad at her. She'd let a drunk man steal her ring.

She drove home and curled up under the covers. Maybe if she got a good night's sleep, this would all be over in the morning. Maybe this was only a bad dream and she would have her ring back.

22

Something wasn't right. Bobby felt it in his gut. He hadn't slept well. He should have checked on Ramona last night, but he knew she was out with her friends and would be going to bed after that. She wasn't expecting him to come pick her up for another couple of hours, but he couldn't wait any longer.

He clenched and stretched out his fist. His entire forearm shimmered as fur formed. He pulled the claws back in and forced his hand to reform. He shook the transformation out of his limb.

He parked behind her little red Scion and clenched his stomach. He prepared for the worst. He was terrified to go inside, terrified that his angel would take one look at him and see him as the monster he was on the inside.

He knocked and then walked in. All was quiet. "Ramona?"

She wasn't up yet.

He stepped quietly into her room. She was asleep. Her dark hair fanned out on her pillow like a cloud of smoke. He smiled. It would be his pleasure to brush that out for her when she woke up. He started to kick off his boots. Everything was fine. He had missed her and let his imagination blow that feeling out of proportion.

She groaned when he lifted her hair to the side. A large bruise covered her shoulder.

"What the fuck?" Bobby felt the wolf surge forward. Taking deep, slow breaths, he forced his anger and his beast back.

He eased in behind her and gently wrapped his arms around her frame. His mouth rested by her ear. "Angel, baby, what happened?"

Ramona twisted in his arms and buried her face into his chest. "I'm sorry, I'm sorry," she sniffled.

Bobby caressed the side of her face and kissed the top of her head. "Sorry for what?"

She was holding on too tightly for her apology to be a breakup. His breathing stopped when her hand stilled his. The ring on her finger wasn't his. Instead there was a dark bruise.

"Do I need to go?" The question about killed him to ask. If she said go, he would. And he would die, but he would leave her if that's what she wanted.

Ramona whimpered. "Please don't leave me. I'm sorry. I couldn't stop him. I'm sorry." Ramona was crying and shaking in his arms.

Every muscle in Bobby's body clenched and froze. He was reading this all wrong. Someone had hurt Ramona, and here he was worrying about her leaving him. It took everything in him not to roar and demand who had scared her.

He took another deep breath. "Ramona, Angel, who did this to you?"

"Coach Shumer. He said I didn't get to wear the ring because I didn't deserve it. I think he broke my finger."

"When did this happen? Where were you? Where were your friends?" The questions rushed from him. How could her friends have let this happen?

"Last night at the Roadhouse, I went back inside for my credit card. So I was getting into my car alone. I know that was so stupid of me. He was drunk and attacked me and took your ring. I'm sorry I couldn't stop him. I tried; he's really strong." She was crying again.

Bobby pulled her in closer, wrapping his arms around her to protect her. Where had he been last night? At the bar when his angel needed him. No wonder he'd felt that something was wrong. It was. "Why didn't you call me last night?"

"I didn't want you to get mad at me."

He adjusted his hold so he could look her in the face. Those big green eyes blinked up at him. He was going to kill Coach. "Why on earth would I be mad at you?"

"'Cause I let Coach take your ring."

"You didn't let him. He mugged you." Bobby carefully took her left hand and examined her middle finger. It was bruised but not broken. Gently he placed his lips to the bruise. It was going to be sore, but no other damage had been done. He started to get out of bed.

Ramona gripped his shirt. "Where are you going?"

"I have to go take care of something. I'll be back soon." *And with your ring.*

"Bobby?" Her voice sounded so frail, so little. "You aren't mad at me, are you?"

In a single swift move Bobby was on his knees next to her bed, his face level with hers, his hand caressing her face. "I love you. Why would I be mad at you? This is on Coach. Now rest, I'll be back as soon as I can."

Bobby broke every traffic law between the long low row of apartments and the Shumer house.

The front door was locked. He didn't bother testing the lock on the back door. He kicked it in. The sound of video games coming from the TV room covered the crashing sound. He followed the sound and pulled the video game controller out of the hands of the teen. He hadn't focused, he was pissed, and this person was going to tell him where Coach was.

The teen screamed.

Bobby stopped. "Where's Coach?" He calmed his voice as much as he could.

"Don't hurt me! I'm calling the police." The boy scrambled back on the couch away from him. He looked like he was going to try to climb the wall.

"I'm not going to hurt you," Bobby barked. "Tell me where Coach is."

"They're gone. They left really early to catch a flight out of Waco. Why? You aren't going to beat me up, are you?" The boy was crying.

"No, I'm not. I'm not going to hurt you. Who are you?" Bobby pulled out his phone and made a call.

"I'm Tommy, their neighbor; I'm house-sitting. Who are you? I'm gonna call the police," he wailed.

Bobby held up his phone. "I already have." He turned his attention back to the phone. "Yeah, Debbie, look, I broke down Coach Shumer's back door. He's lucky he's not here."

"Why are you there, Bobby?" Debbie asked.

"He jumped Ramona last night. I'm gonna come swing by the station. But if you get a panicked 911 from"—he turned to the teen again—"what's your name again?"

"Tommy."

"If you get a call from Tommy, I scared him pretty good."

"Yeah, but Bobby why are you there?"

"I was going to beat the crap out of Coach. He hurt my girl."

～

Ramona tossed her duffel bag in the trunk. It closed with a satisfying *click*.

"So you'll be sleeping over next door at the Hamilton's with the other boys."

Bobby carefully placed the box with the pies on the floor of the back seat. He slid into the driver's seat and looked at her. "You weren't joking when you said there was a boy house and a girl house for these things?"

Ramona shook her head. "No, I wasn't. It all started when my sister and my cousins started bringing boys home for Thanksgiving. And the Hamilton boys could have girlfriends over and their parents would know their virtue was safe, at least after dark. Our folks have been doing it ever since."

"But separate houses?"

"It was the best way to keep the hormones contained. Even married couples split up for the big sleepover party this has become."

"It sounds like fun. I'm sure it will be okay. I get to sack out in a sleeping bag with a bunch of testosterone junkies. Sounds like the camp I never went to as a kid."

His eyes twinkled when he smiled at her like that. How could Ramona tell him she was afraid this would be the family weirdness that had him changing his mind? Should she warn him about her cousin Jo so that he had his guards up and didn't accidentally slip back into his old ways?

"I have to tell you about Devon," she blurted before she chickened out.

Bobby made a low grumble sound in his chest. "Devon was the guy who..." He growled again.

The sound was menacing. It raised the hairs on the back of her neck. It was sexy as hell because he growled for her.

"Yes, that Devon. He's gonna be there, so please play nice."

"I have to have a sleepover with the ass who cheated on you, and you want me to play nice? Ramona, I should be defending your honor and ripping him a new windpipe."

She slid her hand over Bobby's thigh. "Thank you," she whispered.

"Keep that up, and I'm pulling into the first sleazy motel I find."

She squeezed and let go of his leg. The idea had some serious merit. They wouldn't be alone for three nights, and it seemed so much longer knowing her parents were going to be there.

"Devon won't be at the sleepover. He's too dignified for that anymore, but you will be at his parents' house. I quite literally fell for the boy next door. He will be there for dinner tomorrow. Everyone knows we were a thing. I'm sure most of them figured out he's why I left town. I just... This can't... Damn. This can't break my parents and their friends up. It was easier to walk away than it was to start a feud. So I'm asking you to please not confront him about it."

Bobby sighed. "Sweetheart, I won't go starting a fight with the man. Now if he starts something, I will end it."

"I can accept that." Ramona gulped. Devon down; that was easy. Now to see if Jo was going to be as simple. She let out a heavy sigh.

"Sounds serious, Angel. Who else am I going to want to take to the mat? Are you sure you're taking me to Thanksgiving dinner and not some kind of tempting smackdown?"

She let out a soft giggle. "Aren't they the same thing?"

"So who is it that I need to check my claws for? Your dad? Your mom? Trust me, I know how to be charming."

"Oh, I know you do. That's not going to be a problem. I don't want you to be too charming around my cousin Joanne. She doesn't do well when I have nicer things than she does. She tends to try to take them from me. Like when she almost convinced Uncle Charlie that I had given her my new bike. He actually had to ask Daddy why I would be giving away the bike I had gotten that summer. They found me, and fortunately Jo wasn't around, so I was able to tell them that I did not give my bike to her. She stole a watch from me once. Borrowed tons of clothes that never found their way home."

"And you're afraid she'll try the same with me?" Bobby laughed. "I'm a person, not a thing to get shoved into a back pocket with an 'oops, I forgot.' She's not going to walk off with me."

Ramona sighed and turned to face out the window. "She walked off with Devon."

She didn't want Bobby to see that it still hurt. It hurt that her cousin, who was supposed to be her friend, had decided that Devon was too good of a catch to be with Ramona, so she went after him. And Devon hadn't loved Ramona as much as he claimed, because he'd had no qualms in letting himself be lured away by Jo. He'd seemed more upset that he and Jo got caught. What twisted that knife in deeper was, they hadn't even stayed together once Ramona was out of the picture.

Devon was part of Jo's catch-and-release program. She wanted to be able to take him away from Ramona; once that was accomplished, she didn't want anything to do with him.

The car bounced as Bobby drove it off the road and onto the shoulder.

She turned to face him, worry lodged in her gut. "What's wrong. Is everything okay?" She hadn't noticed if the car was making any odd noises or if they had blown a tire.

"I should be asking you that." Bobby cut the engine off, unfastened his belt, and turned to face her.

He caught a long strand of her hair between his fingers and lifted it toward his face. He closed his eyes and breathed in, smelling her hair.

"I'd feel better if I had my ring." Jo would see the ring and know that Bobby was seriously taken, and hopefully not act up.

"I know, sweetheart. Coach had already left town by the time I got to his place this morning. I will get your ring back. Debbie already has your report and took pictures of your shoulder. Derrick said he'd let us go in and get the ring when they arrest Coach so you can have it. I'm sorry I wasn't there to help you last night."

"Yeah, some vigilante rescue wolf you turned out to be. Can't even save your girlfriend." She hid a sniffle behind her laugh.

"Honestly, half the time that's not me. There really is a dog in town that randomly seems to go around saving people."

"I'm joking, you know. It's just... I... I'd feel better if Jo could see the ring, She couldn't ignore that."

"Angel, I cannot be tempted from you. Your cousin can try her best, but nothing, and I mean nothing, would make me want to leave you. I'm sorry that Devon was such an asshole and hurt you. He has no idea what he gave up. Are you sure you want to do this? You don't have to, you know. You are an adult. There is nothing that says you have to go to your family's on Thanksgiving. We can go out, or we can go home and I'll cook for you." Bobby trailed a knuckle down the side of her face. She leaned into the caress. "And it's crushing me that Coach laid a hand on you and hurt you."

"It's time you met my parents. This is the easiest way to get you to meet everyone. My sister, Lorena, and her family will be there, and so will my nan. I want to show you off. Hell, I'll be rubbing you in Devon's smarmy face. It's just…"

"It's just nothing, Angel. Those two people hurt you, and everyone there is basically taking sides if they let them stick around."

"That's part of the problem, Bobby. No one knows. Devon and I had been on again, off again since I was nineteen. And yeah, everyone knew we were on again, but we hadn't told anyone we were engaged. And Jo had never gone after him before. And no one knows."

A stupid tear escaped. Bobby swept it away with his thumb.

He nodded his head slowly. "Okay, I'm good with secrets. No one will find out from me, but if he crosses the line in any way, it's WWE SmackDown time. And don't worry about your cousin. My roving days are far behind me."

Ramona sniffed. "She's really pretty."

"And you are my beautiful angel." The press of his lips soothed her rattled brain. He was right; she didn't need to worry about him.

"She's still going to try."

"Then we'll keep track of her attempts, and have a good laugh over it later. You better?" He looked into her eyes and gave her a half-quirked grin.

She returned the smile and nodded.

Bobby buckled back in, started the car, and continued their way into the suburbs of Dallas.

23

Even though Ramona knew she had nothing to worry about, she worried.

Her mother had been nice enough about taking the pies Bobby brought. She had given Ramona the eye, knowing she hadn't made them. "No, Mami, I didn't buy them. Bobby made them."

Her mom's eyebrows shot up under her bangs. "This Roberto can bake?" she asked as they watched Bobby unpack the box.

"Ma'am, it's just Bobby. On my birth certificate that way." He gave her mother a slight smile.

She could feel her mother judging him. Compared to her petite mother, he was huge. His hair was pulled up into a messy bun, and his jaw was covered with his perpetual two-day scruff. He wore jeans and a T-shirt. And Ramona knew nothing about him was even remotely similar to what her mother expected her to bring home. Nothing about Bobby said *refined*.

"He's a really good cook, Mami."

Her mother muttered something in Spanish about

having more pies in case these were no good.

"It's a good thing you have extra pies coming, from what Ramona told me, these will barely make a dent in what you're gonna need."

Ramona felt her eyes go wide. Mami's lips pursed, and her cheeks flushed before her face relaxed into a grin. "Mija, you could have said something."

Ramona knew he spoke the language. Heck, they even spoke it to each other, phasing in and out of one language to another, much as she did with her mother at home. It hadn't occurred to her to say anything. Just as she typically didn't introduce her mother to people by prefacing how many languages she spoke.

"Ma'am, I run a bar with a kitchen in Texas. I'd be a fool not to know at least some Spanish."

Her mother nodded. And just like that her mother's opinion of Bobby changed. She no longer gave him a side-eye, instead she smiled broadly and conscripted him into helping her in the kitchen.

Ramona almost felt offended when her mother shooed her out. Bobby grabbed her in for a quick hug and a kiss to the temple before she left. Why was she worried again? If he won over Mami this fast, Daddy would be a cinch.

She took a deep breath: parents conquered. Now to survive the onslaught of everyone tomorrow.

Ramona hauled her bag back to her old bedroom. It hadn't been her bedroom for a very long time, but she still instinctively hauled her stuff back into the same room. Her father was sitting at his table winding a fly.

She tossed her bag onto the futon that let the room serve as a guest room when she visited.

"Hey, Daddy. We're here," she announced.

"Hello, darling girl." Her father didn't look up. She didn't expect him too. She leaned over and watched as he wound thread around and around, adding in small bits of feathers and fluff to make a fly lure. The collection on the table next to him was all the same. He had a pile of green and black knots that, from a distance, really looked like a pile of dead flies.

"Looks like you got an order?"

"Yup. Some junior's competition in Mississippi wants all the kids to have the same fly. They ordered fifty nymphs. I'm almost done. These will go out in Friday's mail."

"I'll let you finish then. Just wanted to let you know we're here."

Graham Campbell stopped winding his thread. "So you brought that young man home with you?"

"Yup, Bobby. I told you I was bringing him to meet everyone. He's already making friends with Mami."

"Your mother?"

"No, my other mami. Yes, my mother. They're speaking Spanish and playing in the kitchen."

Her father turned away from his work and stared at her over his reading glasses. His forehead crinkled up in interest.

"Oh, don't look at me like that. You'll have to come meet him. But finish your flies or you won't be able to focus on anything else."

Ramona skipped out of the room after giving her father a squeeze on the shoulders.

She wasn't needed in the kitchen and knowing her mother, probably not welcome. She would get in the way. Big meals were her mother's domain, and she did not share the kitchen well during these times. Of course Ramona was dying to see how Mami was getting along with Bobby. The woman wouldn't let her own children in the kitchen around Thanksgiving.

Ramona slid the pass-through shutters open so she could lean in from the living room and watch the happenings in the kitchen. Neither Bobby nor her mother glanced over at the sound.

Mami directed Bobby to bring down some dishes from the top shelves of the cabinets. The flutter in Ramona's chest spread into a happy tingle. No wonder her mother was happy to keep Bobby in the kitchen. He could reach the top shelf. This was a first. Her mother and father not arguing over which dishes she wanted him to pull down as he balanced on the rickety step stool.

It was a solution easily solved by the purchase of a new step stool, but that was the type of solution that went against every bone in Daddy's hyper-frugal body. Daddy was as stereotypically Scottish as they made them.

Her mother sorted through the stack Bobby had just placed on the counter. He stood by as she decided which dishes she would want. And then, with a nod from Mami, he handed the pile back up into the cupboard. Ramona loved watching him reach up. His whole torso stretched, and she could see the muscles shifting under his tight shirt. He palmed a stack of dishes, and she missed his hands palming her.

Jesus H, this is going to be a long, long weekend. Why had she agreed to stay for three nights?

The doorbell rang.

"I got it," Ramona called out as she pushed up from the counter.

Her sister, laden down with a collection of bags, and her nephew Todd were clamoring in the door. "I told you we don't need to ring the doorbell at Mami and Papi's."

Ramona reached forward and took a bag from her struggling sister. "Hey, guys. Hey, Toddy, how you doin'?"

Todd looked at Ramona with a bit of wide-eyed terror before pushing into his mother's side. She rubbed the back of his head.

"He's excited to be able to do the big boy sleepover for the first time."

Her father came down the hall and stooped. "Where's my big buddy?" He clapped his hands and held his arms wide. Todd bolted from his mother's side and into his grandfather's arms.

On Lorena's heels came her husband carrying the infant car seat.

Her mother stepped out of the kitchen and made cooing noises at the contents of the car seat. She took it from Ryan and carried it to the couch. She sat and continued to sing at the baby inside.

Ryan sighed. "They're in. Now for the rest of it."

Ramona let go from hugging her sister and turned to give Ryan a quick hug.

Caught up in the chaos that entered with Lorena's family, she didn't notice Bobby leaning on the doorframe until Lorena's husband stuck out his hand. "I'm Ryan, Lorena's husband."

"Bobby, good to meet ya. Do you need some help? Are we done in the kitchen, Mrs. Campbell?"

"Oh Bobby, go help Ryan. We can finish up later." She turned her attention back to her grandchild.

Lorena grabbed Ramona by the upper arm. "He's cute, Mona, and big. You didn't mention you were bringing the Hulk home."

"Behave, Lorena. Bobby is a good boy. It's nice to have someone tall enough to reach things in the kitchen."

"Oh yeah?" Lorena hadn't even begun to put her things down yet, and she was already digging into Ramona about the new boyfriend. "What do you think about him, Papi?"

Her father shrugged. "I haven't met him yet." He turned his attention back to the toddler he was swinging back and forth. "Are you ready for our big campout?"

Todd squealed.

The two men came back in from the car, hauling more bags and a portable playpen-crib. They deposited all the packages inside the living room.

"You made it with perfect timing. We should be heading over to the Hamilton's now. Let me grab my kit, and we can leave." Her father grabbed Todd's hand, and they walked down the hall to her parents' bedroom.

Bobby looked at Ryan. "So you did this when you first started coming to Thanksgivings here?"

Ryan nodded and laughed. "Sure did. You'll get used to it, even start looking forward to it. This year will be interesting since Todd will be joining us. The old man might not give you the whole are-you-good-enough-for-my-daughter speech. He'll be distracted with the kid."

"I heard that," her father announced as they reentered the living room. He walked straight up to Bobby and looked up at him. "You're a big one, but don't think you're getting away without me having a reckoning with you."

"Don't worry sir, I already know I'm not good enough for Ramona." Bobby didn't even crack a sarcastic grin.

Ryan kissed Lorena and went and put his face in the infant carrier. Her father followed suit, except he kissed the baby and then her mother on the cheek.

Bobby started to follow the other two men out the front door when Ramona grabbed his hand.

"It'll be okay. I'm a team player, remember?" He leaned

in and kissed her on the temple. "I'll see you in the morning."

Ramona glanced back at her mother and sister. They were occupied with the baby. She tugged on Bobby's arm, pulling him down closer. She quickly slid her lips across his. "Good night. I'll miss you."

Bobby wouldn't tell her what her father had said to him the night before. All she knew was her father seemed to have been charmed by him. Which was good.

Lorena was too busy with baby Noah to have been able to give Ramona too much guff. To be fair, it would have been easier for Lorena to stay at home with the infant, but they had promised Todd, and good parents that they were, they'd kept their promise.

Todd was already racing around, excited for the day. People arrived in droves. Her mother conscripted Bobby into setting up tables, chairs, and getting more dishes down from high places. He did everything with a grin.

Tables were set up in a giant L shape through the formal living room and into the dining room, with the kiddie table at one end.

Ramona breathed in a deep sigh. Jo hadn't arrived yet. Devon was acting as if she were a total stranger and had gone to hang out in the rec room. Bobby was charming her nan, a frail little white-haired old lady with a thick Scotts accent and a sharp tongue. Nan and Uncle Charlie had followed her father to the states after he married Ramona's mother.

Everything was going well until it was time to sit down and eat. Bobby, ever the gentleman, escorted Nan to the table and took the seat next to her. Before Ramona could slide in next to him, Jo was in the seat. *Damn it, when did she get here?* Ramona sat across from them so she could keep an eye on her cousin. Her heart sank when Devon sat next to her.

"Hey, Ramona. So how's teaching in a rural community? Do you have any textbooks?" He sneered. He knew perfectly well that he had driven her away from the posh school district. But what he didn't know was how much better of a school environment RavenCroft was.

"It's pretty fabulous."

"You teach remedial math. How can it be any fun teaching two plus two to a bunch of meatheads who need to pass so they can play football?"

Had he always been such an elitist snob? Probably. She had repressed how much he bad-mouthed students. That behavior would get any other person in the district fired, but not Devon. He was the superintendent's personal "golden boy."

"Those meatheads she's teaching ranked top five in the state this year. I wouldn't go knocking the school's football team if I were you." Bobby's voice wasn't a grumble but a nice conversational tone.

Devon shot him a glare before changing his expression from annoyed to superior. He gave Bobby a sneering once-over. "You look like you know a thing or two about football."

"Oh, do you play?" Jo finally found her opening, and she batted her lashes at Bobby.

Ramona's insides churned in a sickening tumble. She was caught between the two people she pretty much hated the most on the planet, and she had to pretend that nothing had ever happened. No one knew, and it wasn't going to be her that destroyed the families that were involved. She knew these people. She would not be the victim for long before she somehow became the selfish bad guy.

Bobby nodded. "Used to, not anymore."

Devon leaned in. "And what do you do now? You're not a rancher."

Bobby smiled around his mouthful of food and nodded while he chewed.

Nan leaned over. "He cooks at a bar."

Bobby finished chewing and swallowed. "I use math, that a teacher very much like Ramona made sure I understood, so that I could play football. And it turns out I use it at work every day."

"You use math in a kitchen?" Devon lifted one eyebrow, an expression that said he thought he was being clever.

"Have you ever cooked anything, ever? Yes, you use math in the kitchen and in a commercial kitchen more so." Ramona sneered right back.

"I use math in the whole bar," Bobby explained.

"So you know how many frozen hamburgers to order?" Devon was a shining example of asshole today.

Why had she been in love with him? How had she let such a jerk break her heart?

"Exactly, so I know how many pounds of ground sirloin to order, and how many pounds of french fries." Bobby shook his head. "Excuse me." He stood and picked up his plate.

Ramona didn't know who to glare at more, Jo for following him over to the food table, or Devon. Devon won. "Why are you being so rude to him?"

"Ramona, he's a big dumb football player. What are you even doing with someone like him? He cooks bar food for a living."

"No." Bobby's big voice cut into their heated whispers. "I own a bar for a living. I run the kitchen as part of that. Do you really need to know how extensively I use the skills I learned in high school math so you can prove a point to Ramona? Because it's not going to prove the point you are trying to make. Teaching remedial math in a rural, football-oriented community has a far greater reach than teaching to rich kids who grow up with Daddy's accountant whipping out a calculator at every turn."

"Hey, Bobby, do you want another slice of pie before this one is all gone?" Jo called out, holding up a plated slice of pumpkin pie.

"Sure." He nodded back.

Jo handed him the pie, and Bobby turned around and handed to slice to Nan. Completely ignoring the huff of indignation Jo gave him. Ramona wanted to laugh. Jo looked like a pissed-off squirrel. When she pursed her lips like that, it made her cheeks puff out; added to it her big, wide eyes with the whites showing all around the iris, she looked more comical than intimidating.

"You said your name was Bobby Cray?" Devon asked.

"Yeah."

"You played for OU back, what, twelve years ago?"

"Maybe a little longer than that." Bobby nodded.

"I remember you now. You were starting running back your first season. There was talk of you going pro before graduation."

Great, so now Devon was a fan?

"Are you playing this afternoon? You're going to massacre us out there."

Bobby chuckled. "It's been a long time since I played. I think everyone has an even chance."

Jo seemed to lean in a little closer.

"You never finished your second season. Weren't you arrested?" Devon kept shifting his gaze to his lap.

Other conversations at the long table stopped. Ramona felt all eyes shifting to look at either Devon, Bobby, or herself.

"Yeah, you went to jail, didn't you?" Devon had an evil smirk on his face.

"Devon!" his mother chastised him from down the table.

"Why bother asking me when you've looked it up on your phone?" Bobby sat back and folded his arms. "Yeah, I blew my chances at playing pro ball by doing something dumb. I trusted someone I shouldn't have for the wrong reasons. I was arrested. I spent ninety days in jail. If you continue to dig, you will find that I was considered an accessory after the fact. I unknowingly drove the getaway car to an armed robbery."

Ramona closed her eyes. Her stomach sank. This was not how she wanted her parents to find this out about Bobby.

"And he was acquitted during an appeal, and released." Ramona's eyes flew open at her father's voice. "Now stop trying to dig something up to shock us all with. He told us all about it last night. That's a noticeable difference between you and him. Bobby here isn't keeping any secrets from us. I can't say the same for you, Devon."

And with that, everyone went back to their previous conversations and eating. Ramona let out a breath she didn't realize she had been holding. She looked into Bobby's eyes. He gave her the slightest nod and a soft smile. He had told her parents, and they still liked him.

Ramona looked down at her plate. She had managed to only eat about half of everything she had put on it. Her stomach was in knots. She couldn't help but think maybe bringing Bobby for Thanksgiving wasn't the best idea. But Bobby wasn't caving under the pressure. And he was under a lot of scrutiny. Then again, maybe it was a good idea. Everyone could see she'd ended up with a good guy with not just physical strength but strength of character.

She felt that she was under the inspection glass with Bobby, only she wasn't fairing as well. She needed the mental support of pie. There was one slice left of Bobby's blueberry pie on the dessert table. She headed over to take it. She wanted a little slice of him at the moment since launching herself over the table and into his arms might be frowned upon.

Suddenly Jo was at her shoulder. "So how do you know Bobby?" Her voice had a predatory purr quality to it.

She didn't know. Ramona considered not saying anything. If Jo was being this attentive and she didn't know Bobby was taken, she would become downright aggressive as soon as she knew that Bobby was here with Ramona. So far Bobby had ignored Jo's flirting. And it would be entertaining if Ramona could just separate her emotions from it. Bobby had been able to laugh it off last night. Why couldn't she? Right, because Jo had successfully taken Devon from her. At the end of all of it, Devon hadn't been particularly sorry anything had transpired. Maybe she should thank Jo for exposing him sooner than later. But it didn't mean she wanted to hang around and watch Jo try to hone in on her man.

"He's my boyfriend."

Ramona smiled as she heard the serving fork in Jo's hand clatter into one of the glass plates. She decided to go lean against Bobby, sort of to claim the right of touching him, but he pulled her down onto his lap. She giggled and fed him a piece of the pie she had.

"Uh, that tastes awful," he joked.

"I know, terrible. The cook should be ashamed." Ramona slid another bite into her mouth. The pie was perfect. Perfect flaky crust, perfect blueberry taste, perfect man who baked it.

"That's rude. You don't know who made that pie. You're going to hurt someone's feelings," Jo harrumphed as she sat down. Her glare tried to cut at Ramona.

"I'm hardly offended. I made the pie, and I used math, in the kitchen." Bobby smirked.

He was big, but he certainly wasn't dumb.

24

Jo bounced on the sidelines like some kind of high school cheerleader. Oh, right, she had been a cheerleader, hadn't she? Did she still need to be one now? And so obviously cheering for Bobby and Bobby only?

Everyone by now knew Bobby was here with Ramona. That fact really didn't seem to have any impact on Jo at all. Ramona missed her big, bulky ring. It would hurt if she smacked Jo with it. She smiled. That thought should have guilt all over it, but it didn't.

At least Devon had finally chilled out. His attempt to undermine Bobby by letting absolutely everyone know he had gone to prison had backfired beautifully.

Daddy made another tackle; he grabbed a blue flag out of someone's back pocket. He cackled. He never had quite figured out flag football, but he always delighted in collecting as many flags from the other team as possible. But not the flag of the person with the ball.

Bobby had the ball, and people were dropping like flies as he ran across the two front yards that made up the playing field. Jo whooped like this was a bowl game.

Devon made a grab for the flag in Bobby's pocket. Bobby stepped back, dodged, stopped, and spun before continuing in his original direction. Devon fell flat on his face. Ramona was pleased to see Devon sputtering as he got back to his feet.

Touchdown! And the end of the game. Blue won, despite her father running around with a handful of that team's flags in his hand. Per usual, Daddy was trying to convince everyone that proper football was played with your feet. Or, since they insisted on the oblong ball, they could go in for rugby. And every year, as predictable as pumpkin pie, Mami told him they lived in the United States now, so they played American football.

Bobby ruffled his hands through his hair, probably trying to get the sweat to dissipate. At least that's what Ramona did when she needed to work sweat out of her hair. It made his golden-brown hair look huge; he looked like some magnificent maned beast as he approached Ramona. His grin told her he had enjoyed himself.

His gaze cut to Jo, who had positioned herself in his path. Ramona felt her smile fade, and her heart sank as she watched Bobby pull his shirt, stained with sweat, over his head. Jo reached out toward his chest. Ramona wanted to chop that hand off at the wrist.

She wasn't normally this territorial about him, but her cousin couldn't be trusted. Bobby nodded at whatever Jo said. He wiped the shirt across his brow, tossed it at her, and then stalked straight to Ramona.

She suppressed a squealed when he picked her up and swung her around. "Hey, Angel." The kiss he gave her curled her toes.

"Hey, show-off." She rested her hand in the middle of his chest.

He kept his arms around her waist after he set her down. "I'm having fun. I haven't scrimmaged in a long time."

"Oh, is that what you called that? I would have called that, let's see if we can get the ball away from Bobby. I think Daddy is the only person who had as much fun as you did."

He laughed. "What's on the schedule now?"

Ramona handed him back the flannel shirt she had kept tied around her waist while he played. "We cover you up so you stop tempting my cousin." Bobby slipped his arms in and buttoned two of the lower buttons. His skin flashed from behind the meager covering. It was distracting. She continued to button his shirt. "More food, TV, naps. There has to be an argument over dishes. Packaging up leftovers for people to take home with them, more TV. Some public shaming about eating more food; then you and Daddy will head back to the Hamilton's for the great Thanksgiving sleepover part two. Mrs. Hamilton and Mami will stay up and watch rom-coms on TV and knit."

She tugged the front edges of his shirt in place and smoothed the fabric over his chest. It was an excuse to touch him. To show Jo that as Bobby's girlfriend, Ramona was the one who could.

He clasped her hands in place and leaned forward for a soft kiss. "You are being very touchy today, Ramona. What's up?" He nuzzled against her ear. "I like it, but it's not like you with people around."

A damp sweat-soaked shirt slapped Bobby in the face. "You forgot your stinky shirt," Jo growled as she stormed past.

Bobby looked after her, eyebrows raised.

"What did you say to Jo just now?" Ramona tightened her grip on his shirt.

"Oh, that?" He laughed. "You don't have to worry about

her, Angel." He draped his arm over her shoulder, and they began to follow everyone else inside.

"What did ya say?"

"She said something like good game; I said thanks. She said, you must be hot. I said, yeah. She said, how about a kiss for the winner. I said, good idea, and came over to kiss you." He shrugged. A smirk pulled at the corner of his lips. He knew exactly what he had done. "C'mon, more food sounds like a good idea."

Ramona felt like a stuffed pig. She hadn't eaten very much in the first round of the big meal, but she made up for it with seconds and then thirds. Bobby had been right. If he hadn't made those additional pies, there would not have been enough to go around. As it was, there was only half a pumpkin cake left. All the pies were gone.

As predicted, there was the standard argument over dishes. However this year it had a new spin to it. Bobby insisted that he and Ryan and her father do the work. And somehow they did it without any fuss. The fuss came from her mother trying to get her and Lorena to do it. Ramona sneaked into her father's study to escape the drama.

Ramona couldn't have moved if the house was on fire. All that delicious turkey and all those carbs; so many carbs.

Her bliss was interrupted by Jo flopping down on the futon next to her. Jesus H, she had hoped her cousin would have left in a huff already, or crawled off to hook up with Devon. He hadn't come back after the football game. Jo could have Devon. That was one thing Ramona had definitely learned in the past year: when a real man professed his love, it wasn't only until the next hot chick came along and hit on him.

"What gives?" Jo slapped the couch pillow onto Ramona's overfull belly.

She groaned. "I ate too much. What gives with you?"

"Seriously, are you paying him or something?"

"Paying who?" Ramona knew full well who Jo was talking about. But why make anything easy for her?

"Bobby. He's in there doing dishes. He kicked me out of the kitchen. He's acting like I don't exist, and..." She harrumphed. "Acting like you two are a thing. He is not your type, so what's the game?"

"The game, Jo, is he is my boyfriend. Stop hitting on him already. He's not Devon. It's not going to happen."

"You're funny. No, really, who is he here with?"

"Joanne, you are a piece of work." Ramona stood up. "You need to leave me alone. You need to leave Bobby alone."

Jo stood and hissed in Ramona's ear. "Until there is a ring on a finger somewhere, he's fair game."

Ramona felt like she'd been punched. Her thumb played with the bandage she had covering the bruise on her middle finger. She had a ring, only Coach had stolen it. "That didn't stop you last time." Ramona narrowed her eyes.

"Game on, Mona. Let's just see who he goes home with tonight."

"According to the rules of Thanksgiving, I'm not going home with anybody."

Ramona and Jo froze and turned to face Bobby. His hair was pulled back into a messy bun. His arms were crossed. He looked tired and aggravated.

Jo sort of sighed and melted into a relaxed posture. Ramona did not; her hackles were still raised.

"Look, Jo, I'm not some toy you can snatch away from your cousin because you don't think it's fair she's got something you don't. I'm not even flattered, because you aren't interested in me for any other reason than I'm with

Ramona. I've been polite enough, and most normal people would have gotten the hint by now. So let me be perfectly clear, in no uncertain terms: I would like you to stop. I am not interested in being pursued by you. I am not interested in being pursued by anyone. I am in a relationship that I find fulfilling, satisfying, and that completes me."

When he laid his hand over his heart and gave a slight nod of his head toward Ramona, she felt the tears burn her eyes. If she couldn't name a hundred ways that she loved him before, she could now, and this was ninety-nine of them.

Jo stood right in front of him. She puffed her chest up, not that it needed the boost. "I know your type. If it's not me, then it's going to be someone else. Mona is too quiet to hold your interests for long."

She tossed her hair and stormed out of the room.

They could hear her false wail as she walked into the living room.

Ramona was so tired of this, so tired of always being the one who got into trouble when Jo pulled these kinds of stunts. She slid into Bobby's arms. She buried her head into his chest. He was comfort. He was her rock. And for a brief moment before all hell broke loose, she was safe.

Before Bobby had time to do much more than wrap his arms around her, Nan was barging into the room, followed by Mami.

"What did you say to Joanne?" Nan demanded.

Ramona turned. Time to face the music.

Bobby dropped his hand on her shoulder. "Ramona didn't say anything. I did."

"Then why is Joanne crying?"

Ramona sighed. "Jo is crying so that you think I did something mean to her."

Bobby cut in. "I asked her to leave me alone. Is that a problem?"

"It's about time someone put her in her place," Mami said. She tapped the older woman on the arm. "Come on, leave them alone. They've had enough to deal with putting up with Joanne all day long."

Nan was still asking why Jo was so upset when Mami closed the door.

Bobby pulled Ramona back into his arms. She wanted to stay there forever.

"Is it always going to be like this?" Ramona asked against his shirt.

"Is what going to be like this?" Bobby stroked her hair.

"Other women wanting to get at you. Me having to constantly stake my claim. Do I have to constantly worry that at some point you are going to get sick of saying no, and you'll go back to sleeping around?"

Bobby stood back, holding Ramona at arms' distance, looking at her. "You are my life, my blood, my air. Women like your cousin are nothing but gnats to me. Gnats are not interesting, seductive, or worth your worry. I love you. Maybe we should drive home tonight so I can demonstrate just how much."

Ramona blinked a few times. Tears burned the backs of her eyes. That had to have been the single most romantic thing she'd ever heard. That and she really loved thinking of Jo as a gnat. Swat it away and ignore it.

25

Ramona gazed over at Bobby. His face was set, his mouth a straight line, his knuckles on the steering wheel white. She could see the wolf in him ripple through his brow as he did his best to control his rage. Five days and he was as angry as when she'd first told him that Coach assaulted her and took her ring. She hated that they'd had to wait until after school, but Debbie had been right, they didn't need to send an officer onto campus and arrest Coach while there were kids around. And they were going to pick him up from Central because they knew he would be there.

Bobby had shown up at RavenCroft before the last bell rang. He calmly explained to Dr. G why she needed to leave campus early, and could Dr. Grover please call Principal Baker to let him know why they were coming over. Bobby told her Dr. G was all smiles and thrilled that she and Bobby were a couple, and "Of course, anything to help out one of my favorite teachers."

She couldn't quite wrap her head around that Dr. G considered her one of his favorites. Maybe that was why he was on her case about so many little stupid things. She shook her head. It didn't matter. She was a nervous wreck. She just wanted her ring back, and for the coach to be held accountable for the assault.

She held Bobby's hand with both of hers as they walked into Principal Baker's office. Debbie's Derrick was already there, in full uniform, waiting for them.

Baker extended his hand to Bobby. "Never expected to see you back in these halls, Cray. This is some bad business, but we'll get things sorted."

He extended his hand to Ramona. "Pleasure to meet you, Ms. Campbell. Dr. Grover had some enlightening things to say about your teaching. Sorry about the circumstances that bring you here." He turned his attention to Derrick and nodded. "Do we really need you, Officer?"

Derrick puffed up his chest. It looked almost as thick as Bobby's, but the difference was a Kevlar vest versus hard muscles. "Yes, this is an assault and robbery case."

"Are you really going to press charges?" Baker asked Ramona. The sneering tone of his voice made Ramona hold tighter to Bobby. This was exactly why victims of assault didn't come forward as often as they should. The system didn't want the trouble. The implication was clear: she was making a fuss.

"Yes, she is," Bobby growled.

"Can you really identify the ring as yours?"

Ramona decided that this principal was a weasel.

"My name is engraved on the band," Bobby said.

A tickle of guilt overcame Ramona. She hadn't noticed his name inside. Then again, she hadn't taken the ring off except a few times.

"Okay then, let's go." Baker indicated the way out of his office.

Bobby knew exactly where he was going. Ramona felt as

if she were reining him back. Preventing him from tearing off, keeping his anger in check. They passed through the center of the school. Only a few students were still around. Derrick and the principal followed behind.

Bobby crashed out the back set of double doors next to the cafeteria and crossed a courtyard with picnic tables. The smell of locker room overwhelmed her senses when Bobby burst his way in through a blue door with the word SPORTS painted above it.

"Get out of my office," Coach yelled without even looking up to see who it was.

Ramona could feel the heat rise off Bobby. His neck pulsed with his increased heart rate. He huffed his breathing through his nose. His eyes blazed an intense gold. He was barely contained.

"Coach," Baker said as a way of announcing his presence. "We have a situation."

Coach Shumer finally looked up from the large paper chart he was examining. He threw his arm up and pointed at the door. "Get that woman out of my office!"

"Give her my ring back," Bobby growled through clenched teeth.

"You can't have it, not if you are gonna give it to some whore. You don't deserve it," the man attempted to snarl back with as much ferocity. It did not work.

"Now, Coach, you can't do that. Give the man his ring back," Baker directed.

"No."

Ramona noticed Derrick had a hand on Bobby's shoulder. The two of them were definitely keeping Bobby from letting loose on the man.

"Coach Shumer, you need to return the stolen property

immediately, or I will have no choice but to get a warrant and search your home and office."

Ramona cut her glance to Derrick. He sounded so authoritative. Something that in her mind she hadn't quite come to grips with, not after all of Debbie's stories about him.

"That's not happenin'," Coach growled. "This is my office, and I want y'all out."

"Not without my ring," Ramona said.

"Fine!" Coach rummaged in the middle desk drawer and threw something at her.

Bobby reached out and snatched the flying object from the air. He looked at it and hurled it back at the coach. The ring bounced off the other man's chest with a *thud*. "Wrong ring, asshole." Bobby growled with a deep beastly rumble.

Ramona felt him coil up even tighter. She stood in front of Bobby, not to protect the coach from him, but to keep him from doing something stupid in front of an on-duty police officer.

The coach pulled out a box and threw it on his desk. It was full of championship rings.

Derrick whistled. "Coach, really? How many of those are actually yours?"

Ramona picked through the box, looking for her ring, the one with Bobby Cray engraved on the inside and a ring guard. She looked up at Derrick. "None of these are his. Look"—she held the box up—"all the names are different."

She continued to sort through the box. She clasped something to her chest. "Found it!"

Bobby reached for her. She handed him the ring. The expression on his face made her insides flip. They locked eyes. He slid the ring on her finger. "This is yours." He pulled her into his chest and held on fiercely.

"You hear me, Coach? That ring is hers. You touch her again, and I swear—"

"You swear nothing in front of me, Cray. I don't want to have to report I witnessed a threat. You got what you came for, now head on home. I'll take care if it from here." Derrick nodded, indicating Bobby needed to leave.

"You're going to arrest him, aren't you? He doesn't get to stay here with just a warning?" Ramona asked, her voice pitched high with fear and anger.

"Now I think we managed to resolve this without any violence. There's no need to arrest Coach." Baker offered his opinion.

Ramona surged forward.

Bobby caught her around the middle. "Violence has already been done." He gently pulled the collar of her dress to the side, exposing the deep purple mark on her shoulder.

Ramona helped him and unbuttoned the top two buttons at the front of her dress so Bobby could expose more of her bruising.

Principal Baker made a low humming noise as if he felt pain.

Coach dropped into his office chair.

Derrick hissed. "Yes, I'm arresting him. Damn it. That's bad. Debbie said he hurt you, but she didn't show me the pictures y'all took on Wednesday. Okay, get up, Coach. I'm taking you in, and I'm taking that box of rings."

"You can't arrest me," Coach huffed.

"I can, and I am. Now stand up." Derrick's tone said not to mess with him. "Bobby, Ramona, you go on ahead. I'll have Debbie call you if we need anything. You've identified Coach Shumer in front of witnesses. I'll take it from here."

Bobby pulled Ramona to his chest. He held her tightly

as he guided her from the coach's office. They walked in each other's embrace all the way back to his car.

~

Ramona sat curled up with an armful of blankets. She wished it was Bobby next to her instead.

"Are you done at work yet?" She tried not to whine into the phone. Bobby's hours running Ray's were miserable during the week. She basically got to see him for maybe an hour after school before he went in until two or three in the morning.

It was hard today. She didn't want to be alone. Coach Shumer was spending the night in jail. Apparently his wife wasn't going to post bail for him. Ramona had her ring back, but she didn't have the comfort of Bobby.

"Rob is already cleaning the kitchen. It shouldn't be too long now." His voice was a balm over the phone. But it wasn't enough.

"Well, hurry up. I want to show you something." She wanted to show him everything.

He chuckled, promised he would be there as soon as he could, and told her to go to bed. If she went to bed, she would miss this, and this needed to happen tonight. The Leonids were peaking late this year, and the moon had already set.

By the time Bobby arrived, Ramona had taken a mini snooze on the pile of blankets in her arms, but now that he was with her, she was wide awake.

"Okay." She bounced up. She pushed blankets into his arms. "Let's go. You drive."

"What are you doing, Angel?" He gave her a tired laugh.

"I don't know where that rock is, and I want to show you something. Come on." She left him standing inside her door as she skipped down the steps and got into his car. The air was chilly on her skin, but she had enough blankets that this should work.

Bobby kept glancing over at her as he drove out into the dark. She was going to have to get him to show her where this place was in the daylight. He pulled over, and Ramona was out of the car, arms full of blankets. Her nerves were dancing a mile a minute as she waited for Bobby to get out and lead the way.

He jumped onto the rock first.

"The rock won't be warm like it was this summer," she announced as she handed up the blankets. "That's why I brought these." She kept one in her arms as she directed him to spread out the first two. Bobby helped her up. They stood together, his arms around her, in the middle of the rock, surrounded by nothing but stars

"Look up," she whispered.

Perfect timing. Meteors streaked the sky.

"Oh, Angel, that's cool." Bobby held her hands as he sat, pulling her down with him.

He lay back, but she did not. Instead Ramona straddled his waist.

"What are you doing?" he asked.

"Something I wanted to do ever since you first brought me out here." She ran her hands over his chest, pushing his denim jacket open. She snaked her hands under the hem of his shirt so she could feel his skin.

Bobby let out a soft, moaning sigh.

She loved how smooth his skin was. Something in his genetics left him with only a smattering of chest hair between his pecs.

Bobby hissed when her fingers found his nipples, but he didn't complain. He kept his eyes on her the entire time.

Jesus H, if they don't glow in the dark.

"You're supposed to be watching the meteor shower," Ramona said.

"I'd rather watch you," he answered with some heavy breathing.

She wiggled against his crotch. He liked this, and she could feel the bulge hardening in his jeans. She scooted back and moved her hands to his belt.

Bobby captured her hands in his. "Ramona, you keep this up, and I will end up making love to you on this rock."

"Under the stars," she finished for him. "That's the plan."

Bobby released her and ran his hands up her leg. He fisted her skirt, pulling it out of the way, and then was touching her skin. His hands ran farther up until he palmed her butt. "You aren't wearing any panties."

His smile right then made her go weak in the knees. Good thing she wasn't standing up. She finished with his belt and continued to free his erection from the confines of his clothing. In the low light of the night his manhood stood tall and proud, ready for her. She leaned over and licked him.

"Oh God." He snaked his hand into her hair.

"Don't close your eyes," she said. "Watch the sky." She took the tip of him into her mouth and laved with her tongue until he was making low growling noises deep in his chest. He was more than ready, and she couldn't wait any longer.

Ramona adjusted and repositioned herself. She pulled a condom pack from her bra and opened it. She slid it over his length before she followed it with her body. She cried out as she took him in, it felt perfect every time, and every time her body went into overdrive with hyperaware nerves.

Bobby dug his fingers into her hips, holding her in place. "You've been thinking about this ever since July?"

She hummed in affirmation. "I wanted to make love to you under the stars that night. I've been thinking of an opportunity to get you to bring me back out here. When I read about the meteor shower running late this year, I knew this was my opportunity." She rocked her hips in emphasis.

Bobby held her tight to him and counter thrust. "No one has ever made me feel the way you do. No one has ever made love to me under the open sky. You are amazing."

Ramona traced her fingers over his features. She brushed his full mouth with her thumb. "I was so in love with you back then it hurt."

"And now?" Bobby sucked her thumb into his mouth and teased it with his teeth.

Ramona could hardly find the words to express the feelings she had for him. "Now you love me back, and it is the most thrilling feeling in the world."

"I was in love with you too, you know. I thought about telling you that night, but I was stupid." Bobby bucked his hips and pulled on her wrists, overbalancing her so she fell onto his chest. He cupped the back of her head and slid his lips across hers while at the same time thrusting into her.

Ramona moaned into his mouth. Her hips rocked against his. Her tongue darted across his mouth and twined with his tongue. The pressure in her core built to a crescendo. She pushed back up for a better angle, deeper penetration. It didn't take much for Bobby to light her on fire, and when he did, she could not get enough of him.

She dug her nails into his shirt and held on as her body

took over. She cried out, not caring if anyone would be able to hear her. Bobby's fingers held on to her thighs, and he took over the driving thrusts. His roar followed her cries as his orgasm followed behind hers.

Ramona lay in a heap on his chest. His heart pounded against her cheek. She rode the waves of his breathing as his chest rose and fell.

Bobby smoothed her skirt over her backside and pulled a blanket over them.

She wanted to stay joined with him like this forever. They couldn't stay out here all night. It was chilly and getting colder. The few blankets she had brought would not be enough, but for now she did not want to move.

"I'm glad you stopped being stupid. I almost didn't bring a condom," she confessed.

"Good thing you did. It would have been a shame to have missed this. Oh, did you see that one?" Bobby pointed up into the sky.

"No, I mean I thought about letting you get me pregnant. Something I read in a book. All the important moments happen under the open sky."

Bobby moved, adjusting Ramona to lie next to him. He propped himself up on one elbow so he could look into her eyes. "You amaze me." He searched her face. He brushed her hair from her brow.

"I don't know what to say. Ramona," Bobby sighed. "When we make babies, and we will—I know you, you aren't going to be happy being pregnant before you're married. You have romantic ideals that I want to make happen. Love, marriage, and then children. In that order."

"So you will make babies with me?" she asked. Her heart sped up, and her nerves thrummed.

"God yes, I want to make babies with you. But when the time is right."

She reached into her bra and pulled out a second foil packet. "Are you up for a little more practice?"

26

Coach Shumer crashed into Ray's. "You cost me my job!"

Bobby looked up from where he was mixing drinks behind the bar. Sooner or later Coach was going to be drunk enough and mad enough he was going to come after Bobby. And here he was. Bobby let out a ragged breath. He had been expecting this. At least the man had come here and had not tried to go after Ramona again.

"No, Coach, you lost your own damn job. Check your team stats for the past three years. You lost your job because you're a lousy coach and a drunk. Now get the hell out of my bar."

Coach slammed into the bar and growled in Bobby's face. "Make me."

"You don't want to go there, old man. You may be bigger and stronger than the women you choose to beat, but you are no match for me."

Bobby ignored him and delivered the drinks order he'd finished.

Bobby shot his gaze around the bar. It was late enough

on a week night that it wasn't terribly crowded. But the people here were definitely paying attention. He could tell by their postures, by the way their eyes darted toward Coach and then back again.

He could hear Coach staggering up behind him. Could sense the man coiling up for the punch before anyone had time to shout, "Watch out!"

Bobby ducked the punch. He spun and sidestepped another swing. In two blinks Bobby was behind the man pinning his arms to his side and bum-rushing him through the front doors.

Coach swung first. He tried to hit him from the back. Bobby had every right to deliver a smackdown on the man. But there were too many people inside, and he would be beating up an old drunk guy.

"I told you once to get out of my bar. Now get the fuck off my property." Bobby shoved the man away from him.

Coach turned and ran to tackle Bobby. The impact barely staggered Bobby. He wrapped his arm around Coach's neck. He balled his hand into a fist and drove it into Coach's solar plexus.

"That's for hurting my girl." Bobby growled low through clenched teeth. "Leave before I forget myself and give you the pounding you deserve."

He let go.

Coach dropped to the ground, gasping for breath.

"Get up!" Bobby ordered.

Bobby glowered as he watched Coach slowly get to his knees and then up to his feet. Coach was still having trouble breathing. He walked, hunched over, to his SUV.

Bobby stood in front of the doors to Ray's until the truck pulled out and turned toward town. He let out another big breath. That man was going to be trouble until he did something too stupid to recover from, or he left town. Bobby shook the encounter from his limbs and went back inside.

Too many eyes were watching him. "Show's over," he announced as he walked back behind the bar.

The bell sounded, indicating that Rob had an order up. Bobby delivered the burgers and onion rings, and everything went back to normal.

Ramona walked in, and her glow caught Bobby's attention. Mate. He liked that. He liked the whole concept that they were ideal for each other. He loved that she wanted his children. He hated that she had been hurt in order for her to come to Haven, but he thanked the fates that sent Ramona his way. She was his other half; with her he was complete.

"My love, my angel, what are you doing out this late on a school night?" He slid his arms around her and kissed her ever so softly. He wanted to kiss her more, taste her more fully, but they had an audience.

"It's not a school night." She laughed. "Winter break, remember? Quiet night?"

She perched on one of the bar stools as Bobby walked behind the bar.

"Mostly. Coach came in. I took him outside—"

"Bobby, you didn't—"

"I didn't beat the living crap out of him like I want to. I decked him pretty good. Hopefully good enough he'll think twice about coming—"

Someone came into the bar. Someone else screamed.

Ramona spun around and gasped.

Bobby looked up. "Fuck me."

Coach stalked into the bar, a pistol held out in front of him. Aimed right at Bobby.

Slowly Bobby raised his hands up to his shoulders. "All

right, you don't want to make trouble for anyone else in here but me, right?"

"You're gonna pay for this, Cray," Coach growled.

"Why don't we keep this between you and me? Everyone else can go ahead and leave the bar right now." Bobby waved his hand, indicating people needed to move.

"I don't want trouble for them. They can git," Coach agreed.

"Okay, you heard the man. Get on out." Bobby raised his voice.

The few patrons he had left the bar in a hurry.

"Rob, that's you too. You need to leave now."

Rob walked fast past where Coach and Bobby stood, a frozen pose of a classic holdup; one man with a gun pointed at another with his hands in the air.

Ramona stared at Bobby, her eyes wide with terror.

He mouthed, *I love you. Go.*

Ramona slowly slid from the bar stool. She cringed as she tried to pass Coach.

He grabbed her hair and yanked her back toward him.

She screamed and reached for her head, where he pulled on her hair.

Bobby started.

Coach shoved the gun at him. He stopped moving. Bobby slowly scanned to make sure no one else was left inside. His voice was low, menacing. "That is a big mistake. Take your hands off her."

"My wife left me because of you. Said it was bad enough I hit her, but she wouldn't put up with it anymore. Your whore deserved it." He shook the hand with Ramona's hair.

She cried and tried to pull away from him.

"Coach, let go of the girl, and put down the gun. I'm not gonna tell you again."

Bobby already felt the wolf surge through his shoulders and down his arms. He held it back, but the second he let go, he would attack. He slowly unfastened his waistband.

"It's all your fau—"

Bobby released his hold on the shift. His shirt tore apart. His pants slid from his hips. No longer human, he was up and over the bar. His jaws wrapping around the wrist holding the gun, sharp fangs sinking into soft flesh.

Coach screamed and dropped the gun.

Ramona cried out and was on the floor. She was moving quickly, crawling away.

Coach tried to hit Bobby. The wolf let go of the arm in his mouth and went for the man's throat. He wrapped his teeth around the man's jaw and held. It took all his will not to complete the bite and crush Coach's face.

Coach fought with little resistance.

"Bobby, Bobby, stop. I've got the gun," Ramona announced.

Coach lay panting on the floor, covered in blood. He muttered something under his breath.

Bobby shook back into human form. He stood. He didn't give the wounded man a second look but went straight to Ramona. He gently took the gun from her shaking grasp and pulled her in for a searing kiss.

"You better get dressed. I can hear sirens." Ramona pushed on his chest. She was right. He needed clothes. He moved back behind the bar and hitched his pants back on. Running his hand through his hair, he wondered out loud, "How do we explain the bites?"

"Rough vigilante rescue dog?" Ramona shrugged. "Oh I know. Hand me a bottle."

Bobby handed her a beer.

"Watch your eyes," she said as she covered her own.

"Maybe we can convince the police this was the result of a brawl."

There was a loud *thunk* against the bar.

Smart woman. Smart but not much upper body strength. Bobby took the bottle from her and cracked it against the bar, scattering glass everywhere.

"Those look like bite marks, not like cuts from a broken bottle. And how do you explain his jaw?" She was smart, but Bobby didn't really think it was going to fool anyone.

"How long are your nails? Can you make them longer? We'll say your nails did that when you grabbed him." Ramona sounded almost desperate.

He focused on his nails. They grew and became more claw like. He shook his head. "I'm not sure. They don't look all that long."

"I don't think we can say they were self inflicted." Ramona laughed. It was a high-pitched laugh full of nerves. "Whatever, it was self-defense. After all he had a gun, and everyone saw it."

The sirens grew louder.

"The cops will be here in a minute."

Coach made some moaning sounds. Bobby glanced over at him. Coach lay in a heap, halfway under a table. He didn't look like he was going anywhere for a while. He had scratches all over his face from scraping teeth, the front of his shirt was shredded from claws, and there was blood ever where from cuts and his bloody wrist.

Suddenly the man moved. He was screaming incoherently and running out the door.

Bobby looked at Ramona, shocked that Coach could even move. He leaped over the bar and took off after the injured man.

Tires spun in the parking lot, throwing gravel. People

who'd evacuated earlier jumped out of the way as Coach sped out of the lot. His SUV turned away from town. Coach wasn't going anywhere fast. The train that chugged away on the other side of Ray's crossed the road less than a block away.

Police cars passed the lot to Ray's, chasing after the truck.

There was a loud squealing of tires and a sickening *thud*, followed by the earsplitting tearing of metal.

Bobby ran out into the road. Others who had been in the parking lot followed him.

The flashing lights on the police vehicles made it difficult to see properly. They were stopped at skewed angles. Bobby couldn't tell, but it looked like the freight train was slowing. Pieces of white SUV were scattered around and trailing off to the west.

Bobby exhaled hard. He jogged back to Ramona. She waited outside the doors to the bar. Three officers stood with her. Bobby ignored them and wrapped himself around her. Her hair smelled like fresh flowers and evening sunsets. He didn't want to think of anything else at this moment but her in his arms.

"You two okay?" Bobby turned to see Debbie running up to them.

"I think so." Bobby stood back and let Ramona hug her friend. It had been a stressful night.

"I just got word from Derrick. Coach didn't make it," Debbie said.

Ramona looked as if she was about to cry. Bobby pulled her back into his arms. "That poor man."

"He won't be bothering us anymore."

27

Ramona's eyes slowly cracked open. She glanced at the clock and closed her eyes again. It was too early. Bobby's warm breath caressed her shoulder, and his arm draped across her midsection, holding her. If this was what Christmases with Bobby were going to be like, Ramona would take them all.

She would miss Mami's traditional breakfast of fresh cinnamon rolls and sausage balls. Something Ramona had had every year as far back as she could remember. She and Lorena would get up early and stare at the tree twinkling with lights. They had never been allowed past the end of the hallway into the living room with the tree until their parents woke. And the girls weren't allowed to wake their parents up until after seven thirty. They would sit at the very edge of the carpet runner, toes barely into the next room, and point and whisper and try to decide if that big box was for them or for Daddy.

Their parents would wake up and Daddy would ruffle her bed head and say, "Wait for Mami," as he headed into the kitchen and started the coffeepot. Typically as soon as the smell of coffee permeated the house, Mami would be up. She would give the go-ahead, and the girls would attack the tree like rabid teenyboppers rushing the stage at a boy-band concert. Mami would curl up next to Daddy on the couch, cuddled around a steaming mug of coffee, and wrapping paper would fill the air like snowfall as the girls shredded into their presents.

After the frenzy of present opening, Ramona would usually pass right back out on a pile of presents and new clothes. Her family would let her sleep among the shredded papers until the nose-tickling scent of hot, fresh cinnamon rolls woke her.

When Lorena started bringing Ryan home, there were no more mornings of anticipation. It was wake up, roll out of bed, make coffee, and put on a Christmas movie DVD until everyone else stumbled into the living room. Mami still made her cinnamon rolls, and they were still the best.

When Devon officially entered the picture, he never headed over until late morning, having spent the night at his parents' house, while Ramona camped out on the futon in her old bedroom.

This was the first Christmas Ramona had woken up in the arms of her beloved. She never wanted to go back to sleeping on that lumpy futon alone. If that meant having to skip out on a few holidays at her parents, so be it. The trade-off would be worth it. They would never let her and Bobby sleep in the same room. Well, not unless they were married.

Ramona snuggled back against Bobby. His even breaths whispered across her ear. She could do that, marry him. He had changed so much since she first met him with his reputation of easy man slut, but did that mean he was the marrying type? He'd already said he wanted to make babies with her. She should ask him. But she wanted to be asked.

For now she would take him any way he was giving himself to her, and so far that had been wholeheartedly, completely.

She could picture living with him. This house was small, but they could make it work. It was larger than her apartment. Of course, when they had kids... She sighed. Bobby would make the most beautiful babies. Would they do that wolf thing he did? How would she manage that? She huffed. One day at a time was how.

And Bobby had told her they had a connection, the Palatine family. Genetic relatives he had met over the summer. A whole family of shifters that would welcome and support them.

Bobby began to make mouth-smacking noises. He would wake up soon. She should get up and start the cinnamon rolls. She had bought all the ingredients, and her mother had reluctantly given her the recipe.

Mami had not been happy. Christmas was for family. Ramona should be home. Ramona had explained over and over again, Bobby had come with her to her family for Thanksgiving, and she was going with him to his for Christmas.

"Why can't you come home and then call him. Or drive back there in the afternoon?" her mother asked.

"Mami, it's not a quick drive back. It would take all day, and I wouldn't be there for Christmas dinner. They are doing a big lunch, and he wants me there to be with his family."

Mami would never fully understand, you didn't have to be married for someone to be family. Or maybe she did and that's what she was worried about.

Ramona opened her eyes again, deciding it was time to go make those cinnamon rolls. She wanted to surprise Bobby and continue a family tradition. She was going to make two large batches. One to have for breakfast before they headed over to Brad and Melissa's and one to take with them.

She slid out of bed and into a pair of sweats. Pulling her hair into a messy top knot, she did a truncated morning routine in the bathroom before heading into the kitchen.

Cat twisted around her ankles, trying to trip her, or just pay attention to her at the most inopportune moment. She let the dogs out.

Flour, sugar, butter, cinnamon, and more butter blended together with some kitchen magic. As she slid the trays into the oven, Ramona was certain she was covered in as much flour and cinnamon as she had put into the pastries. Timer set, coffee brewing, she checked the clock. It was eight thirty. Time to call home.

"Merry Christmas," she said to the groggy voice that answered.

"Hello, darling girl!" her father replied. "How are you this Christmas morning?" He cleared his throat, and the morning frog dissipated from his voice.

"I'm great. I'm making Mami's cinnamon rolls, and it smells like Christmas."

"Did that young man of yours give you a decent present?" he asked.

"We aren't exchanging gifts until we are over at his brother's house. This way we get to have an opening frenzy with his nieces and nephews," she explained.

"Is he from a big family?"

"Not really, his brother and his kids. I got them some fun presents. How's Mami?"

"She is busy with Noah right now. But she's good. You want to talk to Lorena?" Clearly he handed the phone to her sister, since Lorena said, "Merry Christmas," next.

"Merry Christmas, Lorena. How is your morning? How is Todd loving it?"

"Oh, he is already crashed out. He had a fabulous morning. So many presents, so many. My house is going to be covered in Legos. How is your morning?"

Ramona couldn't tell her sister how fabulous it was to wake up wrapped in Bobby. A loud yawn alerted her to Bobby being awake. She rotated to look over the back of the couch. He shuffled into the bathroom and closed the door. It was hard not to croon. "My morning is great. I'm making Mami's cinnamon rolls. Bobby is heading over for breakfast." It wasn't a direct lie; he was going to head out of the bathroom at some point. Her sister didn't need to know how short his traveling distance was. "And after that we'll head over to his brother's."

"I'll tell Mami. Ours are in the oven now. Sounds like you're going to have a fun day," Lorena said.

"I hope so," Ramona confessed. She expected it would be a good day. She liked Bobby's family, and they seemed to like her. She always had a good time with them.

"I'm gonna let you go. Noah is getting fussy."

"Give everyone a big hug, and let Mami know I'll call her later. Love you," Ramona said.

"Merry Christmas, Mona."

She let the phone drop into her lap. The oven timer binged. Ramona slid the tray from the oven. The heat hit her face like a wave. The rolls smelled divine.

"Good morning, Angel." Bobby wrapped his large sleep-warm arms around her and buried his face into the nape of her neck. "Merry Christmas."

She pulled the oven mitts off and dropped them on the counter. Turning in Bobby's embrace, she wrapped her arms around his neck. "Merry Christmas."

His lips were warm and soft and perfect.

"Are those done?" Bobby glanced over at the pastries.

She nodded.

"Good." He scooped her up into his arms. "You look like a present I want to unwrap, and I don't want to get into trouble for burning the rolls."

"Bobby," Ramona called out, exasperated. But she didn't put up a fight or resist. He looked like a present she wanted to unwrap too, even if she knew exactly what package he had under those boxers.

Ramona sat on the couch, wedged in between Sophie and Abby. She and Bobby had arrived a little later than planned, but it had been so worth it. He had given her the best Christmas present over and over and over again until she screamed.

Melissa served the cinnamon rolls, which everyone ate with lots of oohs, ahs, and yums. The first present was opened, the giant dress-up box for all the kids was a huge success. It contained everything from tutus to butterfly wings to dragon tails. Bobby sat on the floor and Princess Pete, in a tutu and full crown, was in his lap helping him to unwrap all his gifts. Abby's Max was also on the floor with Tyler in his lap. This was a happy family, and all the kids made Christmas that much better.

It had definitely been the right decision to stay here with him for Christmas. Brad and Melissa gave Bobby some practical tools for working on his house. Which he seemed delighted with. But not nearly as delighted as the kids were when they each opened their very own Slinky. There was a reason the classic toy was still popular.

Melissa handed Ramona a box to open. "This is from me and Abby. We figured this was your style, but if it isn't... I kept the receipts. You can return it."

Ramona creased her brow, intrigued. She figured it was probably another T-shirt. She already had a pile of them that each of the kids had drawn something on for her. Ramona ripped the paper from the top of the box. She tossed the lid to the side and lifted out a gold-tone cotton dress covered in a print of vines and leaves.

"We know how you wear those cute flower dresses all the time, and it's just so pretty," Abby said.

"And that green is the color of your eyes," Melissa added.

"It's lovely," Ramona said. She stood up to hold it in front of her. It was the kind of dress she liked to wear for work, and it was the right size. Bobby's eyes flashed an intense gold when he smiled up at her. He liked it too. They had paid attention to her, better than she had paid attention to them.

Not exactly certain what to get either Melissa or Abby, Ramona had opted for massage gift certificates. This way she could also support her friend Khendra's salon and spa. Melissa practically moaned in anticipated delight. Okay, so she hadn't messed up on their gifts.

Brad was harder to buy for. He didn't wear ties, and he managed a tire shop so car toys were not something he would need. The six-month subscription to Craft Beers of the Month, however, seemed to be well appreciated. She knew nothing about Maxfield, so she contributed to the set of rims Abby wanted to get him for his new car.

Bobby hadn't opened his gift from her yet. She had considered giving it to him before they came over, but they had agreed, unless it was risqué or too personal, they would exchange presents with the family. She pointed at the large cube shape. "You open that one next, Bobby."

He crawled over and pulled the gift back with him to where he was sitting.

"I probably need to confess this was kind of selfishly motivated," Ramona said as he opened his present.

He let out a bark of a laugh as he finished pulling the paper from the box. He held it up, showing off the present to everyone. "A tankless water heater." He read the side of the box. "And it's rated for outdoor use. For the tub. I guess that means you'll keep using it?"

Ramona felt a blush warm up her face. "I hope so." She held his gaze and hoped he clued in that she would be using it with him in the tub with her.

Bobby directed one of the twins to grab a large tube from behind the tree and hand it to Ramona. "This one is a little selfishly motivated too."

She looked at the cardboard poster tube. It wasn't wrapped, but it had a large red bow stuck to the side. She pried one of the plastic end caps off and slid out the rolled-up sheets of paper. Bobby helped her to spread them out on the floor at her feet.

"House plans?" she asked.

Brad leaned over the plans. "These aren't the same plans you had before." He pointed at an area of rooms next to what looked like stairs. "You didn't have these rooms or an upstairs before."

Ramona didn't understand. Bobby was giving her the plans for expanding his house.

"Yeah, well, I hadn't thought I would have a family to raise in that house before," Bobby told his brother.

Ramona's gaze snapped up to Bobby's face from the

drawings in front of her. She felt confused. His smile baffled her even more.

He lowered down to one knee.

Melissa gasped. Ramona looked at her expecting something to be wrong.

Ramona returned her attention to Bobby. Where had that little red box come from?

"I thought I would start expanding the place next week if you said yes." Bobby opened the small box, and a diamond ring sparkled up at her.

Ramona felt her cheek twitch. Her mouth went dry. She opened her mouth, but words wouldn't come out. Tears flooded her eyes, and she forgot to breathe. Finally with a hiccup of air she managed a nod.

"Is that a yes, you'll marry me?" Bobby asked as he lifted her hand and slipped the ring on her finger.

She squeaked and fell off the couch and into his arms. She was kissing him before she regained her voice. A crumpling of papers under her pulled her from the kiss. "I'm ruining the plans," she said as she stood up.

"No, the plan worked perfectly. You said yes."

"This calls for champagne," Brad said as he left to go into the kitchen.

"Oh Bobby, I'm so happy for you." Melissa came over and gave him a hug before pulling Ramona in for one as well. "I'm so excited you said yes. Let's see the ring."

Ramona held up her hand, fingers splayed. The ring looked tiny next to the championship ring on her middle finger. Melissa captured her fingertips and tilted her hand back and forth. "Beautiful, classic." She tilted Ramona's hand so Abby could see the sparkle coming from the diamond solitaire.

The ring winked. The sparkle fell from Ramona's hand,

and she was left with a plain gold band with an empty setting.

Nobody said anything. Ramona stopped breathing. A squeal and a yell headed toward them as Petey ran toward the diamond.

"Nobody move!" Melissa yelled in a deep growl.

The kids froze in their tracks. Petey looked pained, as if it was the worst thing his mother had ever said to him, but he held still.

Ramona inhaled a shuttering gasp. "Bobby?"

"Okay, don't move. I see it." Bobby reached between Ramona and Melissa and picked something up from the floor. He showed Ramona the stone. It wasn't a big diamond, but on the back of her hand it had looked plenty big. In his palm it was a tiny pebble of a sparkle. "Damn it. The setting was supposed to be temporary until I could get you back in the shop to pick out something you wanted. It wasn't supposed to fall out. You're still gonna marry me, even if I have to take the ring back already?"

Ramona pulled the empty ring from her finger and placed it in Bobby's palm next to the diamond. "Of course I am. I just won't have a ring to show off right away." The elation of being engaged settled a bit when she thought about the ring. But it spiked right back up to the highest peaks when she returned to the thought that Bobby had asked her to marry him, and she'd said yes.

She watched as he tucked the stone and ring back into the box. "I don't like you not having a ring. And I don't have anything else I can give you right now."

"Bullshit." Everyone turned to Brad. "She's already wearing your championship ring."

Ramona wiggled the ring off and poked at the ring

adjuster in the back. She slid it on her ring finger. It was still too big.

"Hold on a minute." Melissa left the room. When she returned, she held up a second ring adjuster band. "Oh here, give me that ring."

Ramona let the ring drop into Melissa's palm. She watched as the other woman clicked the second band onto the back of the ring shank. "Maybe two of them will make it fit."

Ramona pushed the plastic how Melissa showed her. "You just happened to have ring sizers around?"

"I have a few left over from after I lost all the weight, before I got my rings adjusted. How's that working?"

Ramona held up her left hand and wiggled it. The ring didn't slip off her finger as it had previously.

"It looks better on your finger than it ever looked on mine," Bobby said. "You don't mind wearing that until I can get this one fixed?"

Ramona studied the ring on her finger. "I actually kind of like this one. It's you. That one was just a ring from a store. Can you return it and let me keep this one?" She bit her lip as she looked up into his eyes.

"Are you serious?"

She nodded. "Do you think we could get it adjusted?"

"You can have whatever ring you want."

"Then I want this one. At least for now."

Bobby pulled her back into his arms and claimed her lips yet again. Yes, staying here for Christmas had been the right thing to do.

EPILOGUE 1

Ramona squatted in the dust and held the twine tight to the stake. Bobby pulled the string at the other end and shifted his stake a little to the left. It was her job to prevent him from pulling the first stake out of the ground. After three hours of marking out the footprint to the renovations on Bobby's home, her home, they were almost done.

Phase one, clearing the ground, took almost three weeks. They did the job themselves in their time off work, only letting the rain chase them inside. Building the house was going to take a while, especially since Bobby was going to do most of it himself. Well, he and Brad. They were capable men, but neither was a carpenter. However, they had done a decent job on his small house. Hopefully they would be able to do as well on the new, bigger design.

A large blue Ford F150 pulled down the drive towing an Airstream.

Ramona stood and watched the truck roll to a stop. Bobby crossed over to her and put his arm around her shoulders.

"Do you know who?" she asked.

He shook his head.

A big man with dark, curly hair stepped out of the truck.

A tall, slender blonde, who looked more like she'd swallowed a basketball than was pregnant, got out of the other side.

Bobby walked up to them first. "You must be a Palatine. You have the look." He stuck out his hand in greeting.

The other man nodded. "I'm Morgan. This is my wife, Honey. You're Bobby Cray?"

Bobby nodded and reached for Ramona. "This is my mate, Ramona," he said, pulling her to his side.

"So what brings y'all to Texas?" Ramona asked.

"Morgan is in construction, and we heard that you were building a house. On your own. So I poked him to drive on down and see if we could help out." Honey rubbed her belly. "And for one last trip with just the two of us."

Bobby pointed into the bed of the truck. It was stacked full of lumber and bags of cement. "I see you came prepared."

A red Dodge Magnum pulled in behind the trailer.

"I brought a work crew too." Morgan gave a hearty laugh as a tall, broad bald man stepped out of the car, followed by a sandy-headed teenager who looked like he'd just hit his growth spurt, all limbs. The kid was followed out of the car by a larger, older Native American boy.

Ramona blinked as two more Native American teens, identical to the first one, rolled out of the car. "You hiding any more in there?" She laughed.

Bobby had said he now had a family of shifters that was willing to support him. She hadn't appreciated the truth of that statement until now.

EPILOGUE 2

Melinda wadded up another piece of paper and tossed it at the trash can on the far side of her office. Her new two o'clock had stood her up. She was allowing herself fifteen minutes of peace and quiet and zero work before making use of the rest of the hour for catching up on paperwork.

Nonsensical breaks were healthy for brain function. She wished more of her clients, hell, more people in general knew this. Take a break; don't do anything. Not focusing on work for a few minutes every couple of hours increased productivity the rest of the time. Too many people, including her best friend Julia, felt that nose to the grindstone was the only way to ensure productivity.

Fifteen minutes, then she would call the man, make sure he was okay, see if he wanted to reschedule. She understood that walking into a therapist's office for the first time could be intimidating. Maybe he needed a videoconferencing option.

Her phone rang.

She swung her feet down from their perch on her desk

and adjusted her posture, aligning not only her core muscles and spine but also her focus. She pushed the intercom.

"Yes?"

"Julia is on line one." The new receptionist sounded nervous. She hadn't been around long enough to know that Julia never explained who she was. She was Julia; Melinda didn't need to know anything more.

Mel thanked the receptionist and picked up the phone.

"I have some interesting news for you," the voice on the other line announced.

"Last time you hit me with interesting news, there were dead bodies involved." Melinda chuckled.

"Not dead but pretty damned close. I checked in with Dr. Kimbro's alpha yesterday. She's healing quite well. Slowly but well. Thi—" Julia's voice stopped before she finished the word.

Mel heard the sigh. Julia had a dead body somewhere.

"Why do you have to involve me with dead bodies? Who died? Or..." She sat up a little more and leaned forward. "Who are we going to kill?"

Julia laughed. Good, laughter. Melinda was glad to be Julia's beta and sidekick, but she really wasn't built to hide dead bodies in the woods. Even though she was certain if Julia asked, Melinda would find a non-traceable way of purchasing body bags.

"He's already dead, basically."

"You didn't kill one of your cousins, did you?"

"Why do you think I go around killing people? I have people who take care of that for me."

The two women laughed their way through the conversation. Julia, a rare female alpha among wolf shifters, handled her enemies by annihilating them through stock shares and corporate takeovers. It wasn't her fault that a few pesky vampires were trying to make things very difficult, and so a few dead bodies had actually turned up. None by Julia's hands. Even though she was perfectly capable of doing so. To be fair, the dead bodies had happened over a year ago, but as best friend and de facto therapist, they had had many discussions about those bodies. Julia was coming to terms with the fact that her family was very capable of some nasty things in the name of defending what was theirs.

Melinda was part of that extended family. She knew that she would go to great lengths to protect what was hers. She was also very glad she'd never had to go that far.

Going that far was hard on a person. She should know—most of her clients were killers, not by choice but by circumstances.

"Let me rephrase this: your favorite dead man is in town again," Julia announced.

Melinda stopped breathing.

Nando was back after a year of hiding out in Argentina.

Thirty seconds of dead silence was broken by a squeal the likes of which wasn't typically heard outside a K-pop boy band concert. Melinda held up the phone and kicked away from the desk, spinning her chair.

"Yes!"

She fell out of her chair with a cacophonous noise.

The door to Melinda's office burst open. The receptionist stared at her with eyes as round as saucers.

"Is everything okay in here?" she asked.

Melinda climbed up from the floor, untangled herself from the phone cord, and adjusted herself to sit professionally at her desk. "Yes, everything is fine. Sorry about that."

She watched the receptionist back out and close the

door to her office. Melinda was going to buy her some coffee to make up for seeming so incredibly unprofessional.

"You owe me tickets, bitch," Melinda stage whispered into the receiver.

"If I recall correctly, I owe you a bit more than that."

"Yeah, you do."

"It's all arranged. Don't embarrass me."

"Embarrass you? Julia, I'm going to fully embarrass myself. I just fell out of my chair. When?" She vibrated with excitement, and they were only talking about meeting Nando, not actually meeting him. When that happened, Melinda wasn't going to need to worry about tripping over her own feet. She already knew her feet and legs would turn to gelatin. Tripping wouldn't be the problem; sliding into a puddle on the floor was going to be the problem.

Sigh, Nando. Long, silky hair, magical fingers. Damn, if he could play guitar the way he did, she could imagine how deft his fingers would feel across her skin. Fingers and then fangs. Damn.

Vampires and shifters did not play well together. Maybe she could be the exception.

~

Melinda would make an exception for Nado, but will he?
Find out in Redemption.

If you didn't start reading Legatum from the beginning, it's not too late. Get Protective, Legatum Book 1 now.

Keep reading for a sneak preview of Redemption.

REDEMPTION, LEGATUM BOOK 6

Fernando del Fuego was created to inherit and take over his father's empire. He has zero interest in the politics of vampires, he would much rather pursue a life of music. People died because of his apathy.

Melinda is strong-willed, and focused. As wolf-shifter and therapist specializing in patients with PTSD, she has the calmness and perseverance to help those who need her.

Drawn to Fernando's ethereal looks, and sublime music, she wants him to play her like one of his acoustic guitars. She knows what he is, vampire. Wolves and vampires have never played nicely together, so Mel is surprised when Fernando shows compassion to a soul who is more tortured than he is.

PREVIEW OF REDEMPTION

Excerpt

"Thanks, you're a miracle worker," she declared as she hopped out of the car. That only took thirty-five minutes. She wasn't nearly as late as she could have been. It was a miracle. She made sure to hand the driver a big cash tip. She didn't trust the program to pay properly on a tip.

Mel hefted her briefcase with her laptop higher on her shoulder and made her way to the front door of the club. If Julia hadn't told her there was a club here, she would have missed it. The building looked like any other small business frontage along this street, except for the ticket booth–looking window next to the front doors. She waited behind a couple as they purchased their tickets.

"Hi, I'm supposed to have a ticket. Melinda Franks. It might be under Mel." She showed her ID and was nodded in.

Inside it took her eyes a few seconds to adjust to the lights. The place was small. She quickly found Julia at a small table with a cocktail in front of her and a beer bottle waiting across the table for Mel's arrival.

"I made it," Mel announced with a huff of air.

Julia looked up and smiled. "That was good timing."

"I swear my driver folded time and space to get me here. Does this place do food? I'm starving."

Mel looked around her. There was a small stage in front of them. The rest of the space was dark and practically invisible. So, not a statement club, but one for performances.

"Did I completely blow it?"

Julia shook her head. "I don't think so. I haven't seen Cyan yet, and she said she would make introductions. His set is supposed to start at eight, so we might be out of luck."

"I guess I shouldn't complain. I didn't even know he was doing this show. Bad fan, right?"

"Hardly. I guess it's some sort of secret place for musicians to play before bigger shows. You have tickets to his big show at the Warfield, right?"

"Yeah, but that's almost two weeks away."

"Excuse me." A deep voice, heavy with a Hispanic accent, interrupted.

Mel glanced up and froze.

Fernando del Fuego stood next to her, asking to be excused by her. The beer in her mouth evaporated, and her tongue turned to dust. His lips quirked into a half grin, and she forgot how to breathe.

Click HERE to continue reading Redemption.

Sign up for Lulu's newsletter to keep up to date with new releases and happenings. And get a free sexy short story.

https://lulumsylvian.com/newsletter/

ALSO BY LULU M SYLVIAN

Check out these other series

Legatum

Paranormal romantic suspense

The World of Wet Waterfalls

Paranormal reverse harem romance

Rockers

Contemporary and paranormal rockstar romance

Holiday Strippers

Contemporary, paranormal, ridiculous, romance

ABOUT THE AUTHOR

 Bio-engineered to be the only redhead in a generation of blonds, Lulu feels that "aliens" may actually be the best answer for a life-time of being asked, "Where did you get that red hair from?"

She did not come into writing from years of scribbling words on paper. Her background is rooted in visual arts and making pictures. Encouraged to make those pictures out of words Lulu began writing just to see what would happen. What happened was two full-length manuscripts in three months.

Lulu cannot ride a horse, a motorcycle, spin a hula hoop, or play roller derby. Yes, she has attempted all of those, even if it has been decades since she's been on a horse or a motorcycle. She embraces the crazy that comes with that one little genetic mutation, and attempts to live up to the reputation that proceeds her. Lulu would like to apologize for her contribution to the hole on the ozone layer from her use of hairspray in the 1980s.

For more information, visit:
www.LuluMSylvian.com

www.ingramcontent.com/pod-product-compliance
Lightning Source LLC
Chambersburg PA
CBHW070554260626
47161CB00002B/607